"Why do you do it, Delilah?" Mick demanded.

Del tightened her hands on the edge of the counter. "The media claims I do it because I like writing about heroes, about guys who can win against all odds, and setting myself up as a heroine."

"Are you?"

"No." It was difficult to think with him so close. "And look who's talking! A man who deliberately takes a bullet in the back for a stranger."

His eyes, when they met hers, were dark, intense. "I couldn't bear the thought of that bullet hurting your soft skin," he whispered. He pressed his face into her throat and held her in a tender, possessive way that made her heart rap hard.

"I don't need you to protect me," she said.

"*Tough.* We've forged a bond, you and I." Tangling his hand in her hair, he tipped her head back.

"What does that mean?" She found it hard to breathe with him watching her as if he could see her soul.

"It means you're mine now."

Dear Reader,

When Mick Dawson first appeared in *Beguiled,* he was a sixteen-year-old stud with a grown-up's sense of responsibility and a heart begging for love. *I* loved him, and many of you must have, too, based on the number of letters I received asking for Mick's story.

Now, in *Caught in the Act,* Mick is all grown up, still very much a stud and, yep, he's still looking for love, whether *he* realizes it or not. Of course, I had just the right woman for him! Between me and Mick's two friends Zack and Josh (pretty hunky heroes themselves), we gave Mick everything he deserved—and more. Poor Mick didn't stand a chance.

I hope you enjoy reading *Caught in the Act* as much as I enjoyed writing it.

And be sure to check back next month for *Treat Her Right,* Zack's story, Harlequin Temptation #852, and then again in November to see what Josh has gotten into in *Mr. November,* Harelquin Temptation #856.

Happy reading!

Lori Foster

LORI
FOSTER

CAUGHT
IN THE
ACT

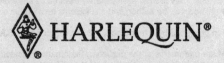

TORONTO • NEW YORK • LONDON
AMSTERDAM • PARIS • SYDNEY • HAMBURG
STOCKHOLM • ATHENS • TOKYO • MILAN • MADRID
PRAGUE • WARSAW • BUDAPEST • AUCKLAND

ISBN 0-373-83469-1

CAUGHT IN THE ACT

I want to give a very special thanks to
Officer LaDon Laney,
who exemplifies the types of heroes I enjoy writing about.
While helping me with my research, Officer Laney
spoke of his family, his community, his co-workers
and his job with admirable love and respect.
His help was invaluable to me.

And to Kathy McCutter for medical assistance,
and Lynda Sue Cooper for answering "cop" questions.

You're all wonderful!

CHAPTER ONE

RAIN DRUBBED THE WINDOW sluggishly, but Mick Dawson could still see out, still see all the different people milling around with colorful umbrellas and hats. He was so intent on watching for her he listened to the conversation with only half an ear. But then, half an ear was the most required when his friends got started on that particular topic.

"See that gorgeous blonde?" Josh Marshall said, deliberately baiting as usual. "The one who just came in? She's wearing a push-up bra."

"Is that right?" Zack Grange kept his tone dry. "How can you tell?"

"I know women." Josh's reply held an overdose of world-weary cynicism. "And I especially know women's breasts." He added, "At your age, I'd think you would, too."

"Yeah, and at your age," Zack retorted, "I'd have thought you'd outgrown your adolescent obsessions."

The three of them sat in the corner booth at Marco's, a casual Italian restaurant they'd first discovered five years ago. It was central to where they each worked, in the downtown area.

They came often, more so every year, it seemed, until now they met almost daily for lunch and often for dinner, too. None of them was married. Josh remained a confirmed bachelor, Zack was now a widower and Mick...well, Mick hadn't met the right woman. His criteria were strict, but to his mind, marriage was forever. He'd seen the worst quite often, marriages made in hell and sustained with sarcasm and cheating and drink. He'd also witnessed that elusive best, unions overflowing with love and trust and support. No way would he settle for less than what he knew could and should be.

Because of their different jobs—each of them stressful—and their lack of romantic ties, meeting at Marco's was about as close to a domestic routine as the three men ever saw.

The restaurant served as a place for celebration— a promotion, a new house, whatever came up that seemed celebration worthy. They also commiserated with each other there, as when Zack's young wife had died and he'd wanted to retreat from life, not seeing anyone, not doing anything except coddling his little girl. Or after Mick had gotten shot in the leg and missed several weeks of work, making him edgy.

Mick's life was all darkness and threats and caution. Ugly. Except here at Marco's, and with the people he trusted—his two friends, his family.

No one else. At least, not yet.

No woman had ever snagged his attention long enough to build a trust, certainly never for anything serious. Until now.

Now he was intrigued.

"Mick, tell this fool that breasts don't lift to the sun like a flower." Josh laughed at his own jest. "If they're damn near touching her chin, she's wearing a push-up bra."

Mick glanced at Zack and grinned. "Josh is an idiot where women are concerned—including his insane fascination with breasts, which, I agree, he should have outgrown years ago."

Josh shook his head in a pitying way. "Men do not outgrow their fascination with breasts. You two are just weird."

"A real woman," Mick told him, "would chew you up and spit you out."

"A real woman?" Zack asked, feigning confusion. "You mean someone with an IQ higher than ten? Why would Josh date anyone smarter than he is?"

Josh said, "Ha-ha. You're just jealous." He grinned and added, "Besides, the ladies have better things to do with their mouths when they're around me. Chewing is definitely out."

All three men laughed. "So," Josh said, "if you two abnormal specimens aren't turned on by a woman's breasts—which should be soft and natural, not shoved heavenward—then what does do it for you?"

Mick groaned. "Didn't we have this discussion back in high school?"

"Yeah, but it's still interesting."

"Bellies," Zack blurted.

Josh raised a brow. "Excuse me?"

For the moment, Mick felt content to just listen.

"I love a woman's belly." Zack leaned back, smiling to himself. "Not all muscled up the way some women want to do these days. Just a nice soft smooth woman's belly." He nodded, confirming his own conclusions. "Very sexy."

Josh considered that, then nodded, too. "Okay, I'll give you that one. Bellies are hot. But not belly button rings."

"No," Zack agreed. "A good belly doesn't need decoration."

"What about you, Mick?" Josh prodded. "Long legs? Great ass? What?"

Mick took another bite of his BLT, almost by rote, not because he was hungry. He considered his reaction when he'd seen *her* for the first time. What had he noticed? What had caught his eye and kept him so interested, to the point he almost felt obsessed?

He glanced out the dim window again. It was a miserable, dank July day, breezy, with fat purple clouds hanging low in the sky.

She should be coming along any minute now.

He'd first noticed her at his old neighborhood. He'd been there to rent out the upstairs apartment of the building he still owned, the same building he'd once lived in as a child. There were a lot of...*unpleasant* memories for him there, along with a few special ones. He kept the building as a reminder to himself that his life had changed, *he* had changed, but he was still a product of his upbringing.

Evidently, she rented from the building next door, because she had come down the walkway to the street and headed toward the post office, letters in her hand. It worried Mick, because no one traipsed around unprotected in that area. To call it rough would be a gross understatement.

But there she'd been, strolling along without a care. He hadn't hesitated to follow her, making certain she remained safe, enjoying the back view of her as she strutted along, her stride long and sure and almost cocky.

The sun was blistering hot that day, shining down on her blue-black, shoulder-length hair, hair so silky it appeared fluid when she moved. Soft, light blue eyes looked beyond everything and everyone, including Mick, as if a great distraction held her. He'd been nearly spellbound by her tall, willowy body with its incredibly long, slim legs and broad, fragile shoulders. Strangely enough, even when she came back out of the post office and went past him, again oblivious to her surroundings, he hadn't noticed her breasts. All his attention had been on her face, with its strong jaw, straight nose, pale eyes.

Mick wondered for an instant what Josh would think of his oversight.

Because he wanted to meet her, wanted to get to know her and have sex with her until he passed out from sheer exhaustion, he wasn't about to discuss her with Josh or Zack. So he merely shrugged. "It's a combination of things, and it's different with every woman."

Before either Josh or Zack could respond to that obscure reply, Mick saw her. Blindly, he laid his sandwich aside and twisted in the booth to better see out the window. Regardless of the drizzling rain, the gray sky, he'd expected her. A little rain wouldn't chase her inside. No, not this lady. She jogged every day around the same time, the same place. Or at least she had for two weeks now. It felt like fate, seeing her first in an area where he owned property, and then here again, where he routinely visited.

Zack, being a reasonable sort, hadn't complained much when Mick had made him move so he'd have the window seat. Josh, though, was unreasonable, always. Outrageous bordering on obnoxious. He'd demanded, all with laughter and taunting grins, for Mick to admit who he was watching for. Mick had refused, but now it didn't matter.

The second he shifted his attention, going on alert, Josh noticed.

"Aha! There you go, Zack. I think we'll get to see this mystery lady any second now."

Mick told him, rather succinctly, what he could do with his speculations. But that didn't deter Josh; if anything, it made him more curious.

Both Josh and Zack twisted around, and they, too, watched through the window. The streets were crowded during the lunch hour. Open umbrellas jumped with the breeze as people milled up and down the sidewalk.

And there she was, weaving in and out of human traffic as she jogged, her head uncovered, her clothes better suited to a bright spring day than drizzling rain. Funny thing was, she went right past them, inky-black ponytail bouncing, rainwater dripping off her nose and darkening her sweatshirt, and still Josh and Zack looked, searching the crowds.

They hadn't realized she was the one.

Mick's body knew that she was. Just seeing her now, bedraggled and wet and distracted, he wanted her. His muscles felt tight, his blood hot, his flesh prickly. Damn, if just watching her jog did this to him, how would it feel to kiss her, touch her, to slide deep inside her and hear her moan out a climax?

He felt the stirrings of an erection and muttered a curse. Insanity, he decided, but it couldn't be helped.

To hide his reaction, he grinned and leaned into the corner of the booth. Now that she'd gone by, he could face Zack and Josh and still keep an eye on her for about half a mile on the long, straight street. He glanced, and saw there was almost no jiggle to her firm little butt in the skintight biker shorts. His large hands would cover that bottom completely, and he'd hold her still, keep her steady for his thrusts....

Josh interrupted his very interesting imagery. "So? What are we looking for?"

"Nothing now." Mick deliberately sipped his coffee, knowing he had to get control of himself. And he had to get her; maybe after he'd made love to her for no less than ten days, he'd be able to get her out of his system.

A comical look on his face, Josh stretched past Zack, nearly knocking his plate off the table, and pressed his nose to the window. He looked and looked and finally said, "Damn it, there's nothing, no one, out there worth staring at!"

Mick and Zack shared a look. Zack shrugged. "If you're only looking for breasts, that could be. Maybe Mick was looking for something else."

Josh frowned at Zack. "No way. You know he's straight. We've both seen him with women."

Mick spewed his coffee. Zack burst out laughing,

and several women in the restaurant looked their way. They kept looking, smiling, flirting, and Mick shook his head. "You're drawing attention to yourself again, Josh."

"Me? I'm not the one laughing like an idiot."

"You don't need to laugh," Zack told him, "to be an idiot." Then slowly, as if speaking to a half-wit, he said, "I meant Mick was maybe looking at a woman who wasn't top-heavy. Just because it's your ultimate definition of what makes a woman, that doesn't mean the rest of us agree."

Josh studied Mick. "That right?"

"That you have strange ideas about women?" He took another sip of coffee and shrugged. "Yeah."

"I meant," Josh said, exasperated, "is she... lacking in the upper works?"

"As far as I can tell," Mick told him, a little annoyed and not sure why, "she's not lacking anywhere."

That only perplexed Josh more.

Mick again peeked out the window, and to his surprise, he saw her turn at the corner, cross the street and start back toward him. There was no more jiggle from her front than there'd been from her back. When she was just opposite the restaurant, she slowed and finally stopped. She rested her hands on her knees while she breathed deeply, heedless of the light rain and his avid attention.

When she straightened again, she stretched her arms high. Her shirt rose, showing a very sweet belly that Zack no doubt would have adored. Captivated, Mick continued to stare at her while a slow heat stirred deep inside him. She walked into the jewelry store located directly across from the restaurant, and Mick made up his mind.

Pushing aside his plate, he stood. So many times over the past few weeks he'd considered following her, initiating a conversation, introducing himself. He didn't want to rush her, but he'd dreamed about her twice, so he knew his fascination wasn't about to go away. Now seemed like as good a time as any to make his move. "I'll be back."

Josh and Zack stared at him, blank faced. Mick was aware of a thread of urgency vibrating through his blood. It had been like that from the second he first saw her, and every moment after when he watched her. He couldn't put his finger on it, couldn't tell anyone outright what it was about her that appealed to him, what pushed him over the edge. He only knew he wanted her. *Bad.*

As he dodged cars and puddles in the roadway, and muddy, slick spots along the curb, he wondered—for about the hundredth time—if she'd been in the area awhile, or if she'd only recently moved in when he first saw her. He'd been buried in work for the past two months, putting in seventeen-hour days, so it was possible she'd been close by for longer than two weeks.

He could get another assignment any day, so he had to take advantage of the opportunity now.

He hoped like hell she was single. Since first seeing her, he'd studied her closely. There weren't any rings on her fingers, but then he knew women who didn't wear them, especially while jogging. Not once in the two weeks of his awareness had he seen her with anyone, definitely not a man, but that, too, could be a fluke.

Mick turned up the collar on his windbreaker and darted across the sidewalk, trying to keep as dry as possible. He didn't have to look behind him to know both Josh and Zack would be craning their necks, their noses pressed to the window, spying on him. It was totally unlike him to chase a woman.

It was totally unlike him to be interested enough to bother chasing.

Thunder boomed, echoing over the street and rattling windows just as he stepped through the jewelry store's ornate front door. Air-conditioning hit him, chilling his damp skin. He brushed his hair back from his forehead and looked around. Glass cases were everywhere, some large, some smaller to showcase a certain piece, and there, in the far corner, she stood. Dressed in her running wear she looked very out of place, conspicuous and unique in the upscale, glitzy store. She also looked sexy as the original sin with her skin dewy from the drizzle and sweat, her cheeks flushed from exertion, her hair as much out of the ponytail as in, wet and sleek.

Damn, he thought, annoyed with himself. She wasn't that pretty, was in fact kind of plain. She wore no makeup, but her lashes and brows were as dark as her hair. Her nails were short, clean. She had a nice body, strong and sleek, fine boned, but not overly curved, not typically sexy.

Not the type of body to make him sweat at the sight of her.

She didn't give out signals or flirt or even pay much attention to men, not that he'd noticed.

His eyes widened. God, maybe she didn't even like men. That'd be a kicker, one he wouldn't, couldn't accept. Not when the mere sight of her turned him on. He didn't just want her; he felt as if he had to have her, just as he had to sleep or eat. It was the damnedest feeling, and he wasn't happy with it or himself.

She didn't appear interested in any particular item as she moseyed from case to case, peering inside, then shaking her head and moving on. For the moment, Mick was content to watch her. He slipped his hands into his jeans pockets, then quickly pulled them out again when he realized that negligent pose might expose the weapon in the waistband holster at his back. Being off duty, he didn't need the gun, but he always carried it.

In this day and age, his cover wouldn't have been believable without it. Drug dealers, prostitutes, gamblers...they all expected you to be armed, and if you weren't, you were considered an idiot, or worse.

Usually, even when conditions didn't call for a weapon, he managed to smuggle in the Smith & Wesson 9 mm in an ankle holster. There were times, though, when he had to go without, leaving him feeling naked, and those were the times when he got most tense, when the adrenaline rush was all but blinding. He always wanted a woman afterward, a way to release all that pent-up energy.

He wanted a woman now.

He wanted her.

Moving closer, watching her, he was amazed that she didn't feel his attention, so acute that it had him half-hard again with expectation. It had always been his experience that blatant staring was felt like a stroke of ice. But then, she was a civilian, and he'd already noted the first day he saw her how heedless she could be of her surroundings. It amazed him sometimes that people could survive with so little caution.

The door chimed behind Mick and more people entered. Two men, dressed much like Mick in jeans and T-shirts, wearing sneakers, one in a ball cap. They appeared to be in their mid-thirties, clean, middle-class. As a cop, Mick automatically took in everyone and everything. He'd already noted the two salesladies, the older couple looking at cocktail rings for an anniversary. He picked up on actions and quiet dialogue and expressions.

Caution was as basic to him as breathing. And because he wasn't a civilian, wasn't oblivious, he immediately detected the sudden charge in the air despite the nonthreatening scene and apparently ordinary people. It had come in like the wind with the men, and Mick didn't like it worth a damn. He had a keen sixth sense, and he trusted it more than he trusted appearances.

The woman looked up, around, made brief eye contact with the two men who'd entered, then again with Mick. Their gazes locked and held for an instant, an instant that made his gut clench with awareness. She gave him a small smile, a simple, friendly smile that nonetheless heightened his tension, before she turned away again.

Senses on alert, Mick followed her, not too close, in no way obvious, but keeping her within reach. Because the shop was small and crowded with displays, the air thick and humid from the rain outside, he could detect her scent. It was earthy and rich, warm woman, damp skin and clean female sweat. His heart punched hard, a little fast; his sex thickened. He'd been too long without a woman, too long without any sexual relief. Sometimes being a contrary bastard was a real pain.

Her wet running shoes squeaked on the ceramic tile floor as she browsed, appearing to study the shop, not just the wares but the structure, the setup. Mick frowned as he watched her, further intrigued and a little distracted. Out of the corner of his eye he saw one of the men reach into his jacket pocket, and a silent alarm screamed inside Mick's head.

He jerked around, but not quickly enough.

"Everyone stay still and calm." The guy waved a SIG Sauer .45 around the room with menacing intent. "No one panic or do anything stupid," he said with a sneer, "and I won't have to kill anyone."

Damn, damn, damn. Mick took a quick, inconspicuous glance around. The elderly woman, clinging to her husband, looked ready to faint, while the salespeople stood motionless, frozen in horror. His movements so slight that no one paid him any mind, Mick edged closer to the woman he'd followed. She stared at the gunman, her blue eyes darker now with fascination, but he saw no real fear.

"We'll do our business," the guy in the ball cap said, "and then leave and no one will be hurt."

Mick didn't buy it for a second; the words sounded far too rehearsed, far from sincere. And there was an anticipatory expression on the man's face.

Things never worked out the easy way—not life, not love, sure as hell not an armed robbery.

The second man hitched his gun at the saleswoman. "You, come open the register and make it quick."

She balked, more out of surprise than rebellion. Mick had a similar sensation. They were surrounded by diamonds and gold of unbelievable value, yet this idiot wanted what little cash might be in the register? The robber had to realize that most sales would be handled with credit cards or checks; his demand didn't make sense.

Mick's hands twitched. He wanted to grab his gun; he wanted to be in control. Right now, control meant keeping everyone alive. It meant keeping *her* alive.

Without warning, the man who'd issued the order shouted, "*Now*, goddamn it!" and everyone jumped, the saleslady screeching and stumbling over her own feet as she rushed to obey.

A predictable panic reaction, Mick thought, to the threat of sudden violence, not something a robber intent on keeping things calm would have instigated. Mick's suspicions rose.

The older woman quietly wept, one saleslady turned white, the other shook so badly she had a hard time working the register. Before she could get it open, distant sirens broke the quiet, making both men curse hotly. Mick tensed, waiting for another outburst, for them to turn and run, for them to retaliate by shooting the saleslady. He'd learned early on that criminals did the most absurd and unaccountable things, often causing death without reason. He prepared himself for any reaction.

But what they did took him totally by surprise.

They didn't yell, didn't run. They focused their blame on the young woman next to Mick.

"Bitch," the guy in the ball cap snarled. "You set off an alarm."

Startled, she blinked, looked around, backed up two paces. "No," she breathed. It was the first time Mick had heard her voice, which quaked with fear, bewilderment. "I don't even know where—"

The man took aim at her and, without thinking, Mick blocked his path. Both gunmen froze at his audacity. He felt the woman's small hands against his back, clutching at his jacket. He felt her face press into his shoulder, was aware of her accelerated breathing, her trembling. She was deathly afraid, and anger surged in his blood.

His voice as low and calm as he could make it, Mick said, "She's a customer. She doesn't know where the alarm is."

He was ignored.

"Everybody get down!" As the guy in the ball cap yelled his order, a car screeched up in front of the shop, motor idling. The customers all dropped to the floor, panicked, including the woman at Mick's back. He felt her jerky movements, could hear her panting in terror.

Mick moved more slowly, his mind churning as he

tried to buy himself some time. If he could get his gun... His elbow touched the woman's wrist, he was so close to her. She, like the others, had stretched out flat, covering her head with her arms, shaking. Mick kept himself balanced on his elbows, ready to move, watching without appearing to watch.

The sudden shattering of glass—again and again as each case was destroyed—caused the older woman to wail, the saleslady to whimper. The woman next to Mick never made a sound. He wanted to look at her, to somehow reassure her, but he didn't dare take his attention off those weapons. The two men grabbed a few large items of jewelry, but it was as if they destroyed the store just for the sake of destruction.

It was by far the most pathetic, disorganized and unproductive robbery Mick had ever witnessed—and that made him more suspicious than anything else might have. By rights, they should have known where the most valuable items would be, and should have concentrated their sticky fingers there. Instead, they seemed to take whatever was at hand without thought to its worth. No one robbed a jewelry store without casing it first, without knowing what would be found inside and where.

The two men finally headed for the door. The tension tightened, grew painful, static crowding the air until it seemed impossible to breathe—and the bastard in the ball cap turned to fire.

Mick moved so fast, he barely had the thought of moving before he was over her, his arms covering her head, his muscular body completely blanketing her delicate one. Though she was tall for a woman, about five-nine, she was small boned and felt fragile to his six-three frame. He was plenty big enough, and more than determined enough, to be her protection.

She gasped at the feel of him on top of her and immediately stiffened, forcing her head up, twisting. "No! What are you doing?"

He jammed her head back down, then cursed when her cheek hit the hard tile floor. Knowing what she likely thought and wishing he could spare her, Mick said into her ear, "Be still."

She wiggled more furiously, trying to free herself, confused and frightened, unsure of his intent. "He's going to—" Mick began to explain, and then it was unnecessary.

The crack sounded loud and startling; the sudden pain in his right shoulder was a lick of pure fire. For only a moment, his arms tightened around her and he ground his teeth together. "Oh God," she whispered, trying to turn toward him.

Mick grunted, but didn't move. No, he wasn't about to move. For whatever reason, they wanted her dead, but they'd have to get through him first.

He felt the blood spreading on his back, sticky and warm; he was aware of the woman squirming beneath him, gasping, crying. But it wasn't until he heard the door open that he rolled and drew his gun at the same time. He blocked the awful pain, any distractions, and got off a clean shot through the glass door, clipping the man who'd tried to shoot her. The hollow-point bullet hit him high in the left thigh before he could get into the car. The leg crumpled beneath him and he went down in an awkward heap, howling in pain, grabbing for the open car door in desperation.

The car lurched away, spewing gravel and squealing tires, tossing the man back. The side of his head cracked solidly against the curb. He lay there unconscious, sprawled out like a wounded starfish.

Surging to his feet, Mick ran out the door. He spotted the car, drew careful aim and fired again. The back window exploded, but the car didn't slow. It careened around the corner on two wheels and disappeared.

Already the streets had filled with onlookers, people too damn stupid to stay inside and away from gunfire. Mick's arm rapidly went hot, cold and then numb; his fingers throbbed. His hand shook as he tried to hang on to his gun, to steady himself.

Josh and Zack appeared, having witnessed the tail end of the robbery from the restaurant. Josh, smooth as silk, slipped the gun from Mick's hand and dropped it into his trouser pocket. They'd arrived just seconds before the police cars. More people from all over the street converged, whispering, curious. Josh caught Mick's upper arm and supported him. "Jesus, man. You're shot."

Zack came to his other side and yelled, "Someone call the paramedics. He needs an ambulance." That made Mick laugh, since Zack was an EMT. Zack shook his head wryly and pulled out his radio, putting in the call himself.

"Here, sit down," he said, and led Mick to the rain-wet curb.

"I don't want to sit in a damn puddle," Mick

grumbled. "I'm fine." Fine enough that he wanted to find the woman. He looked around, and when he didn't immediately see her, terror started to take hold. He located the elderly couple leaning against the brick building. The old woman clung to her husband and cried, while he peered around in dismay and impotent anger. Mick saw the two salespeople, huddled together, dry eyed but white as snow, apparently in shock. Cops swarmed everywhere, separating the witnesses so they couldn't share stories. Two police cars took off to give chase, while another radioed in the call. An officer headed Mick's way.

Where the hell is she?

When the cop reached him, frowning, his hand resting on his holster, Mick said quietly, "I'm Mick Dawson, Vice." He started to reach inside his jacket for his badge, but his arm wouldn't cooperate and he cursed.

Josh said, "I'll get it." He retrieved the badge and flipped it toward the officer, who nodded and yelled for someone to get a blanket.

Frustrated, Mick could do no more than stand there, getting weaker by the second, while Zack gave instructions into his radio and Josh more or less held him upright.

Zack told the officer, "The ambulance is on its way. I'm an EMT. I'll see to him until it gets here."

The officer, frowning in worry, handed Zack the blanket and then set off to clear the street.

Mick started to pull free, desperate to find the woman and make certain she was okay, but just then she stepped around the elderly couple. Her face, her beautiful face, was creased with worry, with disbelief. From a slight distance, they stared at each other, and there was no distraction in her gaze now, no oblivion. The horror of what had just happened darkened her eyes to midnight.

A bruise discolored her cheekbone from when he'd pushed her head down. His stomach cramped with that realization. She trembled all over, and Mick shook off Zack to go to her, needing to hold her, to apologize, though he didn't even know her name, had no idea who she was or why the robbers had wanted to kill her.

Zack, who'd been looking at the wound in his shoulder, drew him back. "Damn it, Mick, you're ready to drop."

Mick started to deny that, but then his legs gave out, and if it hadn't been for Josh and Zack supporting him, he'd have been sitting in the middle of the sidewalk instead of on the curb with a folded blanket beneath him. His vision swam, closed in.

"You're losing a lot of blood," Zack said in his calm, professional voice, but Mick heard the concern, the anger, as his friend began first aid.

"Don't let her get away." Mick meant to say it loud and clear, an order that couldn't be ignored. But the words emerged as a faint whisper, and that infuriated him. He'd finally met her—sort of—and he sounded weak, looked weak.

At the moment, he was weak. Too weak.

But she'd felt so good beneath him for that brief, charged moment, adding to his adrenaline rush, further arousing him though they'd been in the middle of a very dangerous situation. It was so absurd, but even as he'd braced for that bullet, he'd been aware of her under him, her ass cuddling his groin, her head fitting neatly under his chin.

He forced his head up and said again, trying for more than a whisper this time, "Don't let her get away."

He knew Josh heard him because he leaned closer. "Who?"

"In...the running clothes. Black hair." That was the very best description he could muster under the circumstances.

Josh looked up, eyes narrowed as he scanned the crowd and then settled on someone. He said, "You've got it, buddy. Now you just rest. I'll take care of it." He got to his feet and stalked forward purposefully, saying in a tone that brooked no argument, "Miss? I need to see you, please."

And Mick blacked out.

CHAPTER TWO

"WHERE IS SHE?" The sound of his own voice, foggy and dark and thin, appalled him. Mick tried to clear his throat, but it was impossible.

"Shh," he heard Zack say. "Take it easy."

Mick struggled to open his eyes, then wished he hadn't. What the hell had they done to him? His shoulder didn't hurt, at least not at the moment, but he felt as if his brain might explode, and every muscle he possessed was sluggish, refusing to cooperate with his brain's commands.

More cautiously this time, he cracked his eyes open and found Zack on guard at his bedside. Where was Josh? Where was *she?*

"The woman?" he asked again, and he sounded like a dying frog.

Zack lifted a glass of water with a straw to Mick's mouth. He wanted to tell Zack to jam the straw in his ear, but he couldn't. He gave in to his thirst and took several quick sips. He started to move his arm, and fire burned down his side. *Now* his shoulder hurt. He ground his teeth, hissing for breath.

"The anesthesia is wearing off," Zack explained. "You'll be groggy a little longer, but overall you're fine. They left the bullet in—that's two for you now, right? Taking it out would only have caused more damage. You lost too much blood already."

Mick was still registering what Zack had said when his friend leaned forward and growled, not two inches from his nose, "You scared the hell out of me! Don't you know if you get shot you should stay down? Swinging your arm around that way just encouraged it to bleed more."

Mick grunted, as much from the pounding in his head as in reply. "Where the hell is she?"

Exasperated, Zack sighed. He didn't need to ask *She who?* "Josh has been keeping a close eye on her, since right before you passed out and bashed your damn head on the ground. Yeah, that's why your head feels like it's splitting. I'm surprised you don't have a concussion, as hard as you hit. If you didn't have to be so damn macho, if you'd just tell someone when you were ready to faint—"

"I did *not* faint." Mick's voice, his words, were gaining strength, and he grumbled, "I passed out from blood loss."

"Yeah, well, they look about the same when you drop right in the middle of a crowd."

It hurt, but Mick narrowed his eyes and said, "Zack? Come closer."

Zack, filled with new concern, leaned down close. *"Where the hell is she!"*

Zack jerked back and grimaced. "All right, all right, you don't have to bust my eardrum. You said, all ominous cloak and dagger, 'Don't let her get away.' Neither Josh nor I knew if that meant she should be arrested, or if she was the lady you'd been watching for.''

Mick jerked—and the sudden movement squeezed the breath right out of his lungs. Damn, he'd forgotten how badly a bullet hurt. Through clenched teeth, he snarled, ''You didn't…?''

''Turn her over to the cops? Nope. They questioned her, of course, but Josh followed them to the station and then picked her up afterward. She's fine, just shook up and babbling about you being a hero—no surprise there, I suppose. She claims you took that bullet for her, and she wants to see you, overflowing with gratitude and all that, but, of course, since we didn't know what the hell was going on…''

''I'm going to kill you.''

Zack grinned. ''We collected her for you, but she's none too happy right now. Josh is more or less, er, detaining her. No, don't look like that. You know he wouldn't hurt her. But he's taxing himself; it's been over four hours, after all.''

Four hours! Mick wanted to groan again, thinking of her waiting that long, Josh coercing her into hanging around….

''No,'' Zack said, correctly reading his mind, ''she didn't want to leave, she wanted to see you. And she's not happy when she doesn't get what she wants. She's actually—'' Zack coughed. ''She's a very determined lady.''

Zack looked at Mick's IV and added, ''Evidently, she wants you.''

That was a revelation, one he could easily live

with. His head pounded, but Mick held back all wimpy sounds of distress and said, "Get her for me."

"Don't be an idiot! You're hardly in any shape to start getting acquainted." Zack stood, towering over the bed. "I assumed once you came to, you'd explain what the hell's going on, we could then explain it to her, and then we'd let the lady go home so you could get some rest."

"Do *not* let her leave here alone." Mick had awakened with a feeling of panic, again seeing that gun aimed at her—just her, no one else, and for no apparent reason. Until he figured things out, he wanted her watched. He wanted her protected.

It pissed him off royally that he had to ask others to do that for him.

"Mick, we can't just refuse to let her leave."

Giving Zack a sour look, Mick said, *"Get her."*

"Damn, you're insistent when you're injured."

"And I've heard more 'damns' from you in the last five minutes than I have since your daughter was born."

Zack shrugged. "Well, Dani isn't here to listen and emulate. Besides, it's not every day I see a friend shot."

"You say I need to recoup, Zack?"

"That's right."

"So how is it going to help my recuperation when I get out of this bed and kick your sorry ass?"

Zack hesitated before giving in with a laugh. "I can't fight you now, because you're already down and I feel sorry for you. If I let you get up and attempt to hit me, you'd probably start bleeding all over the place again and rip your stitches, and I'd have to let you win.'' He held up both hands. ''Stay put. I'll find out how soon you'll be moved to your room and when Delilah can join you.''

Pain ripped through his shoulder as Mick did a double take. ''Delilah?''

Zack stared. ''Don't tell me you didn't even know her name.''

''So?'' Learning her name hadn't been his top priority. Touching her had, and he'd accomplished that while also protecting her. A nice start, except for the fact that someone wanted her dead, and had shot him trying to accomplish the deed. But he'd figure that one out eventually. In the meantime, he had no intention of letting anyone hurt her.

''So you took a bullet for a complete stranger?''

Very quietly, Mick asked, ''Wouldn't you have done the same?''

And because Zack already had once, long ago, he turned and walked out.

The second Zack pushed aside the curtain and left, a nurse stepped in, ready to check Mick's vitals and reassure him. She lingered, and Mick couldn't help but smile at her, despite his discomfort and his current frazzled frame of mind. She was about five years older than he, putting her in her early thirties. She was attractive even in sensible white shoes and a smock. She smoothed his hair, her fingers gentle, while she explained that he'd be there overnight, but would likely leave in the morning, and that they'd put him in his own room very soon.

Still being polite, Mick was careful not to encourage her. He wanted to meet Delilah, wanted to talk to her, hear her voice when she wasn't frightened, see her smile again. She was the only woman he wanted at the moment, and he was relieved when the orderly showed up and announced it was time to take Mick to his room.

Any minute now he'd meet her, really meet her. And he promised himself that not long after that he'd kiss her...and more. He didn't know how he'd manage that, all things considered, but he would. He had to taste her, had to stake a claim in the best way known to man.

He discounted his wound. It wouldn't slow him down; he wouldn't let it slow him down.

He needed her.

"I'M CAPABLE OF WALKING on my own."

Josh, the man "escorting" her to Mick's room, gave a disgruntled sigh and removed his hand from her arm. He'd been pushy and demanding, a total stranger insisting she follow his orders. She'd done so, once she realized he was a friend of the man who'd protected her.

But she didn't like him, and she definitely didn't like the distrustful way he loomed over her. He pretended gentlemanly qualities, but she knew he held on to her so she couldn't get away. She'd already told him a dozen times that she had no intention of leaving.

Not that Josh paid any mind to what she had to say.

He had "slick" written all over him, from the way he held himself to the way he noticed every single female in the vicinity. She understood his type. Josh was one of those men who felt superior to women, but covered that nasty sentiment with charisma and a glib tongue. No doubt, given his good looks and out-rageous confidence, women regularly encouraged him.

Del just wanted to get by him so she could meet the other man, the one who'd risked his life for her.

Josh slanted her one of his insulting, speculative looks. "I hope you don't go in there and give him any grief."

When she didn't answer him, he added, "He did save your sorry, ungrateful little butt, after all."

She could hardly ignore that! Del whirled and stuck a finger into his hard chest. "I know. I was *there*," she snapped. Her control, her poise and any claim to ladylike behavior were long gone. Today had been the most bizarre and eventful day of her life. "You're the one who doesn't seem to understand that I need to see him, that I should have been there with him all along, to thank him—"

He glared at her, rubbed at his chest and walked away. Del had to hurry to catch up to him. A few seconds later they turned a corner, and Josh pushed a door open. "Here we go," he said. And then under his breath, but not much under, she heard him mutter, "Thank God."

Through the open doorway, Del could see the oc-cupied hospital bed, and she drew up short. Heavy emotion dropped on her, making her feel sluggish in the brain—which was a first. Her breath caught. Her stomach flipped. Her heart fluttered.

He lay almost flat, his long, tall body stretching from one end of the narrow bed to the other. She remembered his height when he'd covered her, pro-tecting her and all but dwarfing her despite her own height. She remembered the power of him, too, the vibrating tension and leashed strength.

His beautiful, dark brown hair now looked disheveled, spikey from the earlier rain and his injuries and... Her bottom lip quivered with her loss of composure.

He was the most beautiful man she'd ever seen, though she hadn't really seen him until he threw himself on top of her and saved her life. At first she'd thought he was with the robbers, and she'd known so much fear she'd actually tasted it.

Instead, he'd taken a bullet meant for her.

Her heart stuttered to a near stop. What kind of man did that? He didn't know her, owed her nothing. She'd barely noticed him in the store before that.

But when he'd chased the bad guys just like a disreputable Dirty Harry clone, she'd looked him over and hadn't been able to stop looking. He'd been all hard, flexing muscle, animal grace and speed.

Now he was flat on his back in a hospital bed. She sighed brokenly, choking on her emotions.

He turned his head at the sound she made, and those deep brown, all-consuming eyes warmed. A slight, heart-stopping smile curved one side of his mouth, and he looked sexy and compelling. In a deep, dark voice hoarse with pain, he whispered, "Hi."

Just like that her heart melted and sank into her toes. There was so much inflection, so much feeling, in that one simple hello. Vaguely, she heard Josh saying, "Delilah, meet Mick Dawson. Mick, Miss Delilah Piper."

Del paid no attention to Josh, her every thought and sense focused on the large dark man in the bed. In the bed because of *her*. No one had ever done anything even remotely like that for her. Her life in the past few years had been, by choice, a solitary one. Even before then, though, her relationships had been superficial and short-lived—nothing to inspire such protective instincts.

The reality of what he'd done, what he'd risked for her, threw Del off balance emotionally, just as the sight of him stirred her physically.

Without another thought, she moved straight to the bed. Mick looked at her, still smiling, but now with his eyes a bit wider, more alert, a little surprised. She sat near his hip and stroked his face. She *needed* to touch him, to feel the warmth of his skin, the lean hardness of his jaw.... Unable to help herself, she kissed him.

Against his lips, she said with heartfelt sincerity, "Thank you."

He started to say something, but she kissed him again. It felt...magically right; she could have gone on kissing him forever. His mouth was firm, dry. Five o'clock shadow covered his jaw, rasping against her fingertips, thrilling her with the masculinity of it. Heat, scented by his body, lifted off him in waves, encompassing her and soothing her. He tasted good, felt good, smelled good.

A little breathless, bewildered by it all, Del said, "I'm so sorry. It should be me in that bed."

"No!" His good arm came up, his hand, incredibly large and rough, clasped her shoulder, and he levered her away. For a man in a sickbed, he had surprising strength and was far too quick.

And he looked angry. And protective.

Excitement skittered down her spine, while tenderness welled in her chest.

The door opened again and Zack, the man who was a little nicer than Josh, started in. He jerked to a halt when he saw them both on the bed, nose-to-nose. Startled, Zack began to backpeddle, only to change his mind once more when he spotted Josh standing in the corner, smirking.

"Uh, Mick?" Zack sounded ridiculously cheerful and vastly amused. "I see you're feeling...better."

Josh chuckled. "I imagine he feels just fine right about now, since she's in here."

Slowly, not wanting to upset Mick, Del stood and cast a quick glare at both men. In her fascination with Mick, she'd all but forgotten them and how they'd bulldozed her, refusing her every request, evading her questions.

"I'd have been with you sooner, but they wouldn't let me," she said to Mick, feeling piqued all over again. "I didn't know what was going on or why—"

"Only family could see him before he got to his room," Zack said, some of his cheerfulness dwindling.

Del had heard the same lame explanation at least ten times, yet Zack had pretty much stayed with Mick, except for when he'd taken a turn guarding her so Josh could look in on him. They were friends, not family, or so they'd told her, so their excuses held no weight. They'd insisted she come to the hospital, insisted she wait around, and then they'd refused to let her do anything useful—like see Mick and thank Mick and...

She brushed her stringy bangs out of her face, still annoyed, still frustrated. "You could have taken my suggestion and told them I was his wife. Then they'd have let me in."

Josh choked; Zack raised one eyebrow and looked at Mick. Mick grinned, then reached out for her hand with his good arm, which meant stretching across the bed. When she took his hand, he said, "I'm sorry you were worried." And in a quieter tone, "Are you all right?"

Dismissing the other two men, she again sat on the bed. She wanted to kiss him some more, but his friends were standing there, not only ogling them, but bristling like overprotective bulldogs. Besides, after her run through the rain, and the burglary, she probably wasn't all that appealing.

"I'm fine."

Mick touched her bruised cheek with gentle fingertips. His eyes were nearly black with concern. "Damn, I'm sorry about that."

His tone made her heart beat faster, made her skin flush and her insides warm. They'd only just met, but she felt as if she'd known him forever.

Catching his wrist, she turned his hand and kissed his palm. Again he looked surprised, and if she didn't miss her guess, aroused. His eyes were hot, his cheekbones slashed with color. He stared at her mouth.

Was it possible he felt the same incredible chemistry?

Del had to clear her throat to say, "You saved me. I'm sorry I freaked. I thought…well, at first I thought you were with them and you intended to…"

"I know." He continued to stare at her mouth, which made her belly quiver, her nerves jump. "I'm sorry I scared you."

The irony didn't escape her. Here he was, in bed, wounded, and he kept apologizing to her. She'd never met a man like him. "You kept me alive," she stressed, which discounted any side effects, such as a small bruise, as unimportant. "I'm the one who's sorry. Well, not sorry that I'm alive, but sorry that you got hurt in the process."

"It's just a flesh wound."

Zack coughed and Josh snorted.

She looked at his two friends, then peered at Mick suspiciously. Was it worse than she thought? But the nurse had told her he'd be okay.

Her ire resurfaced and she said to Mick, "I wanted to come in and see you, but they wouldn't let me. Waiting was awful. When we found out how long it would be, I planned to go home and shower and change, and try to make myself presentable, so when you came to I wouldn't be such a sight, but he—" she directed a stiff finger at Josh "—wouldn't be at all reasonable about any of it."

"Don't blame Josh," Mick said, smiling just a bit. "I asked him to keep you around."

"You did?"

"I was afraid you'd disappear and I wouldn't get to see you again."

His words were so sweet, she forgot about her sweat and ruined clothes and stringy hair. "I wouldn't have done that, I swear! I would have come right back."

Again she leaned down and kissed him, but this time he was ready for her and actually kissed her back. His tongue stroked past her lips for just a heartbeat, then retreated. Her breath caught and she sighed. *Oh wow.*

With a numb mind and tingling lips, she heard him rumble in a low voice, "I want to see you, Delilah."

She lowered her voice to a mere whisper. "I want

to see you, too. I just wish I'd had time to clean up. I'm all sweaty and I have mud on my feet and my clothes are limp and wrinkled. I smell like a wet dog.''

His hot gaze moved from her eyes to her mouth and back again, his expression devouring. "You smell like a woman."

She almost slid right off the side of the bed. Much more of that and she'd be sweating again, that or she'd self-combust.

He was just so darn sexy! The dark beard shadow covering the lower part of his face made him look dangerous. After witnessing him in action that afternoon, she knew he *was* dangerous. His brows were thick, his lashes sinfully long, his high-bridged nose narrow and straight, his mouth delicious. And those dark eyes… This man had singled her out and risked his life to save her. It was beyond comprehension.

It was the most exciting thing that had ever happened to her.

Only a thin hospital gown and a sheet concealed his entire gorgeous, hard body from her. She looked him over, saw the width of his chest, the length of his legs. His feet tented the sheet, and as her attention slid back up his body, she noticed something else was beginning to tent, as well.

She returned her gaze to his, saw the burning intensity there, and froze. He wasn't embarrassed and made no attempt to conceal his growing erection.

Using his left hand, Mick lifted her fingers and caressed them gently. His eyes were direct, unapologetic, and when she glanced at the other two men, it was to see them looking out the window, at the ceiling, anywhere but at the bed.

She was unimpressed with their show of discretion after everything they'd already put her through. It didn't matter that they'd directed their attention elsewhere; they were still in the room, their presence noticeable. They'd more or less forced her to stay, at Mick's request, but it was obvious they still didn't want her alone with him.

If they'd really been polite, if they'd trusted her at all, they'd have left the room. But no, they weren't ready to budge an inch. She supposed they didn't know her well enough to trust her and, after all, he'd just been shot, but still...

Mick looked vital and strong and all-male, and his effect on her was beyond description. She'd long since decided men weren't worth the effort, but oh, she hadn't met this man yet.

"Are you sure you're going to be okay?" She gripped his hand hard, trying to accustom herself to the unfamiliar feelings of tenderness and worry and explosive desire. It had been forever since she'd felt so much awareness for a man. Well, actually, she'd never felt it—not like this. Which was the main reason she seldom dated anymore. Men didn't appreciate her emotional distance.

She felt far from emotionally distant now. "The nurse said you'd be fine, but..."

"Yeah." His voice was rich with promise. "I should be out of here soon."

"Tomorrow," Zack said, still keeping his eyes averted, "as long as you agree to take it easy. They'll send you home with antibiotics and painkillers, but knowing you—"

A noise in the hall alerted them to more visitors. Mick released his hold on Del and bunched the blan-

kets over his lap to hide his partial erection just seconds before a man and woman pushed through the
door. They entered in a rush, heading straight for
Mick.

Not being much of a people person, Del faded
aside, inching into the corner opposite Zack and Josh.
Mick frowned in displeasure at her retreat, and Josh
said, "No worries. I've got it covered." When he
moved to stand between Del and the door, Del realized he meant that he'd continue to keep her around.

As if she'd leave now!

Del's attention snagged on the pretty blond woman
now hovering over the bed, kissing the top of Mick's
head, his high cheekbone, his chin. "Thank God
you're all right!"

The woman's lips were all over Mick, and Del
didn't like it at all. But she knew she had no right to
complain.

"I made Dane drive like a demon to get us here."

"Angel," Mick protested, all the while grinning
widely so that Del knew he didn't really mind her
attention at all, "you didn't need to rush. I'm fine."

Del wondered if Angel was her name or an en-
dearment.

The woman pressed her cheek to Mick's. "But you
were shot!"

Zack laughed. "I told you on the phone he'd be
all right."

"I had to see for myself."

Josh crossed his arms over his chest and smiled. It
was apparent to Del that they all knew each other,
that these were more of Mick's friends. These people
Josh trusted; she could see that.

Feeling like an outsider, or worse, an interloper, Del frowned.

"According to the doctor," Josh said, addressing Angel, "he'll need some baby-sitting."

Zack nodded. "Luckily the bullet hit at a tangential entry. It was expended enough that the force didn't carry it into the chest cavity, which could have injured his lung, or in a through-and-through injury that could have caused more damage to his arm."

"Yeah," Mick mumbled, tongue in cheek, "I'm real lucky."

Del's heart ached for him. This was the most she'd heard, and it hadn't been revealed for her benefit. Rather, the information was for the new arrivals, especially the woman with the lips.

The female who was trusted.

It all sounded so horrendous, worse than Del had imagined. If the shooter had stepped just a little bit closer, if his aim had been a little higher... She closed her eyes, fighting back a wave of renewed fear and impossible guilt. Mick could so easily have been killed.

Her eyes snapped opened when she heard Angel say, "You'll come home with me, of course."

Del had no real rights to jealousy or possessiveness, but she felt them just the same. Who was this beautiful woman who felt free to kiss and touch Mick?

And then the thought intruded: was he married?

Del's stomach knotted. She tried to see Mick's hand, but couldn't with both people crowded near his bed.

The man with Angel said, "The kids would love a chance to fetch and carry for you. They adore you, you know that."

With incredible relief, Del realized that if they had kids, they must be a couple. Which meant Mick was safe from any romantic entanglement with Angel.

Del was just beginning to relax again, feeling on safer ground, when yet another couple pushed through the door. This woman was lovely, too, but the man with her held her close to his side, leaving no doubt that they were together. He was large and dark and so intense he looked like Satan himself. Del stared, but no one else seemed alarmed.

Mick even rolled his eyes. "Angel, did you drag Alec and Celia down here, too?"

Angel touched his face. "They were visiting when we got the news. Of course they insisted on coming."

The room was all but bursting with large men. Josh and Zack were big enough, but their physical presence was nothing compared to Dane's and Alec's, both of whom were in their prime and exuding power.

And Mick, even flat on his back and wounded, was a masculine presence impossible to ignore. He had an edge of iron control, of leadership, that couldn't be quelled by an injury. All in all, the men made an impressive group. Del expected the walls to start dripping testosterone any moment.

She watched them all, memorizing names and studying faces as they shared familiar greetings. The women were all-smiles, and even Dane looked somewhat jovial. Alec, however, looked capable of any number of nefarious deeds.

Just as Del thought it, she saw his piercing gaze sweep over Mick from head to toe, and he grinned a surprisingly beautiful grin, making his black eyes glitter and causing Del to do an awed double take.

"I knew you wouldn't go much longer," Alec

drawled, and even his deep voice sounded scary to Del, "without getting yourself shot again. It's a nasty habit."

"I'll try real hard to keep that in mind," Mick said.

"Zack tells me you got shot on purpose this time." Alec crossed his massive arms. "At least I try to avoid it when possible, and when Celia isn't around."

Celia, slim and elegant, leaned over Mick's bed and kissed his forehead. To Del's way of thinking, there was far too much kissing going on, and far too many visitors. At this rate, she'd never get him alone.

But that concern was secondary to another. Judging by what Alec had said, this wasn't the first time Mick had been shot. Del looked at Josh and Zack, to judge their reactions to that news. Their expressions were impassive, leading her to believe they already knew Mick had been shot before this.

"Don't let Alec tease you, sweetie," Celia said. "He's glad I got him shot. Otherwise we'd never have ended up together."

Alec looked very dubious at her statement, whereas Del was completely floored. What in the world did these men do that they took turns catching bullets?

Celia continued, saying, "If you stay with Angel, then we can visit you."

Del knew that any second now Mick would agree to Angel's offer, and then she'd lose her chance. She took a deep breath, unglued her feet and tongue, and declared, "I'm taking him home with me."

The room fell silent, and as one, all eyes shifted her way. The women and two men stared, as if seeing her for the first time.

Mick smiled.

Under so much scrutiny, Del squirmed. Thanks to

the rain and her long jog and the events at the jewelry store, she looked like something out of a circus sideshow. But determination filled her. She wasn't a coward and she wouldn't start acting like one now.

Moving out of the corner, she edged in around Angel, who kept kissing Mick's forehead. Del got as close to him as she could, then stated again, "I'll take care of him." She made her voice strong, resolute.

Angel blinked, looked at the other people, then back at Del. "You will?"

"Yes. After all," Del explained, "it's my fault he's hurt."

Everyone's gaze shifted from her to Mick. Expressions varied from male amusement, astonishment and fascination, to female speculation.

Del wanted to wince, to close her ears so she wouldn't have to hear what Mick might reply to her appalling assumption. They were strangers in every sense of the word, but he'd claimed to want to see her again. What better opportunity would there be than for her to take him home? She'd never played nurse to anyone before, but how hard could it be?

She stood by his bed, refusing to budge, blocking Angel and her lips, in particular, and waited in agony.

Expectation hung in the air, along with a good dose of confusion.

Mick grinned, managed a one-shoulder shrug and addressed all six people at once. "There you go. Looks like it's all taken care of."

"WHAT DO YOU KNOW ABOUT her?"

Josh looked down at Angel and shrugged. They stood in the hallway outside Mick's door, which was as far as Angel would go. "Not a damn thing," he said, "except that Mick is in a bad way."

Angel pressed a hand to her chest, looking as if she'd taken the bullet herself. "The wound?"

Josh knew how close she was to Mick—practically a surrogate mom even though only nine years separated them. Mick's real mother, from what he understood, had been plagued by too many personal weaknesses. She'd died long ago, and Angel and Dane's family had become Mick's. "I'm sorry, I meant that he's been acting...infatuated."

Relieved, Angel bent a chastising look on him. "Mick is a grown man, a very levelheaded man. He doesn't get infatuated."

Josh knew that, which only made it more baffling. Beautiful women flirted with Mick and he hardly noticed. But this one... Josh shook his head. "Call it what you want, but today he chased her down, took a bullet for her without even knowing her name. And according to Zack, the first thing he asked about, even before he got his eyes open, was Delilah."

A slow smile spread over Angel's face. "This is wonderful!"

"Did you hear me?" Beyond respecting her a great deal, Josh knew Angel was one of the chew-'em-up-and-spit-'em-out women Mick had mentioned during their lunch, so he carefully measured his words. "Today, just a few minutes ago, is the first time he officially met her. Before that, he just watched her jog every day." Josh thought about Mick's preoccupation with Delilah and added, "She's not even all that eye-catching."

Angel smacked him on the shoulder. Not hard, but it still stung.

He refused to rub it.

"Looks are nothing, and you should know it by now. Besides, I think she's cute."

Dane, carrying two colas, strolled up behind her. He handed one to his wife and asked, "Who's cute?"

"Mick's woman."

Grinning, Dane said, "That little dynamo in there telling him she won't leave now that he's awake, not even to go home and get a change of clothes? And if she does leave, she absolutely will not take a body-guard with her?" Dane laughed as he sipped his drink. "Both Alec and I offered, at Mick's insistence. Alec even promised her we wouldn't leave him alone, that one of us would be sure to stay with him until she returned. But she's not convinced. If anything, that seemed to have the opposite effect on her."

"I wonder why."

"Because she likes being difficult," Josh pointed out, disgruntled.

Dane grinned. "Actually, I believe she's jealous of Angel."

Angel frowned. "Of me? But Mick and I are like…"

"You don't have to convince me," Dane told her. "But then I know you both well. She doesn't."

"Why would she need a bodyguard?" Angel asked, changing the subject. Dane spent a few minutes explaining about the bizarre aspects of the robbery, and Mick's concerns.

"For whatever reason, I don't think Mick has told her that he's a cop," Dane said. "He tried telling her she could be in danger, but she's blowing the whole thing off as nothing more than a fluke, or a coincidence. I get the feeling he'll have his hands full with that one.''

Josh glared toward the closed door. ''After spending several hours with her today, I can tell you that she's about the most contrary woman I've ever met. All she did was bitch at me.''

Dane raised both brows. ''Let me guess, you tried treating her as you do most women, flirting, teasing—''

''Condescending,'' Angel added.

''I was charming!''

''—and,'' Dane continued, ''she was too smart to fall for it.''

''She wants to do things her own way,'' Josh grumbled, still amazed that she'd taken exception to his manner, ''and damn the consequences. She's far too...independent and stubborn for my tastes.''

Barely stifling a chuckle, Dane clapped him on the shoulder. ''It's good for you, teach you a little humility around the ladies.''

Josh wasn't interested in learning humility, thank you very much. He and the ladies got along just fine. Delilah Piper—well, she was just an aberration, a woman who couldn't be swayed with sound male logic, smiles or compliments. In fact, she'd been rude enough to scoff at his compliments, as if she'd known they were false, which, of course, she hadn't because he was damn good at flattery when he chose to be.

Josh felt renewed pique; no woman had ever scoffed at him before. ''Do you want me to go drag her out of there?''

Dane's expression filled with anticipation. ''Oh yeah, I'd love to see you try.''

True, Josh thought. Knowing her—and, after

spending hours closed up with her in the waiting room, he did indeed feel that he knew her—she'd probably kick him someplace dirty. His groin ached just thinking about it. She'd threatened to do him in once today already, when he wouldn't agree to label her Mick's wife, just so she could sneak in and see him sooner. Obstinate woman.

And besides, brute force wasn't something he'd ever used on a female. He'd only been mouthing off because he'd used up his other tricks on her without success. "I'll see if I can dredge up some diplomacy," he told Angel and Dane, and sauntered into the room with all the enthusiasm of a man headed to the gallows.

One look at Delilah and he was again filled with confusion. What was it about her that had Mick going gaga? The woman was...*lanky.* That's the only word he could think of that described her. Her arms and legs were long, her body slim, her breasts small. She appeared delicate when he knew she was anything but.

He had, however, noticed that she had a very nice tush, not that it made up for the rest of it.

And now she watched him, on alert, as if he had no right to be in the room seeing one of his best friends. His gaze met Alec's and Alec shrugged. Celia stared wide-eyed.

None of them were used to Mick being thwarted. Most times, he told people what needed to be done and they did it. Mick had an air about him that demanded obedience. Women especially went out of their way to make him happy. Not that Mick took advantage of his appeal to women. Just the opposite, he seemed unaware of how they gravitated to him and he was the most discriminating male Josh had ever known. Beautiful women came on to him, but more often than not, Mick showed no interest at all.

Until now.

According to Angel, Mick had been that way since he was sixteen. Always a take-charge guy, always irresistible, but at the moment he looked ready to pull his hair out.

With flagging patience, Mick said, "I want you to be comfortable, Delilah. Go home and take the shower you mentioned earlier. Change your clothes if you want, get something to eat."

"I'm not hungry and I'm used to the clothes now." Her every word exuded stubbornness, though an edge of desperation could be heard, too.

Alec and Celia stood at the foot of the bed. Celia shook her head and Alec narrowed his eyes in contemplation.

Mick looked tired and frustrated and pained as he said, "I don't need you to baby-sit me, Delilah."

Josh decided enough was enough. Mick wasn't in top fighting form or the conversation never would have gone on for so long. He hated seeing his friend this way, wounded and weak.

Josh had handled plenty of women in his day. This one was no different—at least not in the most important ways.

"Of course you need a damn baby-sitter." Josh leaned against the wall, ready to take on Delilah and win. "Good God, Mick, you were dumb enough to get shot in the first place, then dumb enough to pass out. I can understand why she doesn't trust you now to do as the doctors and nurses tell you. You'd probably yank out your IV, wouldn't you? Or get up and parade around the room until you keeled over again. If she doesn't stay right here like a good little mother hen to make sure you behave yourself, you might even—''

Predictably enough, Miss Delilah exploded. She went stiff as a spike, sputtered, then practically shouted, ''Don't you talk to him like that, Josh!''

Celia jumped a good foot at Del's explosive outburst. Alec coughed to cover a laugh. Zack, always laid-back and calm, watched the drama unfold with interest. But then Zack knew Josh and likely suspected his motives.

''Well,'' Josh reasoned, extravagant for the sake of their audience, ''why would you refuse to go home and change out of your rumpled clothes unless you didn't trust him to act intelligently?''

Delilah fried him with a look before bending down to Mick. She said very sweetly, ''I'll be right back.''

When she stalked around the bed, both Celia and Alec scurried to get out of her way. Josh didn't know if it was the scent of mud and sweat that motivated them, or the intent look on her face.

As she passed Josh, she snagged his shirtfront and dragged him out after her. Biting back a victorious laugh, Josh looked over his shoulder in time to see Mick chuckling. Josh sent him a salute.

Once in the hallway, Delilah rounded on him. She opened her mouth to speak, but he beat her to it. ''You need to shower. I can see sweat stains under your arms, and I can smell you.''

Her face flaming with color, she kept her gaze glued on Josh, then turned her head the tiniest bit and sniffed. She wrinkled her nose and frowned.

Josh almost laughed. Truth was, Delilah smelled

kinda nice, like shampoo and lotion and woman, not that he'd ever tell her that. Calmly now, because he didn't want to offend her, he said, "Mick needs you here. I know that. Hell, you're all he's talked about since he came to."

"Really?" She looked skeptical, and hopeful.

"Yep." Seeing her uncertainty, Josh softened. Most of her aggression had been on Mick's behalf, so he couldn't really hold it against her. "He'll be uneasy if he thinks he's imposing. You don't know him like I do. He's not used to relying on anyone. Do you really want to start a relationship that way?"

She stared down at her muddy sneakers and mumbled, "No."

Such a small voice for Delilah! And he noticed she didn't deny the relationship part. Good. At least that meant she was as interested as Mick. Josh would hate to think his friend was the only one smitten.

"He also doesn't want you to be alone. He doesn't worry about women often, so you could show a little gratitude and go easy on him."

Seconds ticked by before she finally admitted, "I didn't—don't—know those men." She looked at him, her eyes troubled. "And I don't want a total stranger waiting around on me while I shower and change. I don't like to impose on others, either."

Josh wanted to curse, to end this awful day by heading home and phoning a reasonable woman, a doting woman who'd give him the comfort of her body and her feminine concern. He did not want to spend more time with this particular woman, who treated him as an asexual nuisance.

But he knew what he needed to do. He drew in a breath and made the ultimate sacrifice. "All right.

Then let me take you home. You can do what needs to be done, then I'll bring you back. You can stay until visiting hours are over. I know he'd appreciate that.''

As if he hadn't made the grand offer, she said, "Maybe Zack could drive me home?"

If it wasn't for Mick... Josh drew a deep breath and reached for control. "Zack can't. He has a four-year-old daughter and he needs to get home to her."

"Oh." Delilah eyed him, apparently liking his plan as little as he did. "I suppose Dane or Alec would be okay...."

He should have said fine, should have let Mick deal with her. Instead, he heard himself say, "Dane and Alec just drove two hours to get here, and I'm sure they'd like to spend their time visiting Mick, not chauffeuring your stubborn butt around town."

Stiffening, she said, "I could take a bus...."

"And Mick would still worry. Someone shot at you today, lady." From what Josh understood, someone had singled her out as a victim. It didn't make sense, and he understood Mick's concern. "You witnessed a burglary and it doesn't matter that you told the police you didn't recognize anyone, that you have no idea what's going on, it's still strange."

She didn't relent, and he said, his patience at an end, "Hell, I promise not to speak to you, all right? I won't even look at you if it'll make you happy."

Using both hands, she covered her face. Her normally proud, straight shoulders hunched and she turned partially away.

Thinking she was about to cry, Josh froze. Damn, but he couldn't deal with weeping women. There was nothing he hated more, nothing that made him feel more helpless. His stomach tightened, cramped. Delilah acted tough and talked tough, but she was still female, delicately built, and she'd been through an ordeal.

But she didn't so much as sniffle. "I don't mean to be nasty," she said from behind her fingers. Her voice was miserable but strong, and devoid of tears. "It's just..." She hesitated for a long minute, then dropped her hands and sighed. "I feel so responsible."

Josh's hostility and impatience melted away. She'd been involved in a robbery, shot at, stuck in the hospital all day in wet, grubby clothes with total strangers. If he'd known her longer, he'd have offered her a hug. But he'd just met her—and so had Mick. Josh was still worried. It wasn't like Mick to fall so hard so fast. He'd never even seen Mick trip. On rare occasions, Mick dated, and then moved on.

Josh couldn't think of a single female, other than family, who Mick would have invited to stay at the hospital with him. Not only would he have found it an intrusion, he was far too private to want anyone around him when he wasn't up to full speed.

In his line of work, Mick naturally had to be careful, and that caution had carried over into other aspects of his life. Or perhaps it had always been there, left over from a less-than-wonderful childhood. But whatever the reason, Josh could tell that for this woman, Mick was throwing caution to the wind.

Settling for a friendly arm around her shoulders, Josh steered her back toward the hospital room. "The last thing Mick would want is for you to feel bad. About anything. As to responsibility, it sure as hell isn't *your* fault those idiots showed up and started shooting. Okay?''

"Thanks." She nodded, and even managed a small smile for him. Josh was struck by that smile, and for the first time, he had an inkling of what Mick felt.

They walked through the door, and she seemed to forget all about Josh the second her gaze landed on Mick. Nonplussed, he watched her hurry back to Mick's bedside. "Josh is going to drive me home, but I'll be right back."

Mick's surprise at the quick turnaround was plain to see as he looked from Josh to Delilah and back again. Josh winked. Oh yeah, he'd have fun ribbing them later with this one. He'd gotten her to do what the rest of them couldn't. He hadn't lost his touch, after all.

"Don't worry, Mick," Josh said, feeling in good humor for the first time since the shooting, "I'll keep a real close eye on her."

That earned him a frown from both Delilah and Mick. Delilah apparently didn't think she needed to be watched, and Mick obviously didn't want any male looking at her too closely. Jealousy, Josh decided, and was glad he'd never suffered such a miserable emotion.

"You really don't have to rush," Mick told Delilah after dragging his attention away from Josh. But it was plain to Josh that Mick wanted her back where he could be the one keeping an eye on her, protecting her, not any other man, not even a friend he trusted. He was also in pain and doing his best to hide it. Damn stubborn fool.

Delilah glanced around the room. "Will your visitors stay all night?"

"No," Mick said, making the decision before anyone else could answer.

Alec coughed again. Celia rushed to assure her. "We'll be at a nearby hotel for the night, but we'll stay here until you get back. How's that?"

As if it was up to her, Delilah nodded. "That'd be perfect. Thank you." Then she bent to kiss Mick again. "I'm going to give my cell phone number to the nurse, just in case." She turned to Josh. "Are you ready?"

"I'll be right there."

She looked suspicious at his delay, but didn't question him on it. She turned and moseyed out.

The door had barely closed before Angel and Dane came back in. Angel propped her hands on her hips and said, "Now that she's not within hearing distance, tell me the truth. Does your shoulder hurt?"

With a crooked grin, Mick admitted, "Hell, yes." Then he turned to Zack. "If you could see about some pain medicine...?"

"The doctor ordered it for when you woke up, but you were too bullheaded to take it."

"It would've made me sleepy."

Josh shook his head. "And God forbid he miss a single second of Delilah Piper's visit."

Zack, always something of a peacemaker as well as an EMT, laughed. "I'll go get your nurse and she can take care of you."

Josh walked over to the bed, where both Dane and Alec now hovered. Josh knew they were dying for some answers. Together the two men ran a private investigations firm, and they could sniff out trouble without even trying.

"The other men got away. The police are still looking, but they haven't turned up anyone."

Mick's curse was especially foul. "What about the one I shot? Did they find out anything from him?"

"The idiot had ID on him. He's Rudy Glasgow, and he's still unconscious." Josh knew that despite Mick's injuries, he'd want to know it all. Still, he hesitated before saying, "It doesn't look good."

Mick dropped back onto the pillow with an aggrieved sigh. "I know my shot to his leg didn't put him under. Was it the head wound from when he fell?"

"Yeah. You two mirror each other—both shot, both with conked heads. Only his was worse. He rattled something in his skull and the docs don't know when he'll come to, which means they don't know when he'll be able to answer questions, if ever. You were lucky that you landed more on Zack than the concrete when you fell."

Not amused, Mick cursed again.

"I also turned your gun over to the officer first on the scene. He insisted, of course, and with you passed out cold..." Josh shrugged.

"That's standard procedure," Mick assured him, not worried. "I'll be issued a new one."

Josh nodded. "I notified your sergeant and he's getting in touch with Internal Affairs."

"Which means I'll have to see the damn psychiatrist, too." He groaned.

"Just procedure?" Josh asked, though he already knew any shooting required a follow-up visit with the shrink, just to keep the officers healthy in mind and body.

"Yeah." Mick looked weary beyond belief. "When she leaves here tonight—"

Dane held up a hand. "We won't let anything happen to her. I promise."

And Josh assumed that meant one or both of them would be tailing her the rest of the night, even after she finished her hospital visit. Delilah wouldn't like it if she knew. But then, Dane and Alec were damn good, so she wouldn't find out unless they wanted her to know.

Alec looked thoughtful, and with his intense, dark features, the look was almost menacing. It had taken Josh some time to get used to him. "So you think the robbery was a sham? Just an excuse to shoot her?"

"They aimed for her head," Mick rumbled in disgust, describing how he'd covered her, and the shooter's angle. He gave details he hadn't given when Delilah was in the room. "They didn't threaten anyone else. Hell, they didn't even look at anyone else."

"But why her?" Dane asked.

"I haven't got a clue. Far as I can figure, she was just a customer, like the other two in the shop."

Though Mick said it, he didn't look quite convinced. Josh didn't like any of it, especially since his friend seemed determined to be in the middle of it all. "I'd better get out there or she'll leave without me."

"She doesn't have a car here, does she?" Mick asked, concerned over the possibility.

"No, but believe me, that wouldn't stop her. Prepare yourself, Mick, because she's about the most obstinate, bullheaded woman I've ever run across." He squeezed Mick's left shoulder. "Take it easy while we're gone."

"You won't let her out of your sight?"

"Just when she showers." He grinned at Mick's warning growl. It amused the hell out of him how possessive his friend had gotten, and how quickly. "Quit worrying. I'll bring her back safe and sound."

CHAPTER THREE

MICK WATCHED JOSH GO, and though he trusted Josh implicitly, he cursed the injury that kept him confined to bed. "She could have been killed today."

Angel sat beside him on the narrow mattress. "Is that why you agreed to go home with her? So you can protect her?"

He nodded, but he saw that both Alec and Dane knew his reasons were more varied than that. And more territorial, more sexual. Protecting wasn't the only activity he had in mind. He'd never burned for a woman before, but now he felt like an inferno ready to combust.

Why the hell would someone want her dead?

Mick remembered the way she'd been looking the place over, the way she'd initially smiled at the men—a smile he'd considered merely polite, stranger to stranger.

Zack came back in, the nurse trailing him. She gave Mick a dose of morphine through his IV, and seconds later the discomfort receded and lethargy settled in.

Mick relished the relief from the searing pain, even while he fought to stay awake and sharp enough to think.

"Relax," Dane ordered him.

"I have to figure out what's going on." A vague sense of impending doom, of limited time plagued him.

Dane shook his head. "No. You're in no shape to start snooping around. Let it go for now. The bastard who shot you isn't going anywhere, and he won't stay out forever. When he comes to, you can question him. Or better yet, let someone else do it."

"No." Even with the morphine clouding his mind, Mick knew he wasn't about to pass up the opportunity to get some answers. "I need to call my sergeant, to tell him I want to stay advised. And I need to talk to the head nurse. I need to—"

Angel pressed her fingers over his mouth. "You need to sleep. I have a feeling when Delilah gets back, you'll be determined to stay awake and alert."

Alec cocked a brow while cuddling Celia to his side. "He wouldn't want to miss a minute of that, as Josh said."

Mick relaxed, thinking of Delilah's emotional strength, her boldness, how she'd kissed him, her taste, her heat. They were right—he didn't want to miss that. In the next instant, he fell asleep.

MICK WOKE TO THE SOUND of quiet tapping. The room was dim, with only one light glowing in the corner. The curtains were all closed, but he could tell it was night. He'd probably slept another four hours or so, and it enraged him. There was a lot to consider, a lot to do, not the least of which would be getting to know Delilah.

The tapping continued, light and quick. He bit back

a groan as he turned his head on the soft pillow and zeroed in on the source. There, sprawled in the room's only chair, a laptop resting across her thighs, was Delilah.

God, she was lovely.

A nurse had evidently brought her a pillow and blanket in an effort to help make her comfortable. The padded lounge chair could have served as a bed in a pinch. Delilah had the back reclined, the pillow behind her shoulders, the blanket thrown over the arm of the chair.

Her rich dark hair, freshly washed, swung loose and silky around her shoulders. The light from the laptop cast a soft blue halo around her. Her eyes looked mysterious, purposeful, as she typed away. Mick watched her, aware of the acceleration in his pulse, the expanding sexual tension.

She'd changed into a pair of baggy jeans and a miniscule, snowy-white, cropped T-shirt. Her sandals were off, tucked beneath the chair, her bare feet propped on the edge of the counter in front of the window. Two flowering plants now sat there, no doubt from Angel and Celia.

Delilah's slim legs seemed to go on forever, and Mick, still only half-awake, pictured them around his hips, hugging him tight while he rode her, long and slow and so damn deep. He visually followed the trail of those incredibly long legs, and when he came to her hips he imagined them lifted by his hands, her legs sprawled wide while he tasted her, licked her and made her scream out a climax.

A groan broke free from him and Delilah jumped, nearly dumping her laptop. "Mick!"

Heat throbbed just below his skin. He was so aroused he hurt, but he'd done nothing more than look at her and give his imagination free rein. What would it be like to actually have her?

He swallowed and said with a drawling, raw deliberation, "I don't suppose you'd like to give me another kiss?"

Slowly, her gaze glued to his, she set the laptop on the floor and stood. "I didn't mean to be so brazen earlier. I just…it amazed me that anyone would do what you did."

"So you kissed me?"

Arching one dark brow, she half laughed. "I wanted to devour you, actually."

The shadows in the room did interesting things to her body. "Do you always say exactly what you think?"

She shrugged. "I guess so. I know I shouldn't, but I'm out of practice when it comes to this sort of thing."

"You can say whatever you want to me, okay?"

She nodded. "You saved my life, and you got hurt in the bargain. I saw you and I just…wanted to kiss you."

That didn't sound right to Mick. "So it was about gratitude?"

"Yes…no. I'm not sure." She made a helpless gesture, then shifted her feet and tucked her silky hair behind her ear. "The thing is, touching you seems…right."

He understood that. Touching her seemed right, too. Hell, devouring her seemed right. He'd have gladly gotten started right that minute, but she stood there, waiting, uncertain, very different now that they were alone. She wasn't as defensive, and there was no reason for her to be protective.

No woman had ever been protective of him. Except Angel, but that was back when he'd been a boy. With Delilah it felt different.

"Everyone else has left?"

"Yes. Angel and Celia gave me the number of the hotel where they're staying so you could call if you needed them. The man, Alec, said you had his cell number if you wanted to make sure he was on duty. Whatever that means."

Mick nodded, understanding perfectly. Alec would wait and watch for Delilah to leave. He'd protect her until Mick could take over. There wasn't a more capable or harder man than Alec Sharpe. Knowing he'd keep his eye on Delilah gave Mick a new measure of relief.

When he didn't speak, she gestured at the flowers and said, "The women bought these in the gift shop."

"That's just like them."

She fidgeted. "They're…friends of yours?"

"More like family. As close as family can be without all the baggage."

"Oh." A mix of emotions crossed her features—confusion and relief. "Josh and Zack said they'd be in touch in the morning."

"I figured as much." She stood there before him, barefoot and fidgety, and Mick used the opportunity to look at her. The loose jeans hung low on her slim hips, showing a strip of pale belly between the waistband and the hem of her shirt. He saw the barest hint of her navel, enough to fire his blood, to make his mouth go dry.

He glanced at her breasts and found himself smiling. She was indeed small, but still so damn sexy he ached all the way down to his toes. As he stared, her nipples tightened, pushing him over the edge.

He needed her closer. Because she looked uncertain, he asked, "You didn't like kissing me?"

"I did!" she blurted, then bit her bottom lip. She twined her fingers together and shifted her bare feet again. "I just didn't want you to think that, you know, just because you were nice enough to save me that you had to..."

"Had to what?" Inside, he grinned, knowing what she thought, but in the mood to tease her.

"You know. Be sexual with me." His gaze shot to her face and she rushed to add, "I wasn't sure if you felt the same way I did. I mean, you're incredible. Gorgeous and sexy and hard and...what woman wouldn't want you? But I'm just me. I didn't know if you wanted to—"

Just that quickly, his humor fled. "I want to."

"You do?"

He was hard, and there wasn't a damn thing he could do about it. "Come here, Delilah."

As if reassured, she strode to the bed and sat beside him, this time to his left. "You want me to kiss you again?"

Unwilling to rush her or scare her off, he didn't

move. He wanted her to be as free as she'd first been, taking what she wanted from him, when she wanted it. Was there a better male fantasy than having a bold woman who knew her own mind and went after what she needed?

Holding himself still, Mick said softly, "I'd love for you to kiss me again."

"You don't need anything first?" She searched his face, looking him over, he assumed, for signs of discomfort. "A drink? More pain medicine?"

I need you. "No."

Tentatively, she laid a hand on his chest. "You're so warm," she whispered, her fingers lightly caressing, edging under the loose neckline of the hospital gown. "I watched you sleep for a while and it made me nuts." She glanced at him, meeting his gaze. "You even look good when you sleep. I had to get out my laptop to keep busy, just so I wouldn't end up touching you. I didn't want to wake you."

Mick had no response to that, other than a rush of heat. The thought of her watching him and wanting him fed his awareness of her, making it more acute.

She touched his throat, then slid her slender fingers over his uninjured shoulder. "I think," she whispered, watching the progress of her hand, "that you're about the sexiest man I've ever seen."

If they'd been anywhere other than a hospital room, he'd have pulled her under him. He shifted, felt the pain deep in his shoulder and cursed.

She quickly pulled away, then poured him a drink of water and lifted the straw to his mouth. "Shh. This will help."

Getting her under him would help, but he didn't say so. He drank deeply, hoping the icy water would cool his urgency, return a measure of his control. It was insane to want a woman this way.

After setting the paper cup aside, Delilah again rested her hand on his chest. Her gaze locked with his. "Your heart is racing."

"I'm horny," he explained, because anything more eloquent was beyond him while she continued to touch him.

Her light blue eyes twinkled and her lush lips curled into a satisfied feminine smile. "No sex for you, at least not until you're healed."

That "not until" stipulation—which pretty much guaranteed he'd eventually have her—about stopped his heart. Without another word she leaned down and touched her mouth to his. She was gone before Mick could respond.

Her blue eyes were warmer, softer, and he rumbled, "Again."

She looked at his mouth, bent, stroked his bottom lip with her hot little tongue. "Do you like that?" she breathed.

He groaned.

Still so close he tasted her breath, she asked, "You're not married or anything, are you?"

"No."

"At first, I was afraid Angel or Celia—"

"No." Using his left hand, he touched her hair. Warmth, softness. "I love your hair." He tangled his fingers in the silky mass and brought her mouth back flush with his.

"Thank you," she murmured, and obligingly gave him the longer kiss he wanted.

Dull pain pushed at Mick, but he blocked it from his mind. It was nothing compared to the feel of her. "Open your mouth."

She did, then accepted the slow, deliberate thrust of his tongue. He stroked deep, taking her mouth, exploring all the textures and heat, and the taste that was uniquely Delilah.

They both groaned.

Delilah pulled back. She touched his jaw and asked, "Did I hurt you?"

He had to stop this or he'd lose it completely. "Of course not."

"I'm not married or anything, either."

Mick, still on the verge of a meltdown, managed to lift a brow at that candid disclosure, and she shrugged. "I just thought you should know," she said, her words coming in soft, uneven pants, "being as we're...well, doing this."

"This?" She stayed close and the scent of her, lighter now and touched with lotion and powder, filled him. He wanted to wrap himself in it, wanted to hold her close to his body until their scents mingled.

"The whole sex thing." She drew a breath, but kept her gaze steady, unwavering. "I assume that's where we're headed. I mean, I'll have you all to myself in my apartment and I want you. I assume you want me, too."

He could hardly believe what she'd just said. No woman had ever come right out and so boldly stated her intentions to have an affair with him. Women sometimes chased him, but they were subtle, never so up front with their motives. They teased, flirted, advanced and retreated.

They didn't advance and advance.

"What is it you do?" she asked, unconcerned with his bemused astonishment—maybe even unaware that she'd astonished him. "I've never known anyone who carried a gun and shot people."

He should have been prepared for that, because he knew she'd ask. But he was still stuck on that affair statement, attempting to get his head back together—a near impossible feat because all he could think about now was starting that damn affair. The sooner the better.

"Mick?"

He wanted to tell her the truth, but he knew nothing about her except that she evidently had an enemy, someone who wanted her dead, someone who would have succeeded if that bullet hadn't been sidetracked by his shoulder. He also knew she was eccentric, a woman heedless of her surroundings, honest to a fault, brazen and stubborn one minute, shy and uncertain the next. And he knew she wanted him, not as much as he wanted her, but enough.

His innate caution warned him against going too fast. Thinking of Dane and Alec, he lied. "I'm a private investigator."

Her eyes widened with unrestrained excitement. "Seriously?"

She looked so comically surprised, he grinned. "Yeah." Starting things off with a lie wasn't the best course of action, but he had few choices until he found out what was going on. If all went as planned, he'd be able to tell her the truth soon enough. She'd understand his reasoning and forgive his deception. He'd see to it.

"Wow." She settled on the side of his bed, her hip against his, her hand still resting on his chest. "I could use you for research."

Mick did a double take, momentarily getting his mind off the idea of pulling her down on the narrow bed beside him. "Research for what?"

She shrugged in the direction of the laptop. "I'm a writer. I'm always looking for easy ways to research. From the horse's mouth is always the easiest."

A writer? Now, somehow that fit. The creative types were always a bit different, as far as he knew. "What do you write?"

"Mysteries." She waggled her eyebrows. "Fun stuff. Whodunits with a few laughs and some racy romance thrown in."

It was Mick's turn to say, "Wow." Then he added, "Have you ever been published?"

"Well, yeah." She seemed to consider that a stupid question.

She'd said it so casually, as if it were nothing. He'd never met a novelist before, and now he planned to sleep with one. "How many books have you done?"

"I've had four published so far, with two more in the works." She nodded toward her laptop. "I'm working under a deadline right now."

"How old are you?" Mick didn't think she looked

old enough to have one book published, much less four. He'd always pictured writers as more seasoned, scholarly types.

His question made her grin. "Twenty-five, almost twenty-six. I sold my first book when I was twenty-three."

Mick eyed her anew. A mystery writer. He had to shake his head at the novelty of it. And here he'd claimed to be a PI. A match made in heaven. "I'll be damned," he said, still dealing with his amazement. "Maybe I could read one sometime?"

"Sure. I'll show them to you when we get to my apartment. By the way, I drove myself here so I could take us both home tomorrow. Your friend Josh was pretty ticked off about it. He was going to tattle, and you should have seen his face when we found you asleep. He looked so frustrated, I thought his head would explode. Of course, for that one, it might be an improvement."

Mick closed his eyes. Some maniac had tried to kill her, and here she'd been on the road alone again, vulnerable. He could just imagine Josh's frustration. "Delilah."

"Del."

"Excuse me?" He opened his eyes again and stared at her. Hard.

"If we're going to be friends, you may as well call me what everyone else does."

"And everyone else calls you…*Del?*" It sounded like a man's name to Mick.

She shrugged. "It's what I've always gone by. Only my father called me Delilah, usually if he was angry, and he died a few years ago. Now I only use my full name when I write."

Mick wondered how her father had died, if she had any other family left.

He shook off his distraction. He'd have time to ask her about her family later. Keeping his tone stern, he said, "Josh was right to be angry. Someone tried to shoot you today. You shouldn't be alone, not until I—" He pulled back on that, quickly saying instead, "Until the police can figure out what's going on."

She flapped her hand at him, waving away his concerns, then let it settle on his abdomen. He nearly shot off the bed. Every muscle in his body clenched and his cock throbbed. He'd never been in such a bad way before.

If she moved her fingers just a few inches lower, she could make him feel so much better. He closed his eyes against the image of her soft hand holding him, stroking him. Too fast, he was moving way too fast.

"I don't think," she murmured, watching her hand on his body, "that they were really shooting at me. Why would they?" She looked up at him, her hand thankfully still. "I mean, they aimed at me, but I think it was just a random thought. They were criminals and they got thwarted because the police showed up, and they were mad, so they wanted to shoot someone."

Nearly choking on an odd combination of explosive desire, frustration and protectiveness, Mick asked, "And you think they chose you, a woman who didn't have a thing to do with anything, a woman just visiting the store? They didn't look rattled or frenzied. They looked like they meant to shoot you—you specifically—before they took off."

Her fingers spread wide and her brow furrowed. "I don't know. I didn't notice anything like that."

Her baby finger was a quarter inch from the head of his penis. His body strained, fighting against his control. He *needed* to lift his hips, to thrust into her hand.

"You," he rasped, "are the person they accused of setting off an alarm, when you hadn't moved and weren't anywhere near anything that could have triggered an alarm."

That made him think of something else, and he forced himself to concentrate on things other than her touch. "How did the cops know? Did anyone tell you?"

She stared blankly at his bandaged shoulder, deep in thought. "The officer who questioned me said someone on the street noticed the guns when he was walking by, and he used his cell phone to call them."

"Honey, listen to me." Mick put his left hand on her bare waist, between the bottom of her shirt and the top of her jeans. Her skin was smooth and warm, her muscles taut. "Did you recognize either of them? Was there anything at all familiar about them?"

"No, of course not." She looked at her hand on his abdomen, then at his erection. He read her thoughts as if she'd spoken them aloud. Instinctively, he tightened, which brought forth a moan of pain from both physical discomfort and sharp anticipation.

"You're in a bad way," she said in a hushed,

husky tone filled with understanding and her own measure of need.

He wanted to howl. He wanted to ask her to go ahead and stroke him, hard and fast, that she use her mouth...

"Delilah..."

"Del," she whispered, and started to glide her hand lower.

Using his left hand, Mick caught her wrist. His hold was tight, too tight, but he felt stretched so taut he was ready to snap. "I'm in worse than a bad way," he rasped. "I'm on the very edge, and if you touch me I won't be able to control myself."

She tilted her head, staring at him as if she didn't quite grasp his meaning.

"I'll come," he said bluntly, then watched for her reaction.

She stayed still, but probably only because he held her slender wrist in an iron grip, refusing to let her move.

"This is difficult for me," he explained, watching her, needing her to understand. He felt more tension than he had at fifteen, when he'd seen his first fully naked female, there for the taking. He'd lost control then; he was ready to lose control now. He ground his teeth and insisted, "I'm not usually like this."

Her eyes, warm and heavy-lidded, looked him over. "You're hurt, in bed. This is a strange situation."

"It has nothing to do with any of that and everything to do with you. I want you bad, and have since the first time I saw you."

He could tell that admission pleased her. "Today?" she asked,

Gently, he lifted her hand away from his body so he could carry on a coherent conversation. He brought her hand to his chest and kept it there. "I saw you two weeks ago, near a building I own. You were heading to the post office."

Her frown reappeared. "I never noticed you," she said. Then, chagrined, she added, "I was probably plotting, and I don't pay much attention then. My mind tends to wander."

He thought about how she'd been examining the jewelry store, studying it, prowling from one corner to the other. "Plotting...what?"

"My book, of course."

She said it as if it should have been obvious to him.

"So," she asked, "you saw me a few weeks ago?"

"And many times since then. I eat at Marco's a lot, and you—"

"Jog by there a lot." Her smile was very sweet. "Whenever I have a deadline, I need to get outside at least once a day to clear my head so I can really think and plot. So I jog. But I've never noticed you before."

"I've watched you almost every day. Today when I saw you actually stop and go into the jewelry store, I decided it was time to introduce myself."

Her countenance darkened. "Instead you saved my life."

They stared at each other. The air was charged, until a nurse started backing in, dragging a cart with her.

Delilah moved so fast, Mick was stunned. She snagged the pillow from her chair and dropped it over his lap. To the nurse she said, "Time to check him again?"

The nurse looked over her shoulder and smiled. "I'll only be a minute." Then she turned to Mick. "For an injured man, you're about the healthiest thing I've ever seen."

Mick was in no mood for small talk. "Is that right?" he asked, while watching Delilah.

"Yep. Great lungs, great reflexes. The epitome of health. I wish everyone would take such good care of their bodies."

Delilah made a choking sound at that observation. "I'll, uh, just get out of your way." She tapped a few buttons on her laptop, closed it and set it on the window ledge. She picked up a large tote from the floor and swung the strap over her shoulder, saying to Mick, "I'm going to run down to the coffee shop and grab a bite to eat. Do you want anything? You slept through dinner."

The nurse said, "We can still get him a tray."

Delilah leaned close and whispered, "It was nasty-looking stuff. I'd pass if I was you."

The nurse heard and grinned. "The coffee shop has pretty good sandwiches and chips and desserts. You're not on a restricted diet, so if something sounds good…"

Delilah started out. "I'll surprise you."

"Delilah—"

"Del," she said, then added, "Don't worry. I'll be right back. We'll pretend we're having a picnic."

And before he could warn her to be cautious, she was gone. Mick sank back against the pillows, the ache in his shoulder receding to no more than a dull, annoying throb. The nurse offered him more pain medication, but he passed. He needed all his wits about him to deal with Delilah Piper. Otherwise, he thought, grinning shamelessly, she'd probably take sexual advantage of him in his weakened physical shape.

He could hardly wait.

The nurse finished her poking and prodding, changed his bandage, and then, at his request, handed him the phone.

He called Josh. A woman answered—no surprise there—and Mick heard her grumbling, heard the squeaking of bedsprings, before Josh came on the line.

"You're either feeling much better or much worse if you're making a call."

"Much better," Mick told him, and he knew it was only a partial lie. "Can you bring me a change of clothes tomorrow? The nurse said I should be ready to get out of here by eleven."

"Sure thing, but it'll have to be early. I'm on duty starting at eight."

As a fireman, Josh worked varying hours, usually four days on, four days off. On his off days—today being one—he spent a lot of time with women.

Zack, an EMT stationed right next door to the fire department, was just the opposite. He spent all his spare time with his daughter and only rarely made time for women, and then only when his hormones refused to let him put it off any longer.

"If it's inconvenient, I can ask Zack."

"It's no problem. I'd planned to check up on you anyway, just to make sure your little woman hadn't done you in."

"You don't like her?" Mick asked, not really caring, but curious all the same. Personally, he found everything about Delilah unique and enticing, even her damned stubbornness, which had earlier about driven him nuts.

"She's...different."

True enough, Mick thought.

"And she took exception to me right off the bat." Mick grinned. That was probably a first for Josh.

"She's not like other women, and she'll take some getting used to. But it appears she's as nuts about you as you are about her, and I suppose that's all that really matters." There was a muffled sound as someone snatched the receiver away from Josh and he apparently wrestled it back. Mick heard him growl, "Just hang on. I'll only be a minute."

Chuckling, Mick said, "I won't keep you."

"S'no problem. She'll wait. So, what's it to be? Jeans? And I guess some type of button shirt?"

"That'd be easiest. I'm sure you can find your way around my house."

A feminine whisper, insistent and imploring, sounded in the background. Mick grinned again. "G'night, Josh."

"Hey, before you go, you should know that Alec

is hanging around, waiting to take care of things for you.''

Mick appreciated the subtle way Josh explained that with his lady friend listening. "Thanks. I'll ring him next.''

He disconnected his call with Josh and punched in Alec's number. He imagined Delilah would return any minute, and he wanted to make sure things were set first.

"Sharpe.''

"It's me, Alec. Where are you?''

"Hanging out in the parking lot.''

"Damn, I hate to do that to you.''

He could hear the smile in Alec's tone when he said, "Celia's with me. It's no problem.''

That made Mick smile, too. He could just imagine the two of them necking like teenagers. Alec was still a bad ass of the first order, but with Celia, he was a pussycat. "Why don't you head out and I'll call you when she decides to leave?''

The door opened and Delilah came through, her arms laden with paper bags and disposable cups of steaming liquid. Mick eyed her cautiously, not sure how much she'd heard.

She set everything down and turned to him with a smile. "Is that Josh?''

"No, it's, uh, Alec.'' He could hear Alec laughing in his ear. He knew they all appreciated the unique effect Delilah had on him.

"Alec?'' That surprised her, he could tell, but not for long. "Well, tell him to go home and go to bed.

I'm not leaving tonight, so I don't need a body-guard."

Mick scowled. "Delilah..."

"Del." She sat on the side of the bed and took the phone from his hand, then said into the receiver, "I'm going to stay the night. But thanks for thinking of me, anyway."

And then she hung up.

CHAPTER FOUR

AT TEN O'CLOCK, the doctor gave Mick the okay to leave, together with a long list of instructions. Del listened intently and felt confident that she could take care of everything that needed to be done.

Angel and Celia, along with their husbands, had come and gone already. They'd been there since early morning, but because Delilah now realized that they were in fact Mick's family, she enjoyed the attention they lavished on him. He treated both women with an avuncular ease, not with the heated awareness he'd shown her.

Unfortunately, Josh had shown up, too, at the crack of dawn. She'd been asleep when he'd arrived, and was forced to awaken to his scowling face. He'd seemed suspicious of her overnight stay, as if he thought she might have molested Mick in his sleep. Stupid man.

Though Josh was uncommonly handsome, and could be witty when he chose to be, she wasn't at all certain she liked him. Whenever he looked at her, his demeanor plainly said he found her lacking. He distrusted her interest in Mick, and showed confusion at Mick's interest in her.

Nevertheless, she did appreciate his friendship with

Mick. Willingly, he'd brought Mick clothes to wear home, then insisted she leave the room while he helped Mick dress. She would have stubbornly re-fused—*she* wanted to help him dress!—except Mick had wanted her to leave, too.

Delilah had already washed her face and brushed her hair and teeth while his family visited. They'd shown up just as Josh was leaving, and she couldn't help but feel a twinge of poignant sadness, seeing how loved he was. He had a good family, loyal friends, and she envied him that.

Hoping to make a better impression on them today than she had yesterday, she'd applied a little makeup and exchanged her slept-in T-shirt for a dark-rose tank top. Though the hospital was cool, out the win-dow she could already see heat rising off the blacktop in the parking lot.

Now that they were alone again, Mick paced around the room, waiting for an orderly to bring a wheelchair. To Del's discerning eye, he looked rug-gedly handsome with his morning whiskers and tired eyes. He also looked a little shaky. She wanted to coddle him, but she'd already figured out that he wasn't a man used to relying on others.

"Does your family live close?"

He glanced up at her, clearly distracted. With his arm in a sling and his eyes narrowed, he looked like a wounded pirate. "A coupla hours away. They'll be back over the weekend, I'm sure." His dark gaze sharpened. "Will that be a problem?"

"To have them visit? Of course not. For as long

as you stay with me, I want you to be completely comfortable. It'll be your home, too.''

He looked undecided, as if there was more he wanted to say, then he just shook his head. ''We need to come to a few understandings.''

''Oh?'' Seeing Mick flat on his back in bed was one thing. Him standing straight and tall—all six feet three inches of him, moving around the room with flexing muscle and barely leashed impatience—was another. He was an intimidating sight. An arousing sight.

''I want a few promises from you.'' He stalked toward her, as if ready to pounce, and she felt her heart tripping.

She was a tall woman, meeting many men eye-to-eye. Not so with Mick. He looked down at her, his dark eyes drawing her in, and without thought Del went on tiptoe and touched her mouth to his.

He froze for a beat, then slanted his head to better fit their mouths together, and caught her with his good arm at the same time. He carefully gathered her close, his large hand sliding up her back to her nape and holding her immobile.

Del was acutely aware of his arm in the sling between their bodies. Her breast brushed against the stiff cotton restraint and she shuddered, trying to keep space between them so she wouldn't inadvertently hurt him.

''Relax,'' he whispered, and then his hand left her neck to coast down her spine, down and down until he was squeezing her bottom, cuddling, drawing her up and in until her pelvis nudged his groin. He made a rough sound of pleasure.

Del pulled her mouth away and rested her forehead on his chest. "This is incredible," she groaned.

"I know." He kissed her temple and asked, "How many bedrooms do you have?"

Her nerve endings jumped with excitement. "I have two, but I was thinking we'd—"

The orderly pushed into the room with the wheelchair and gave them a cheery greeting.

Del felt heat flood her face, more so when Mick gave her a scorching look of understanding. He started to pick up the small bag of items he had to take home, but Del rushed to beat him to it.

"You just sit," she said, trying to regain some composure, "and I'll get this." Mick kept her so flustered, she could barely think, and she almost left her laptop behind. Without preamble, the orderly plopped nearly everything into Mick's lap and started out the door. Del hustled after them.

"It's stupid to ride in a wheelchair when I'm perfectly capable of walking."

"And smooching," the orderly said in agreement, even more cheerful now that he knew what he'd interrupted. "But it's hospital policy."

Mick stayed silent until they got into the car and were on their way. He seemed inordinately alert, watching everything and everyone, and he soon had Del on edge.

"Do all PIs act like you?"

Mick didn't bother to glance her way when he said, "Yeah."

"Are you going to do this the whole time you're with me?"

Again, he said, "Yeah." But then he turned to face her. "You were shot at, Delilah. I wish I could blow it off as bad luck on your part—being in the wrong place at the wrong time—but I can't. Not yet. Not until the police have a chance to talk to the guy I shot, and that can't happen until he comes to."

She bit her lip. "Do you think he'll die?"

"I doubt it." He turned to look back out the window, hiding his expression from her, but she heard the contempt in his tone when he added, "But don't feel bad if he does."

"I wouldn't. I mean, I don't. He could have killed someone."

"That's about it."

Given his surly tone, she decided a change of topic was in order. They stopped at a light and she looked Mick over. His hair was thick and shiny and a little too long. The whiskers on his face, combined with the tiredness of his eyes, made her heart swell. Today he wore the softest, most well-worn jeans she'd ever seen on a man. They hugged his thick thighs and his heavy groin and his lean hips and tight buttocks.

Her pulse leaped at the thought of that gorgeous body beneath the clothes. Tonight, she'd get to see all of him. She'd make sure of it. She was so wrapped up in those thoughts, she almost missed the light turning green.

She eased the car forward, while her thoughts stayed attuned to Mick.

The shirt Josh had brought him was snowy-white

cotton, buttoned down the front, and looked just as soft as the jeans. The thick bandage on his shoulder could be seen beneath, as could the heavy muscles of his chest, his biceps. "The doctor says you can shower," she told him with a croak in her voice. "But he doesn't want you to soak."

"Right now, a shower will feel like heaven."

"Will you need anything in particular? I could run by your place after I drop you off and pick you up anything you need."

"Josh grabbed me a change of socks and boxers. Angel's taking care of the rest later today. For now, whatever soap and shampoo you have will work." He glanced at her, smiling just a bit. "Do you use scented stuff?"

"No."

His eyes went almost black. "Good. I love the way you smell. I'm glad it's you and not from a bottle."

Del tightened her hands on the wheel. Boy, much more of that and she wouldn't make it home. Luckily, he stayed silent for the rest of the ride, and Del didn't bother trying to draw him out again. Her heart couldn't take his idea of casual conversation.

She pulled up to the garage in front of her building. She had to pay extra to park her car there, but she knew if she left it on the street, it'd likely get stripped. She said as much to Mick as she turned off the ignition.

"Yeah, I know. I told you I own that building next door, right?"

Del rushed around to his door to help him—and got a disgruntled frown for her efforts. He was suddenly in an oddly defensive mood, and she didn't understand him.

"You told me. I wasn't sure if you meant the building to the left or the right."

He grunted. The building to the left was a shambles. His building was nicely maintained. "Alec used to rent from me, before he married Celia. The agency where he works is located between here and where he lives now."

Del cocked a brow. "If he doesn't live *here* now, why did he follow us?"

Mick jerked around. Wary, he asked, "What are you talking about?"

She rolled her eyes. "Your friend is pretty hard to miss, looking like Satan and all. I saw him a few cars behind us. I suppose this is more of your protection?"

Tilting his head back, Mick stared at the heavens. "Something like that." When he looked at her, she could almost feel his resolve. "I don't have a gun right now. The cops confiscated it as evidence."

Del gasped. "They're not going to accuse you of anything, are they?"

"No, it's routine to take any weapon used in a shooting. I'll get another one before the day is out, but until then, I wanted someone armed to keep an eye on things."

Fascinating. He spoke about guns with the same disregard that she gave to groceries. "This is all really extreme, you know."

"It's all really necessary, as far as I'm concerned." Then he added, "Trust me, honey. This is what I do, and I'm not willing to take any chances with you."

That sounded nice, as if he might be starting to like her. But maybe, Del thought, all private detectives were as cautious as Mick. She had no comparisons to go by; she'd never known a PI before.

Shrugging, she decided not to fight what she couldn't change, and hefted out her laptop. She put the leather strap of the carrying case over her shoulder along with her tote, and then reached inside for his bag.

Mick caught her shoulder with his left hand. "Something we need to clear up."

Del peeked up at him. He looked too serious, almost grim. Getting to know this man, with all the twists and turns of his personality, would be exhilarating. "Yes?"

He relieved her of his bag, then her laptop, holding both casually in his left hand as if they weighed no more than a feather pillow. "I'm not an invalid."

Her temper sparked. "No, of course not. But you are wounded and you're not supposed to strain yourself."

Without warning, he leaned down and gave her a loud, smacking kiss. His expression was amused and chagrined and determined. "It doesn't strain me, I promise."

"But you can only use the one arm."

Slow and wicked, his grin spread. "I can do a lot," he whispered in a rough drawl, "with one arm."

Her stomach curled at the way he said that and what she knew he inferred. She cleared her throat. "I see."

"Good. Now lead the way."

She didn't want to. She wanted to insist that he let her help him. He'd done enough already, more than enough. Too much. The man had a bullet in him, thanks to her.

She turned and marched toward the front stairs. The entry door was old and heavy, and she hurried to open it, anxious to get Mick settled inside.

Together they climbed the steep stairs to the upper landing, where she used her key on both of the locks for her apartment door, one of them a dead bolt. Being a runner, she made the climb with ease, breathing as normally as ever when she reached the top. She half expected Mick, with his injuries and his load, to huff at least a bit, but he didn't.

He did, however, keep a vigilant watch. "I'm relieved to see the landlord keeps the place secure. Not all the buildings in this area are safe."

Del looked at him over her shoulder as she reached inside and flipped a wall switch. She didn't tell him that she'd had the dead bolt installed recently. The front door opened directly into her living room, and one switch turned on both end-table lamps. She said only, "I'm not an idiot. I wouldn't endanger myself."

She tossed her tote onto the oversize leather sofa to her right and reached for her laptop. Mick, who'd been looking around, taking in her modest apartment, held it out of reach, lifting it over his head as if he didn't have a bullet in his other arm, as if the pain wasn't plain on his face. His strength amazed her.

"Where do you want it?"

Sighing, Del pointed to her desk in the corner, where a half wall separated her kitchen area from the rest of the room. Her desk was the only modern, truly functional piece of furniture she had. A computer occupied the center of the tiered piece, with a fax machine, a printer and a copier close at hand. There were file folders and papers stacked everywhere, notes, magazines, interviews she hadn't yet put into the file cabinet behind the desk. Reference books littered the floor.

Mick lifted a brow and boldly glanced at her papers as he set the laptop down.

His curiosity would have to be appeased another time, Del decided. She took his arm and steered him toward the narrow hallway on the opposite side of the room. "The bathroom is this way. You can shower while I change the sheets. Are you hungry?"

He'd never admit it, she knew, but he looked ready to drop, pain tightening his mouth and darkening his eyes. Twice she'd seen him rub at his temples when he didn't know she was looking. The doctor had told her that he was as likely to have headaches from his fall as pain from his wound. Del had a hunch the two were combining against him.

"After you finish," she said gently, but with as much authority as she could summon, "you'll need to take your medicine."

Mick stopped in the bathroom doorway and caught her chin with his hand. His gaze burned, touching on her mouth, her throat, her breasts. "After I finish," he said, his fingertips tenderly caressing her skin, "I intend to see about you."

Her knees almost went weak. "Me?" It was a dumb question; she knew exactly what he meant.

Nodding slowly, he said, "All that teasing you've been doing, all that talk about starting an affair, and your bold touching. I'm beyond ready."

She really did need to learn a little discretion, she thought, now wishing she hadn't told him all her intentions. But she was used to going after what she wanted, and he'd been irresistible, a man unlike any she'd ever known. Everything about him turned her on, from the protectiveness she'd never received before, to his strength and intensity, to his rough velvet voice and drool-worthy bod. The man was sexy emotionally and physically, and she wanted him.

She caught his wrist and kissed his palm. "Mick, you need to rest. There'll be plenty of time for..."

He carried her hand to the thick erection testing the worn material of his jeans. Her heart dropped to her stomach, then shot into her throat.

"You think," he whispered roughly, his eyes closing at the feel of her hand on him, "that I can rest with that? The answer is no."

Her palm tingled and of their own accord her fingers began to curl around him. He lifted her hand away, leaned down and kissed her. "I just need fifteen minutes to shower and shave."

Carrying his bag into the room with him, he turned and closed the door, leaving Del standing there with her lips parted and her eyes glazed and her muscles quivering. She sucked in a breath and let her head drop forward to the door, bracing herself there until she stopped trembling.

His effect on her was startling, almost too much to

bear. She'd given up on men as too much trouble, with not enough payoff. But with a mere look, Mick could make her hot, and when he touched her, or she touched him, the need was overwhelming.

She heard the shower start and realized she hadn't reminded him to be careful. She leaned close and said loudly, "Don't soak your shoulder! The doctor said that was a no-no."

Just as loudly, he retorted, "I was there, Delilah, remember?" And then she heard the rustling of the shower curtain and knew he was naked, knew he was wet....

She turned and hurried away.

When he'd answered her, he'd sounded distinctly irritable. Well, hell. Heaven knew, he was likely to be doubly so when he found out she had no intention of making love with him today. It would be too much for him, and there was a good chance he'd injure his shoulder anew.

No, she couldn't let him do that.

She also couldn't let him go unsatisfied. She closed her eyes, feeling wicked and sinful and anxious. There was only one thing to do. Granted, *she* was likely to end up the frustrated one, but that was a small price to pay to a man who'd played her hero, a man who'd saved her life. And she had no doubt he'd make it up to her later. She may not have known him long, but she knew that much about him already. The man wanted her—more than any man ever had.

It was a heady feeling. She liked it.

She especially liked him.

MICK FOUND HER in the kitchen, staring into her refrigerator as if pondering what to fix. A glass of iced tea sat on the counter.

He shook his head, not yet announcing himself. Foolish woman. How could she possibly think he'd want food when she stood there looking more than edible? Oh yeah, he wanted to eat her up. And he would, slowly and with great relish. "Delilah."

She whirled around, first appearing guilty, then abashed when she saw his naked chest. He'd done no more than pull on snug cotton boxers; he had no need of the sling right now, though he kept his right arm slightly elevated to relieve his shoulder of pressure. The bandages there were made to withstand showers and would dry soon.

Any clothes he would have put on would just be coming off again, so he hadn't bothered with them, either. By look and deed she'd made her willingness, her own desire, clear. It didn't matter that he hardly knew her, not when everything about her felt so right.

He braced his feet apart and let her look her fill.

Her eyes widened and then traveled the length of him. Twice. She touched her throat. "If I looked as good as you, I'd have skipped the boxers."

Though he appreciated the sentiment, Mick was too far gone with lust to manage a grin. "Want me to take them off?"

She shook her head and said, "Yes. But not yet. If you were naked now, I'd forget you're hurt and do something I'd regret."

"Like what?" She continued to stand there, her gaze returning again and again to his straining hard-on, which the snug cotton boxers did nothing to hide.

"Like throwing you down on the floor and having my way with you."

He did grin this time. "The bed is right around the corner. Why don't we go there now?"

Just that easily, he saw her resolve form, harden. He may have only known her a day, but he already knew that look.

"You need to take your medicine. Good as you look, I can see that you hurt."

The pain in his shoulder and head were nothing, certainly not enough to make him want to wait another day to have her. "I'll take a pill after I've sated myself with you."

Her gaze locked on his. "Oh boy, you don't pull any punches, do you?"

"From what I remember last night in the hospital, neither do you." And to encourage her, he added, "But I like it when you speak your mind."

She nodded. "Okay, yes, I want you to sate yourself with me. I want to sate myself with you, too." Her expression was one of worry, regret. "But I figure that'd probably take me hours, maybe even days, so we should maybe put it off until you're not likely to die on me."

Damn, her brazen words mixed with the sweetness of her expression and the obvious worry she felt for him was an aphrodisiac that fired his blood. She was a mix of contradictions, always unique, sometimes pushy and too stubborn. Mick took two long steps toward her, ignored the continual throbbing in his shoulder and head, and gathered her close.

He wasn't prepared for her stiffened arms, which

carefully pushed him back again. Shakily, she said, "We have to make a deal."

The need stalled, replaced by innate suspicion. What possible deal could she need to make at this moment? Thoughts flew through his head as he remembered numerous deals offered to him by prostitutes, drug dealers, gamblers, people from his youth and the people he now came into contact with every day of his life.

He also thought about the robbery, about her uncommon interest in the jewelry store, her interest in him, her willingness to bring a near stranger into her home and have sex with him.

By nature, he was overly cautious. From his upbringing, and then working undercover, he'd become suspicious of almost everyone and everything.

Because of his background, he often doubted the sincerity of women in general.

Dropping his hands so he wouldn't accidentally hurt her with his anger, Mick growled, "What kind of deal?"

She blinked, confused by his temper. Carefully, her words no more than a whisper of sound, she explained, "I can't stand seeing you in pain. I want you to take your medicine first, then we'll go to bed."

Mick made sure no reaction showed on his face, but once again she'd managed to take him off guard. Her deal was for him, not for her. "The medicine makes me too groggy."

"Not for fifteen minutes or more. I've watched you after you take it. It doesn't kick in right away, and you only go to sleep when you let yourself."

Still not touching her, he said, "What I have in mind will take more than fifteen minutes."

She inhaled sharply at his words, then touched him, her hand opening on his chest, her fingers splayed, sifting through his body hair. The reflexive clench of his muscles brought a sharp ache to his temples, his shoulder.

"You're welcome to stay here until you're completely recovered," she said, still stroking him with what seemed like acute awe, probably attempting to soothe him, when in fact each glide of her delicate fingers over his muscles wound him that much tighter. "There'll be plenty of time for both of us to indulge ourselves."

He didn't answer right away, trying to figure her out in the middle of an intense arousal that kept rational thought just out of reach.

"Please," she added, both hands now sliding up to his shoulders. One edged the bandage that came over his shoulder from the back. "I won't be able to enjoy myself for fear of hurting you."

He didn't want that. He fully intended for her to experience more than mere enjoyment. He wanted her ripe with pleasure, numb with it. He wanted to give her the kind of explosive release she'd have only with him.

Yet, she was right. In his present condition, it wasn't likely to happen. With her insistence, she was probably helping him to save face.

Mick brought her close and said against her hair, "I'm sorry. I'm not used to wanting a woman quite this much." He wasn't used to wanting to *trust* a woman, either. But he wanted to trust Delilah. He wanted to involve himself with every aspect of her life. He needed to tie her to him in some way.

Nodding, she said, "I know the feeling. You blow my socks off."

He tilted her back so he could see her face. Her honesty humbled him, and pleased him.

"We haven't discussed it," he said, thinking now was as good a time as any, "but I want you to know the nurse was right, I come with a clean bill of health—in all ways. Not only have I always been discriminating, but I'm very cautious, too."

That brought a beautiful smile to her face. "Same here. I can't claim to have been a recluse, but I haven't met many men that I wanted to get involved with. Not like this, not enough to let them interrupt my life. And men take exception to that. They don't like to be neatly compartmentalized."

"Is that right?"

She nodded. "You may not have noticed, but I get really wrapped up in my work, and most of the time I'm not even aware of men around me. At least, not for long."

Mick grinned. "I noticed. At first I wondered if maybe you were a lesbian."

Her mouth opened, then closed. She frowned at him, her pale blue eyes burning bright. "I'm not."

His grin widened. "I noticed that, too."

Still scowling, she said, "Not that there's anything wrong with—"

"Of course not. But I have to tell you how glad I am that you're interested in men."

"I'm interested in *you*."

He appreciated her clarification. "Which means I'm one lucky bastard."

She snorted. "If you were so lucky, you wouldn't have gotten shot." She turned and grabbed up the pills. "Take these."

He downed them in one gulp, washing the bitter taste away with sweetened tea.

"Are you hungry? You really didn't eat that much yesterday, and you hardly touched your breakfast."

He'd been too caught up in his thoughts, in mentally organizing all the things that had to be done that day, to concern himself with breakfast. And the truth was, he felt hollow down to his toes. He could probably eat two meals, but not yet. "No. I just want you. And now that I've swallowed the damn pills, time's wasting."

Her eyes warmed, the vivid blue darkening. She took his hand and turned to lead him down the hall. Without looking at him, she said, "Let me see if I can help you to sleep soundly for a few hours."

It took a great deal of resolve not to turn her against the wall and enter her right there, standing up, without the benefit of a soft mattress. At twenty-six, he'd known lust, but he'd never known anything like this, an all-encompassing need to devour a particular woman.

Her bedroom was small, holding a bed that would barely accommodate his size. The beige spread was tossed half off the bottom of the mattress, pooling on the floor and showing matching beige sheets. Across from it sat a triple dresser with a mirror, the top cluttered with papers and candles and receipts.

A wooden rocker sat in front of one window. The other window held an air conditioner, softly humming on low, keeping the room pleasantly cool. Over the bed a ceiling fan slowly whirled, barely stirring the air but making the room comfortable.

The building didn't have central air, of course. None of the buildings on her street did. Some of them didn't have heat, either. Thankfully, Delilah's apartment building was kept up, just as Mick kept up his building next door. And she wasn't on the first floor, so she could open her windows without fear of intruders.

Her bedroom wasn't what you'd call neat, not with laundry piled on the chair and shoes tossed haphazardly over her closet floor, but it was orderly. He had the distinct impression Delilah could walk into this room and find anything she needed without effort.

She went straight to the bed and propped up the pillows. "Sit here."

Bemused, Mick allowed her to take control. She always seemed less reserved when she was the aggressor, as if taking control gave her more confidence. He wanted her without inhibitions, so he gladly let her lead.

He settled himself, easing his injured shoulder back against the headboard. Delilah stood in front of him and unsnapped her jeans. The sound of her zipper sliding down nearly stopped his heart. Transfixed, he watched her disrobing in front of him. There was no false modesty, no timidity, but no real brazenness, either. She revealed her body with a no-nonsense acceptance that touched his heart; she wouldn't flaunt, but neither would she cower. Mick tightened his fists in the bottom sheet and held himself still.

He'd been half-afraid he was rushing her, moving too fast. But judging by her willingness now, she was finally as ready as him.

But then, he'd been ready from the first moment he saw her.

CHAPTER FIVE

DELILAH'S JEANS DROPPED, and she smiled at him as she stepped away from them, using one foot to nudge them aside. "I'm not as perfect as you," she stated, again with that simple acceptance of her own perceptions, "but somehow I have a feeling that won't bother you."

Oh, he was plenty bothered, on the point of going insane. Her comments weren't geared toward gaining compliments, but he could only give her the truth. "You're the sexiest woman I've ever seen."

Her mouth twitched and then she laughed. "Yeah, right. With small boobs and a straight waist and gangly limbs?"

He wanted to correct her, to point out everything he found enticing, yet when she caught the hem of her tank top and tugged it over her head, he went mute. His heart struck his rib cage, his breath caught.

The bra she wore had no shoulder straps, and the cups only half covered her. When she flipped her hair back, he could have sworn he saw the edge of a mauve nipple.

He swallowed hard. "This is insane. Come here."

"In a minute. Don't you want me naked?" she teased.

"God, yes." He shifted his legs. He was uncomfortable, drawn tight, ready to come from just the sight of her. "I want to touch you, too." *And taste you and bury myself deep.*

Reaching behind her back, she unhooked her bra and let it drop. Her breasts were round and firm, with small, tightly puckered nipples now darkened with desire.

She left her miniscule panties on and walked toward him, her gait long and sure and purposeful. Without reserve, she climbed into the bed and straddled his lap. Mick groaned as her rounded bottom nestled on his thighs and her breasts came even with his face. He reached for her.

"Shh," she said, catching his right arm and holding it still. "Let me. You just sit back and relax."

Blood rushed through his head. He gritted his teeth and nodded. He didn't tell her that relaxing was out of the question.

"Tell me what you want." As she spoke, she looked at him and touched him, and his vision narrowed to only her.

"I want to taste you."

Her eyes smoldered, encouraging him even as her hands attempted to ease him. It was a wasted effort. Each soft stroke of her hands—over his chest, his uninjured shoulder, his waist, his throat—inflamed him.

He saw the pulse fluttering in her throat when she asked huskily, "Where?"

"Everywhere, but for now, I want your nipples."

Her thighs tightened around his, giving her away.

She wasn't nearly as detached or in control as she pretended. He didn't quite understand her forceful determination, but he knew at least part of it was inspired by reciprocal lust.

She drew a shaky breath and slowly, so slowly the anticipation damn near killed him, she leaned forward.

Mick struggled to stay calm. He couldn't stop himself from bending his knees, forcing her farther forward, couldn't stop the flexing of his cock against her tantalizing ass. But he made certain to gently kiss the rounded softness of her breasts, to nuzzle against her until she moaned. He teased her, licking close to her nipple but not quite letting his tongue touch it.

She twisted, attempting to hurry him, but Mick held himself in check. She needed to catch up to him—if that was possible.

With a rough, impatient sound, she finally murmured, "Mick, please…"

He placed a wet, soft kiss directly over her nipple, briefly drawing her into the heat of his mouth with a gentle suction, and then releasing her. It wasn't easy, considering he wanted to feast on her.

She moved against him, one small jerk on his thighs before she stopped herself. Panting, she said, "I like that."

"I thought you would." He did it again, then again and again until she gasped for breath, until her hands settled in his hair and her nipples were tight wet peaks. Likely with more force than she realized, she brought his mouth to her breast, saying without words that she now needed more.

And he suckled her, strong and deep and long.

The combined sensations rocked him: the taste and feel of her on his tongue as his mouth tugged at her, the heat of her sex pressing insistently against his abdomen, her scent and softness and her unique determination.

The physical bombardment on his senses was enough, leaving him confused and wild with need. But the emotional storm also overwhelmed him. He wanted to consume her savagely, brand her as his own, hear her cries and feel the bite of her nails. And he wanted to hold her gently to his heart, to let her feel protected and know that he'd take care of her. Basic, elemental instincts rolled through him in a way he'd never felt before.

As he continued to tongue and suck, her back arched and she released a ragged moan. Then she moved against his thighs, a riding motion that rubbed the damp silk of her panties along the length of his shaft.

He replaced his mouth with his fingers and said harshly, "Kiss me, Delilah."

She did, stealing his breath as her tongue licked in to tease his. As wild and out of control as he felt, she was more so.

"Let's get these panties off you," he murmured, knowing he couldn't last much longer.

She pulled away, trembling, gasping for breath. Her head dropped forward. After a moment, she dipped down and kissed his throat, her mouth open and hot and wet. Mick wanted to protest, but he loved the feel of her mouth on him.

The pills had muddled his mind some and it took more effort than he could dredge up to stop her as she sank lower, biting at his chest, hotly licking his own nipples, tasting and teasing him.

His arm hurt like a son of a bitch and his head continued to throb dully, but raging lust and crushing need overrode it all. Using his good arm, he tangled his fingers in her silky hair, letting it slide over his chest and then his abdomen as she moved lower and lower down the length of his body.

When her tongue dipped into his navel, he nearly shouted with the pleasure of it. "God, Delilah," he managed to rasp, "baby, you have to stop."

She ignored him. Her hand crept up his tensed thigh, higher and higher until she cuddled his testicles for a brief, heart-stopping moment before grasping his erection and slowly stroking.

He stiffened, all sensation, hot and thick, rushing into his groin. Her mouth, still gentle but hungry, kissed him through the cotton boxers, and the pleasure-pain was so excruciating it blocked everything else.

He cursed, feeling himself sinking, out of control. He had to stop her, but he didn't want to. He wanted her to—

As if she'd read his mind, she eased the boxers down.

"No," Mick protested with a long groan, knowing he sounded less than convincing. The damn pills had melted away his determination, made him forget all his plans. He could only focus on Delilah, on what she did, how she touched him.

"I've been thinking about this all day," she breathed.

He opened his eyes, needing to watch. The look on her face mirrored his own emotions of fire, need, possession. She watched her hand driving him to distraction, her grip firm, her thumb curling over the end of his erection with each long stroke, pushing him closer and closer....

Mick felt a surge of release and desperately fought it off, but she saw the drop of fluid at the head of his penis and leaned forward.

He shuddered, cursed, held his breath—then shouted in reaction when her mouth closed over him, not tentatively, as he'd expected, but sliding wetly down the length of him, taking all of him in, sucking.

Maybe if he hadn't taken the damn pills, maybe if it had been any woman other than her, he could have controlled himself.

But from the moment he'd seen her he'd wanted her, and he couldn't hold back, couldn't stop himself from coming. His fingers knotted in her hair and he held her head to him, not that it was necessary because she didn't pull away. She drew him deeper and made a low sound of pleasure that he felt in his soul. He tightened, surged, and experienced the strongest release of his entire life. He growled with the force of it, his body taut, arching, his mind going blank.

His only realization in that turbulent moment of rioting sensation was that no other man would ever touch her; she was his, and he intended to keep her.

MICK DIDN'T SLEEP LONG this time, probably no more than an hour, but he awoke half-frozen. The air conditioner, on the highest setting, hummed loudly, and the ceiling fan whirled overhead. He felt his hair blowing, felt his skin prickle with goose bumps.

He'd passed out just as she'd left him, half propped against the headboard, his legs now limp, his shoulder cushioned by a soft pillow. At least she'd pulled the spread up to his waist, he thought, a bit disgruntled.

He felt like an idiot as he looked around and realized the room was empty. He cursed. Then cursed again when he pushed the spread away and became racked with chills. It was like sleeping on the wing of an airplane, for crying out loud!

He swung his legs to the floor, stood—and nearly fell. Weakness had invaded every muscle. The pain pills had no effect on his aches, not after that mind-grinding orgasm, where every muscle in his body, clear down to the soles of his feet, had knotted in pulsating pleasure. She'd wrung him out—no doubt that had been her intent.

He grunted, unable to believe what she'd done, and unwilling to accept that after she'd done it, he'd had the gall to fall asleep.

If the room hadn't felt like a meat locker, he'd probably have been hot with embarrassment.

He glanced down at his boxers, still around his thighs, and shook his head. It was too much, far too much.

He straightened his underwear, whipped the spread off the bed and around his shoulders to ward off the cold, then went to the window to turn the unit down. The air conditioner sputtered and died with a sigh.

Forcing himself forward on shaky limbs, Mick left the bedroom. The apartment was quiet, other than the rattling of pans in the kitchen area. On his way down the hall, he decided to take the offense. Delilah knew he'd wanted to make love to her, but she'd taken the choice away from him. *How* she'd taken it away had been beyond incredible, but still, she needed to know that he wouldn't be so easily manipulated. Not ever again.

He was appalled that he'd proved so easy this time. But then, maybe that's why she'd given him the pills, to weaken his resolve. He'd be sure to ask her that.

When he reached the arched kitchen doorway, she had her back to him, stirring a pan of something on the stove. Whatever she was cooking smelled good, as did the coffee in the coffeemaker. She'd pulled her tank top back on, but not her jeans, and the sight of her bottom in the silky panties did a lot to obliterate his other concerns.

Before he got distracted, he asked, "Did you talk me into the pain pills so you could keep us from having sex?"

She yelped, dropped her stirring spoon and jerked around to face him. Their gazes locked.

The sight of her face made his mind go blank, his heart trip. *She'd been crying.*

"Delilah?" he asked around a sudden lump of emotion. Damn, that bothered him. He didn't get lumps of emotion. In his job, he saw the worst life had to offer and he handled it dispassionately, with a distance that could be applauded. Always, from the time he'd been a young boy, he'd kept his emotions in check.

But God, she looked like hell with her eyes swollen and wet, her cheeks blotchy, her nose red. Seeing her made his heart thump.

She bit her bottom lip and turned to the stove again. He heard her sniff. "Yes."

Mick shook his head. He wanted to hold her, to comfort her. Yet she'd turned her back on him. "Yes what?"

"Yes, I gave you the pills so you wouldn't complain when I...eased you. It was the only thing I could think of. I didn't want you to strain yourself, and the doctor said it was too soon for you to have sex."

Talking with Delilah was like wading through syrup. He kept getting stuck, but damn, it was sweet. He cleared his throat, forcing the emotion away so he could think and react clearly. He slowly approached her and stood at her back, close enough to breathe in her sexy scent and see the enormous pot of spaghetti sauce she stirred. "You spoke with the doctor about us having sex?" Her initiative amazed him—and aroused him.

"Yes. Right after I bought the condoms."

Mick paused. *Bought the condoms?* Before he could ask, she said, "I snuck them into the bedroom, in the nightstand drawer, just in case you didn't go to sleep after you came."

She spoke as bluntly as any man, but then, she'd done that from the first, speaking her mind with candor. Unlike other women he knew, she didn't measure her words. She was so female she made him crazy, yet she didn't always act female. Damn if that didn't arouse him, too.

Hell, everything she did aroused him. Just moments before he'd thought himself fully satisfied, but now... "The hospital sells rubbers?"

She glanced at him over her shoulder, and he watched one fat tear track down her cheek. "Yeah, of course they do. It's a hospital, and they understand about unnecessary risks."

She'd managed to distract him, after all.

Mick shook his head and wrapped one arm around her waist. Resting his chin on top of her head, he asked, "Why are you crying, sweetheart? Did I hurt you?"

"Of course not." She leaned into him, then pushed back with a frown. "You're shivering." Twisting, she put her hand to his forehead in a maternal gesture of concern. "Are you sick?"

"Just cold." He turned her back around and laced his hands over her middle. Her bottom pressed into his groin. "The room was like ice."

She nodded. "I figured you'd like it cold. Most men get warmer than women, right?"

He had no idea, but he doubted any man would relish the igloo accommodations she'd provided him. She'd obviously had some sexual experience, and she was comfortable with her body, with her sexuality. But she was far from knowledgeable about the opposite sex. Mick shook his head at the added contradictions. "Why are you crying?"

She shrugged and leaned back against him. "I'm

just a little sad. I'm sorry you have to see me like this. I'm a terrible crier. Very ugly. The news just took me by surprise."

"What news?" He rubbed his chin against her hair, spread his hand over her belly. He loved the feel of her, her softness, her sleekness. She was so feminine, but not in a frail way.

"A guy I know died. I just read it in the paper."

Mick stiffened, caught between conflicting reactions. He wanted to comfort her from any upset, and he wanted to jealously demand information about the guy who'd made her cry. He must have been important to her to bring on the tears.

It shouldn't have mattered. They'd only just officially met, and hadn't officially consummated their relationship yet. But it did matter. A lot.

"Who was he?" Mick asked, keeping her pressed into him by his hand on her belly.

After a long, shuddering sigh, she put the spoon down and turned into his arms. Her face nuzzled into his chest and she whispered, "Just a guy who helped me with research." He felt her wet cheek on his pec muscle and groaned.

"I'm sorta known for my research methods, you know," she continued. "They've become part of my publicity." She leaned back to stare up at him earnestly, and in case he hadn't understood, she clarified. "For my books, I mean."

"How is research a publicity stunt?"

She lifted one shoulder. "People are amazed by the strangest things. But whenever I write about something in a book, I try to experience it first so that I get it right. When I can't experience it, I try to talk to someone who has.''

"So what type of research did this guy help you with?'' Mick hoped like hell it wasn't a love scene. He could handle anything but that.

Turning away, she reached for a napkin and mopped her eyes. Mick heard another loud sniff. "He was a small-time criminal. I had a scene in my book where a guy stole a car. I couldn't really steal a car—'' she glanced at him and added "—not without getting arrested, I'm sure.''

"Better not to try it,'' he agreed, smiling.

"That's what I figured. So I hired this guy, and he took me through all the ins and outs of car theft. For a criminal he was a really nice guy.''

Mick glanced at the coffeepot. "Mind if I have a cup?''

"Oh, of course.'' But she didn't let him get it himself. "Sit down and I'll pour it for you.''

Since his knees were still shaking, Mick sat. More than most things, he hated being weak, and for now there was nothing he could do about it. He pulled out a chair at the black, wrought-iron parlor table and gratefully dropped into it.

"Cream or sugar?''

"Black, please.''

She set the steaming mug in front of him. His first sip made his body hair stand on end, and he nearly spat it back out. His throat raw, he rasped, "Damn, that's strong.''

Delilah didn't take his comment as a complaint. She smiled, looking adorable in her skimpy top and panties, her nose bright red. "I figured you being a man and all, you'd want it strong."

It was a wonder new hair hadn't sprouted on his body. He coughed, and because he didn't want to hurt her feelings, he said, "I think I'll take the cream and sugar, after all."

She happily got them for him, then went back to the stove to check her sauce. To Mick, it looked like there was enough to feed an army. Hopefully, she didn't expect him to eat it all—because he was a man.

Making sure she didn't notice all the sugar he dumped into his coffee, he asked, "So where did a nice woman like you meet a car thief?"

"In prison."

The mouthful of coffee—still too bitter to enjoy—got spewed across the table. He continued to choke as Delilah grabbed up a dish towel and patted his back.

"Mick! Are you all right?"

He wheezed, trying to regain his breath enough to speak. With his eyes squeezed shut, he finally demanded, "What the hell were you doing in prison?"

Tilting her head, she smiled. Given her swollen eyes and the tear tracks on her cheeks, it didn't have the usual effect on his libido. "More research." She chuckled. "You didn't think I meant I'd been serving time, did you?"

Actually, he had, but he wasn't dumb enough to say so. Relief warred with confusion. "Of course not. But can you explain all this research for me?"

She pulled out her own chair at the table. "Okay, but don't let me forget the spaghetti sauce. Your friends are coming over for dinner and I want to impress them.''

"Josh and Zack?''

She snorted. ''I meant your other friends, the ones you said were like family.''

"Dane and Angel are staying for dinner?'' He didn't like putting her out, especially since she was so upset.

"I invited them. Angel called and said she had your things, and wanted to know when it'd be a good time to drop them off. I know she's still worried about you, and she doesn't exactly trust me, so I thought this would be a way to make her feel better.''

Cautiously, Mick asked, ''What makes you think Angel doesn't trust you?''

Del made a face. ''I'm not dumb.''

Mick let that go. He'd have to talk to Angel first to see what had been said. He knew Angel would never insult Delilah, but she was protective. ''Why do you want to impress them?''

"They're like your family. I like you, so of course I want them to like me.''

Mick almost told her it didn't matter what anyone else thought, that he intended to make her a part of his life. But he'd never gotten so deeply involved with a woman, and to do so now, at Mach speed, was just plain foolish. He liked her, all her quirks and unique qualities. He liked her different way of viewing things and her outspokenness mixed with occasional glimpses of uncertainty. And God knew, the sexual chemistry between them was explosive.

But most of her background was still a mystery to

him. So he forced himself to be cautious, to go slow.
He tucked a tendril of her silky hair behind her ear
and asked, "Are you sure you're up to a dinner
party?"

"Why wouldn't I be? You're the one who got
shot."

"*You* were the target. And you've been crying."

She waved that away, ignoring his first comment
and only responding to his second. "I'm overly emotional about the people I care for. There aren't that
many. Being a writer keeps me isolated, so I don't
get into the social swing of things often. Neddie became a friend as well as a teacher. We had a lot of
fun hot-wiring my car."

This time Mick just stared. She gave an impatient
sigh and went on. "It's true. We were alike in a lot
of ways, reacting to our place in society. Neddie became a misguided criminal, just trying to fit in. I became a writer."

"It's hardly the same thing."

"Of course not. I just meant that we understood
each other. Neddie was wrong, and he knew that. But
he always said he never hurt anyone who didn't deserve to be hurt. Anything he did, he did among other
criminals, including stealing cars. And from what he
told me, I believe him."

"Criminals always have excuses, Delilah."

"Well, he was a nice criminal, okay? And very
patient. We took my car to a deserted lot and practiced on it for hours. Once I got the hang of it, Neddie
timed me."

Mick's left hand, resting on the tabletop, curled

into a fist. "You went to a deserted lot with a convict?"

"Can you imagine how the cops might have reacted if they'd seen me hot-wiring a car around here?"

She needed a keeper. *She needed him.* He drew a calming breath, something he found himself doing often around her. "Back up and tell me what you were doing in prison."

"I had a character in a book who had spent a good portion of his life in prison. I couldn't very well write that without knowing what the inside of a prison was really like."

"Ever heard of research books?" he asked dryly.

She laughed. Though he knew her humor was aimed at him, he was glad to see her mood lightening. "I use research books when I have to. But I think it's always better to get firsthand, in-person information whenever I can."

"You said that's part of your promotion?"

"Yep. It didn't start out that way. But then this one reporter got wind of it when my last book hit the *New York Times* bestseller list. She interviewed me and asked me all kinds of questions about my research, and since then the media is real accommodating. They always make a fuss about my way of researching."

His head throbbed. "Media?"

"Yeah. Silly, huh?"

His tongue felt on fire as he sputtered, "You're a celebrity."

Delilah wrinkled her nose and with a note of dismissal said, "To some people, I guess."

"You do this often?"

She shrugged. "Often enough. I was on a talk show once, and not too long ago I got featured on the news."

"The news?"

"About my newest book, and my research for it. It was fun."

In that moment, a thousand questions went through his mind. What the hell was a celebrity doing living in this neighborhood? How much money could she possibly make and what other types of research had she done?

Could any of that have to do with the incident at the jewelry store?

Before he could start on his interrogation, and that's what it would have been because he fully intended to get a lot of answers, she said, "We better get a move on. Everyone will be showing up in about half an hour. I still need to shower and change and make the bed and boil the spaghetti and fix a salad—"

Mick caught her hand as she rose. He tugged her between his legs. "I can help."

This time her laughter had the desired effect. He got hard as a stone. "Mick," she said playfully, and cupped his neck in both hands. "I think I can handle a shower on my own."

Damn, that brought an irresistible image to his mind. Delilah naked and wet, water streaming down her body, over her belly and between her thighs....

He released her hand and curled his arm around her waist, keeping her close when she tried to impatiently edge away. "I meant," he said, his voice now hoarse, "that I can handle spaghetti or a salad."

"No," she said in that unrelenting tone he already recognized. Delilah was used to making all the decisions, and used to holding her ground.

He'd have to work on that flaw.

She leaned down and quickly kissed him. "Not one-armed, you can't, and the doc specifically said you shouldn't use your right arm."

Mick was ready to explain a few things to her, but she added, her voice sweet and cajoling, "Please, Mick. Just let me take care of you, okay?"

He opened his hand on the small of her back, then slipped it down her spine to her bottom. He filled his palm with one firm cheek. "All right," he agreed. "But on one condition."

Her eyes narrowed. "What?"

"Tonight, after everyone is gone…" He let his fingers drift lower, pressing in to touch the heat of her, pleased with her gasp and small moan. "Tonight you'll let me show you exactly what I *can* do with one good arm."

Breathless, she said, "Sex is—"

"I know, not on the agenda." His fingers caressed her. "But I can return your favor of today."

Her lips parted, her eyes glittered and her cheeks looked warm. Several heartbeats went by, then she whispered, "Yes, okay."

Mick felt like a conquering warrior now that she'd given in to him at least a little. He grinned and smacked her butt. "I'm glad you can see reason. Now go get your shower. I'll pull on my jeans and park myself in front of the TV."

"And you won't lift a finger?"

He stood, kissed her forehead and replied, "Not until tonight."

With a comical look on her face, she turned the sauce down to warm and left the room. Mick flexed his aching shoulder, winced and decided to make a fresh pot of coffee while Delilah was otherwise occupied. He could only imagine Dane's expression if he took a gulp of that thick, bitter brew. It would probably prove amusing, but then Mick would have to drink it, too, which would negate all the fun.

So far, her coffee, her air-conditioning and her lack of discretion in dangerous situations were the only things he had trouble with. Those things aside, Delilah Piper was one hell of a woman. With each passing minute, he fell a little harder.

CHAPTER SIX

IT TURNED OUT TO BE a hectic evening, and Delilah was glad to see it winding down. Not only had Dane and Angel come to dinner, but Alec and Celia had called, and she'd invited them along. She figured she might as well get the family gathering over with. She was used to people not understanding her, to assumptions that her preoccupation with her stories was sheer daydreaming, motivated by lack of intelligence or attention.

She wasn't used to caring, to going out of her way to be accepted, and she'd felt on edge. Added to that was her urge to write. She had a deadline looming, and her mind kept wandering to her story.

Then Zack had dropped in with his four-year-old daughter, Dani. She was about the cutest thing Delilah had ever seen, and strangely enough, writing took second place to other thoughts. Dani had blue eyes like her father's, but her hair was blond and curly, and she had dimples when she smiled.

It took only a moment for Del to see that the little girl adored Mick. With her father's admonition to be careful of Mick's injury, she'd rushed to him, climbed into his lap and kissed his cheek as if he were a favorite uncle. Then she'd given him three more kisses to "make him all better." Mick had claimed to feel much improved on the spot, which prompted Dani into giggles.

Something about seeing Mick with a little girl in his arms made Del's heart swell. It was an incongruous sight, Mick so strong and darkly handsome, holding such a delicate, fair child. But it also looked very right, as if Mick were made to be a father.

Del frowned at that. Their relationship, started only a day before, hardly warranted thoughts of parenthood. She shook off the strange aberration and concentrated on being a perfect host.

She wasn't used to entertaining and she definitely wasn't used to so much company. But she didn't resent the intrusion on her writing time. In fact, it was all really nice.

During dinner, Josh phoned, and minutes later another man called for Mick, though he didn't introduce himself and Mick didn't tell her who it was. During his whispered conversation, she saw Alec and Dane share a look.

Her small apartment felt like Grand Central Station. Celia kept watching her closely, as if she was waiting for something, though Delilah had no idea what. Both she and Angel were cautiously nice.

Other than Mick, Del hadn't entertained a man in ages. And she'd never entertained a man's family before now. She had no idea if she was doing things right.

Mick caught her alone in the kitchen getting ready to make more coffee. He wore the sling again, but he still managed to drag her close for a kiss.

"Dinner was great."

He sounded sincere, and she smiled against his mouth. "Thank you." It had been a guessing game, trying to figure out how much sauce and spaghetti to make. After she'd done her best calculation, she'd doubled it for good measure. And that was a good thing, because the men had eaten far more than she'd ever anticipated. "Everyone is so nice. I like them."

"Even Zack?"

"His daughter is wonderful."

Mick laughed at that careful evasion. "You still holding a grudge?"

That sounded infantile, so she shook her head. "No, of course not. I understand why they were so protective of you."

"They were protective of *you*, Delilah."

She didn't agree, but saw no point in arguing. "I suppose for Zack to have such a sweet daughter, he must be a good father."

"He is that." Mick stroked her hair, then added, "Zack likes you. He told me so."

Staring at his chest, Del asked, "What about the others?"

He tipped up her chin. "Angel is cautious because I don't normally get involved with women."

Del wasn't at all certain she understood that. "You're not a virgin."

He choked on a laugh. "No."

"Then what do you mean—"

"I mean I'm real choosy. I already told you that, right?"

"The same is true for me, but maybe for different reasons. I've never had much time for men."

"You're making time for me."

There was no denying that. But Mick was... different. Well worth any effort.

"And," he added, still explaining Angel's reserve, "we've been moving pretty fast."

Delilah chewed over that obvious bit of information. "She's afraid I'll hurt you."

His eyes warmed, and his hand on her cheek was so gentle. "She's afraid you could, and that's a first." He kissed her again. Then once more. "Damn, I have to quit that or they'll wonder what we're doing in here."

She didn't want him to quit. "We're just kissing."

"I want to do a lot more."

So did she. "Tonight, I wouldn't mind—"

His hold tightened. "Tonight," he growled, "it's your turn."

Her heart tripped. She was still aroused from the afternoon. She'd been aroused since the second she saw Mick in that hospital bed.

Knowing he wanted to touch her and...do things to her made her whole body feel tight and too hot and somehow empty. Sighing shakily, she said, "All right."

"An agreeable woman," he teased, and took her mouth with a kiss that curled her toes and made her breasts tingle.

A knock sounded on the wall behind them. Mick lifted his head and turned.

Del groaned, then went on tiptoe to peek over his

shoulder. Celia stood there smiling. Alec stood next to her, looking amused.

"I—I was just about to make more coffee," Del stammered.

"Why don't you let Alec do that?" Mick suggested, putting his good arm around her shoulder.

That idea didn't sit right. "But he's a guest."

Alec raised a brow and gave Mick a curious glance. "I don't mind. Coffee is my specialty. Besides, I think my wife is dying to ask you something."

Celia elbowed him, then stepped closer. She looked anxious, her hands clasped together, and she kept glancing from Del to Mick and back again. Finally she blurted, "Are you *the* Delilah Piper? I mean, I saw some books on your shelves and I know it seems crazy, but..."

Mick looked at Del with surprise, and Celia stood there holding her breath. "That's me," Del said.

Mick frowned. "You've heard of her, Celia?"

"Are you kidding? She's fabulous! One of my favorite authors."

That got Del's attention. "Thank you. You've read me?"

Celia rushed closer. "Each and every one. Ohmigosh, that last one had me on the edge of my seat. When the car went off the bridge into that river..." She shivered, as if remembering the scene.

"I did that, you know," Del told her. When Celia stared wide-eyed, Del nodded. "It's true. Of course, I took some lessons first, so I wouldn't drown myself, but then we found this old bridge that no one uses anymore, and the instructor and I took the car right off the side.''

Beside her, Mick growled, ''What the hell are you talking about?''

And in an awed whisper, Celia said, ''Angel didn't believe me that it was you. I mean, that you're the author who really did all those things.''

''The coffee will be done in a minute,'' Alec said, interrupting another angry outburst from Mick. ''Why don't we go back in the living room and Celia can grill you like I know she's dying to?''

Del loved talking about her work, and she allowed herself to be tugged into the room. Mick held her hand tight, and as soon as her backside found a couch cushion, he demanded, ''What the hell do you mean, you drove your car off a bridge?''

Angel gasped. ''Then it's true? It's really you?''

Mick didn't give her a chance to answer. ''Delilah, what's going on? What are they talking about?''

''You don't know?'' Alec asked, then shared a look with Dane. To Del, all those shared looks felt like a conspiracy. Regardless of her attempts, she was still an outsider in their group.

''Know what?'' Mick's gaze narrowed on Del, dark and almost…predatory. A hush fell, everyone watching with expectation.

Del turned in her seat to face Mick, unsure of his sudden change in mood. He sounded angry for some reason, and he looked more than a little disturbed.

Maybe he needed another pain pill, though he kept refusing them. ''I explained how I do my research, and about the interviews, Mick.''

"You said you visited a prison, not that you drove your car into a river."

She took exception to his tone, especially in front of their guests. She wanted the visit to go well, not be ruined by an argument.

Attempting to sound reasonable in the face of his growing ire, she explained, "I knew what I was doing. I took diving lessons and a class that teaches you how to keep from panicking. I learned all kinds of neat things. You see, under murky river water you sometimes get disoriented because it's so dark." She shivered. "Really nasty, if you want the truth. But if you let out just a little of your breath, the bubbles will rise and show you the way to the surface."

Mick groaned.

"Also, if you stay calm, your heartbeat is slower and you use less oxygen, so you can hold your breath longer. I wasn't very good at that part of it, though. I couldn't hold my breath long at all. Still, it was pretty exciting to—"

"Drive your car," Mick rasped in an ominous voice, "deliberately off a bridge?"

Del frowned. Unlike Angel and Celia, Mick didn't seem at all impressed with her career. Not that she expected or needed him to be impressed. In fact, it was kind of refreshing that he didn't seem in awe.

She was used to a variety of reactions, most of them gushing, some fascinated, even disbelieving. But not angry. That was a reaction she'd never encountered. "It was kind of neat."

"*Neat?*"

That one word held a wealth of scorn and incredulity. Del lost her temper, too. "I may have done a lot of...eccentric things, but it's my life and I can damn well—"

"What other eccentric things?" he demanded. "What else have you done?"

She heard Dane mutter something, and Alec chuckle in return. Those two seemed to find everything amusing, and this time Del had the distinct impression they were laughing at her, or rather her predicament.

Indignant, she gave them each a look of censure, not that it had any visible effect; Dane winked at her, and Alec continued to smile. *Men,* she thought, and decided to ignore their misplaced humor.

Though her heart hurt and embarrassment threatened, Del stood and walked to her bookcase. She pulled out her first book and addressed the women, while deliberately disregarding the men—Mick especially. "For this story I learned skydiving."

"I've always wanted to try that," Dane admitted.

Despite her resolve to ignore him, Del glanced his way. "I learned how to do it without a chute. Another jumper passed me one in midair."

Mick closed his eyes and groaned. He definitely sounded in pain this time.

"For heaven's sake," Del said, thoroughly exasperated. "I *had* a chute! I just pretended I didn't. And there were plenty of other people jumping with me, trained for that sort of thing. Rescue jumpers were there in case something went wrong. Besides, we practiced a lot first in simulated jumps before I actually did it."

Angel piped up and said, "I remember the villain in that book had to steal a chute off another man. That man almost died, but being the male protagonist, he didn't."

"I never kill the male leads." She looked at Mick. "That would ruin the romance aspect of the books."

He groaned again.

Celia, like a true adventurer at heart, asked, "Did you take a chute off someone else?"

Alec immediately hauled her to his side and wrapped his brawny arm around her shoulders. "Don't even think it," he warned, and he looked deadly serious, his expression fierce. Celia just smiled.

"I didn't want to go that far," Del said, a little distracted. It fascinated her the way Celia and Alec interacted. He looked so savage, so menacing, yet Celia wasn't the least threatened by him. Just the opposite; Celia cuddled closer. "I learned how to put a chute on in the air."

Mick bolted to his feet. He looked ready for a full-fledged rage. The only other time she'd seen him like that was the day of the robbery, when he'd rolled to his feet after being shot, and raced out the door. That day his eyes had been nearly black with rage—as they were now. His jaw had been clenched tight, too—as it was now.

She wasn't quite sure what to make of him.

Lifting her chin, Del pulled another book off the shelf. "In this one, I learned how to navigate through an underwater cave."

"That was the creepiest scene," Celia whispered.

"There were sharks and poisonous snakes. It gave me nightmares." Then she added, "It was also my favorite book."

Del went to her desk, pulled out a pen and signed both books. She handed one to Celia and one to Angel. "Here, a gift."

Celia clutched the book to her chest. For a long moment she was speechless, then she blurted, "Thank you!"

Angel looked amazed. "You don't have to do this."

Del shrugged. "I get some copies for my own use." She hoped to change the subject so Mick would quit scowling. It didn't work.

Attempting a relationship was hard work. Now she remembered why she'd never much bothered. Of course, that was before Mick, with guys who were easy to dismiss.

She couldn't dismiss Mick.

Angel scooted to the edge of her seat. "Where do you get your ideas?"

She'd been waiting for that question; without fail, it always got asked. She smiled, then for almost half an hour answered questions and explained about her work and laughed and had fun. Mick didn't appreciate hearing about her research techniques, but the women, especially Celia, hung on her every word.

When Del admitted that she had a looming deadline and intended to put in a few hours of writing that night, Alec pushed to his feet. "We need to be heading home. It's getting late and Celia—" he gave his wife a cautious look "—is getting ideas."

Dane also stood, saying in an aside to Del, "Alec is a worrier."

Del looked at the big dark Alec, towering protectively over his petite blond wife. He looked like a marauder, not a worrier. "If you say so."

Angel leaned against Dane and sighed. "We'll let you get to your work."

Del blushed. "I didn't mean to run everyone off."

"Not at all. Dinner was wonderful and the company was even better. But the kids will be getting antsy at their grandmother's."

"You have children?"

"We have two," Angel told her. "Grayson, who's twelve, and Kara just turned ten."

"Our Tucker is nine now," Celia said, "and looks just like his daddy."

Alec's frown lifted into a smile of pride. "The kids would love to meet you, Delilah."

Mick forestalled Del's reply by saying, "I'll tell you all about them tonight."

Del seemed to be the only person who heard his lingering undertone of annoyance.

Angel bent a fond look on Mick. "He does love talking about the kids, so prepare yourself."

"That's because they worship him," Dane added. "It's almost nauseating how they fawn all over him. Especially Kara. The boys aren't quite as bad as she is. But as you probably noticed with Zack's daughter, females love Mick."

Angel elbowed Dane hard, which made him grin and kiss her mouth. Del had already noticed what an affectionate bunch they were, always touching and teasing and kissing.

Mick obviously loved these people, and they loved him, but now, rather than making her feel excluded, the sight of them all together touched her heart and made her yearn for things she'd never considered before. They were wonderful people.

At the moment, though, Mick was busy throwing them all out.

Del watched as Mick herded everyone toward the door. She had the distinct feeling he wanted privacy so he could yell at her. Not that she'd let him. No one had yelled at her since she was a little girl, and she wasn't about to let Mick start now.

Celia surprised her by giving her a hug and telling her she'd cherish the book. Del felt a little silly. It was only a book, but she enjoyed Celia's enthusiasm.

Angel followed suit and hugged Del, too, whispering in her ear, "It's so nice to see Mick confused by a woman." She leaned back and grinned. "Thank you for taking such good care of him."

"My pleasure."

Angel's mouth quirked. "I can see that it is."

Mick stood at the door until everyone had gone. Del didn't wait around for him to start complaining or questioning her. She gathered up the coffee cups and carried them to the kitchen.

He stepped up close behind her. "Delilah."

She could feel the tension emanating off him in waves. It made her tense, too. "Call me Del."

Her hands shook. She refused to turn and face him,

choosing instead to rinse out the cups and put them in the dishwasher.

He ignored her order. "Why," he asked in a barely audible growl, "do you do all this crazy stuff?"

"You mean like bringing strange men home to my place? I was just wondering the same thing."

She'd meant to distract him from his grievances, but her ploy didn't work.

"Hell, yes, that's part of it. Don't you have any sense of self-preservation at all?"

She tightened her hands on the edge of the counter. "I learn what I need to know and I don't take unnecessary risks."

He stepped closer, crowding her against the sink. His anger was there, pulsing between them. But there was something else, something more. Her skin prickled with awareness as she felt his erection nestle against her bottom. Her breath caught.

"Tell me why you do it, babe."

She swallowed hard. "The media claims I do it because I like writing about heroes, about guys who can win against all odds, solve twisted mysteries and get the bad guy every time. They psychoanalyze that I'm setting myself up as a heroine."

"Are you?"

"No." It was difficult to think with him so close, and so aroused. "My parents say I've always been too creative and too frenetic. I'm not content to sit idle."

His hot breath touched the side of her throat as he spoke. "I can see that." He nuzzled her, making the fine hairs on her nape tingle, her breasts swell.

"You've got more energy than any woman I've ever met. And you don't think about things, you just act."

"You're…you're complaining?" His words sounded disgruntled, but his touch was so gentle, so exciting.

His good arm came around her waist and squeezed her. "The things you've claimed to do are insane, Delilah."

"Look who's talking! A man who deliberately takes a bullet in the back." She forced enough room between them so that she could turn and face him. Her hand trembled from a mix of anger and excitement as she reached up and touched his jaw. "What if that bullet had hit something vital? A lung or your heart or your spine? You could have been killed."

"I'm trained to react."

She snorted at that bit of idiocy. "They don't train you to get shot, do they? I thought PIs did sleuthing, not gunplay."

He looked away from her gaze and focused instead on her mouth. "We do what we have to do."

"And that includes nearly getting killed for a stranger? At least I take every precaution when I do my research."

His eyes, when they met hers again, were so dark, so intense that Del felt consumed by him. "I couldn't bear the thought of that bullet hurting your soft skin," he whispered. He leaned lower and kissed her, tiny biting kisses from her throat to her ear, to where her neck met her shoulder.

Del shivered, then forced herself back in control.

"I can't change who I am, Mick. This is what I do, what I enjoy doing."

He pressed his face into her throat and simply held her. It was a tender, possessive embrace and made her heart rap hard.

"Not since before Angel married Dane have I felt the need to protect someone."

She slipped her fingers through his silky hair, over his neck and the hard joint of his shoulder. "I don't need you to protect me," she assured him softly. Then, touching the bulky bandage on his back, she added, "I don't even want you to try to protect me. Especially not when you get hurt in the bargain."

His head lifted and he stared at her hard. "*Tough.* We've forged a bond, you and I, whether you like it or not." He tangled his hand in her hair and tipped her head back. "You *did* take me in, not just into your home but into your bed. If you didn't mean it, you shouldn't have started it."

"Mean it?" She found it hard to breathe with him watching her so intently, as if he could see her soul. "What…what does that mean?"

"It means you're mine now."

He continued to study her, probably waiting for her to refute his claim, but Del had no intention of doing so. No one had ever wanted to protect her. No one had ever wanted to claim her.

She swallowed. "I was going to clean the kitchen—"

"Leave it," Mick ordered.

"—but I'd rather go to bed with you."

His jaw hardened and his pupils flared. He caught

the back of her head and drew her up for his kiss. He tasted so good, and she leaned into him until she heard him groan.

"Mick..." Very gently, she pushed him back. "You should take your medicine."

"Not this time, sweetheart."

"Your shoulder—"

"Will be fine. I promise." He took her hand and started toward the bedroom.

Del admitted to herself that she wanted to let him have his way. Never in her life had she felt so hungry for a man. Never had a man been so hungry for her.

The bedroom door closed behind them and Mick leaned against it. "In the morning," he said, "we're going to talk. Without distractions."

Del had no problem with that plan. "You'll tell me more about the kids and how you and Angel met and about your background?"

There was only a slight hesitation before he nodded. "All right."

"I'm curious about you, Mick."

His gaze moved over her, hot and anxious. "We haven't had much time for talking, but we'll catch up. For now..."

"For now, I want what you want."

He pushed away from the door, his smile slow and lazy. Hot.

"As long as you don't hurt yourself," she qualified.

Mick again caught the back of her neck and lifted her to her tiptoes. Against her mouth he said, "You can help me out by taking your clothes off."

She smiled. "And yours, too?"

"God, yes."

MICK KNEW HE SHOULD HAVE put off the lovemaking in favor of getting a few things straightened out, but he seemed to have little control around her. That in itself was a worry. He was used to an icy indifference in most situations, an iron discipline that never wavered.

Especially where women were concerned.

Too many things didn't add up, and now that he understood the lengths she went to for research—his blood nearly froze every time he thought of it—new questions were beginning to surface about the robbery. He couldn't let lust make him lose sight of the possibilities.

She kicked out of her sandals while unbuttoning her blouse, and his discipline shattered. She didn't undress slowly to tease him. Rather she tore her clothes off as if she felt the same burning urgency as he.

Mick braced his feet apart to keep himself steady while she stripped bare. Her frenzy fired his own.

Tomorrow they would talk. But tonight, he'd make her his in every way.

CHAPTER SEVEN

IN NO TIME, Delilah stood before him wearing only a lacy bra and skimpy panties. He was so hard he hurt. He could feel the hot pulse of blood through his veins, the heavy, rhythmic beating of his heart.

Slowly, savoring the moment, Mick walked to her. With just his fingertips he touched one taut nipple straining against her bra. "Don't move," he whispered, and bent to take her in his mouth.

Her moan was raw and real and satisfying. Mick took his time, suckling her, teasing with the tip of his tongue, the edge of his teeth. He felt the heat rising from her slim body, her restless movements, her heavy hot breath.

"Mick, please." Against his instructions, she tangled her fingers in his hair and tugged. He straightened and began working his own buttons loose.

He held her gaze as he asked, "Are you wet for me right now, Delilah?"

Her pupils dilated, she shook her head. "I don't know."

"Check for me."

Her lips parted. "But..."

"Put your fingers between your legs," he urged, "and tell me what you feel."

Her pulse thrummed wildly in her throat. She swallowed hard, her gaze locked with his, and when her hand moved between her thighs, Mick had to bite back a groan. He locked his knees against the wash of raging lust.

"I...I'm swollen. And hot."

Triumph exploded through him. "And?"

Trembling, she whispered, "And wet."

He cursed low. The damn shirt pulled at his shoulder as he tried to wrest it off. Delilah stepped up to him, her entire body quivering. "Let me."

With gentle hands she eased the shirt from him, then went to her knees to work on his jeans. *Not this time,* he told himself, seeing her on her knees, knowing how ready she was for him.

He let her get his jeans unsnapped and unzipped, then he stepped away. "Stand up, Delilah."

"But—"

"It's your turn tonight, remember?"

Staring at his erection, she licked her lips with blatant insinuation and said, "I know."

Mick laughed, a harsh, hoarse sound. She looked as if she wanted to make a feast of him, and that nearly cost him his control. "You are such a tease." Then, with more command in his tone, he said, "I want you to finish stripping, then sit in the chair."

Startled, she cautiously stood and looked over her shoulder. The chair was piled with clothes, positioned in front of the window. Her bewildered gaze met his. "The chair?"

"That's right." He looked at her breasts, straining

against the lace. "Take off your bra. I want to see your nipples."

She glanced again at that straight-backed, hard-seated chair. A shiver ran through her before she reached behind herself to unhook her bra. The position thrust her breasts out more. Mick hardened his resolve, doing his best to remain unaffected by the luscious sight of her. Looking at him, Delilah dropped the bra. Her breasts rose and fell with her accelerated breathing.

"Now the panties," he said, feeling sweat dampen his back and shoulders. His hands shook with the need to touch her, but instead he went to the chair and removed the clothes, dropping them onto the floor. He turned to face Delilah—and she was breathtakingly naked.

As if she was overwhelmed, her head hung slightly forward, her hair shielding her expression. Her long legs were pressed together, her knees locked. Her hands flexed, opening and closing in small, nervous movements.

Mick was caught between wanting to stand there and look at her forever, and needing to be inside her now, this very instant.

Her nipples had flushed a dark rose, puckered tight. The black curls between her thighs looked silky, shielding her secrets.

"Don't be shy with me, Delilah."

Her head lifted, their gazes clashed. "I want to throw you down on the carpet. I want to strip your jeans off you and taste you again." She licked her lips, panting. "I don't understand it, but I'm not shy with you at all. I just want you. A lot."

Mick held out his hand. "Then come here. Let me help you."

She strode to him, her small breasts jiggling, her silky dark hair swaying. He caught her and held her away, but tipped up her chin so that she looked at him. "I want you to sit in that chair and let me pleasure you."

She blinked hard and a slightly worried frown pulled at her brow. "Couldn't we just—"

"No." Mick moved her to the chair and urged her onto the hard seat. He smiled at the way she sat so straight and proper, her spine erect, her knees together and her hands in her lap. But not for long.

Going down on one knee, he sat back on his haunches. "Open your legs as wide as you can, Delilah."

Her shoulders stiffened and color rushed into her face. "What are you going to do?" she asked, both breathless and excited.

"I'm going to kiss you." He glanced at her face, then back to her sex. "Here." Pressing his fingers between her thighs, he cupped her in his warm palm and felt her spontaneous jerk. Though she was tense, her breathing suspended, he could feel her, soft and wet, just as she'd said.

Shifting slightly, he stroked her, his fingertips opening her more, touching her distended clitoris. "Relax for me," he murmured.

Instinctively, she curled forward before catching herself and, with some effort, leaned back in the chair.

She took several deep breaths, and her thighs went limp, yielding to him as he pressed her legs wide. "Scoot to the edge of the seat."

Her head tipped back and her eyes closed. He saw her throat move as she swallowed audibly. "Mick, I feel...exposed."

"You are exposed," he whispered, watching as she slid forward in a delectable sprawl. "I wish I had two good arms right now so I could touch you everywhere."

Her eyes snapped open. "You're not hurting, are you?"

"Shh. I'm fine." He moved between her thighs and leaned forward to kiss her mouth, taking his time, enjoying her while he breathed in the spicy scent of her arousal. She curled her fingers around his upper arms and held on, making no move to push him away.

He could feel her impatience and drove her as far as he could, wanting her to remember this night forever. When she couldn't stop squirming beneath him, he cuddled her breast in his left hand. He wanted to hold both breasts, but his right arm and shoulder felt numb with pain.

He teased her nipple, stroking with his thumb and carefully tugging until her back arched. "Give me your other breast."

Her eyes slowly opened. "What?"

"I want you in my mouth."

Understanding dawned and her look turned equally hot and gentle. She cupped her breast and raised it high. At the same time her other hand went to the back of his head and brought him forward.

At the sight of her offering herself so sweetly, Mick growled. He kissed her softly at first, plucking with his lips, lapping with his tongue. She moaned, pressing herself into him, and he suckled greedily, unable to get enough of her taste, her incredible scent. Delilah moaned and writhed and managed to raise herself enough to rub against the fly of his jeans.

Mick cursed the injury that kept him from taking her in all the ways he wanted.

"Mick!" She cried out, straining against him.

It was too much. He moved back and opened her legs even more. Her pink flesh glistened, wet and ready, and he leaned forward to taste her deeply, his left hand curving around her bottom and holding her still.

Delilah raised her hands and covered her own breasts, crying, moving with his mouth. He loved the taste of her, so hot and sweet. He pressed his tongue into her, slow and deep, then stabbed with quick motions, swirled and licked and teased, and when he knew she was near, when he felt the tremors going through her slender thighs, her belly, he caught her clitoris and drew on her gently.

Her contractions were so strong she nearly escaped him. Fingers biting deep into her soft ass, he held her close and did his best to block the pain of his injury, enhanced by her thrashing.

With one long, last, shuddering moan, she stilled. Her breathing remained ragged, loud, and she seemed boneless in the narrow chair, her long limbs sprawled for him, around him. Her hands dropped to her sides.

Shaken, Mick put his good arm behind her and

rested his face on her belly. Though he stayed perfectly still, which eased his physical aches, his mind still reeled and his emotions rioted.

Damn, he thought. This level of connection was more than he'd expected, more than he'd even known existed.

It scared him spitless, because he wasn't a hundred percent sure he could trust in it, in her. He just knew he wanted her now, and he couldn't bear the thought of any other man with her like this.

His arm tightened and he forced himself to say lightly, "You okay, sweetheart?"

"Maybe."

He raised up to smile at her. "The taste of you is enough to make me insane."

Her eyes remained closed, but she smiled. She took several deep breaths to calm her racing heart and said, "Know what I'm thinking?"

He lightly kissed her belly button, then nuzzled the soft skin of her stomach. "Vague, soft, happy thoughts, I hope."

"I'm thinking I want you inside me."

Mick clenched his jaw. He wanted to be inside her, but he didn't see how he could. Much as he hated to admit it, he wasn't invincible. His arm hurt like a son of a bitch, more so with every breath.

Her position in the chair had taken a lot of the physical stress off his arm and shoulder, but her soft moans had caused his muscles to tighten, to flex, and now his pain felt very real.

Delilah sat up. She cupped his face in her hands and said, "Did I tell you I took riding lessons?"

His shoulder screamed a warning, but his erection was more than willing to listen. "On a wild stallion, no doubt?"

Her smile was still softened by her climax. "No. As a little girl, my parents gave me riding lessons. C'mon." She pushed at him gently until he moved back and gave her room to stand. She reached a hand down to him, and with a laugh, Mick came to his feet.

"First," she said, "a pain pill for you. And no arguing. I promise to make it worth your while."

Mick pulled her up short. "You don't have to do this, sweetheart."

"But I want to." Her expression clearly showed her confusion. "I'm not doing you a favor by making love to you. What you just did...it was so wonderful. I had no idea."

Mick wanted to know which part had surprised her, but he kept quiet.

"The only thing is that now I feel empty." She flattened her hands on his chest and stared up at him. "I meant it when I said I want you inside me."

Holding her gaze, he slid his hand down her belly. "My fingers would probably do," he said, and matching actions to words, he pressed two fingers deep inside her.

"Oh, God." Still sensitive from her climax, she dropped her head forward and curled her hands, clutching at him. They both breathed hard. "That's...that's wonderful," she whispered, delighting him with her honesty, her openness.

Her hand moved down his body and curled around his hard-on.

Mick had to fight to keep from coming the second she touched him. He felt primed to the max, and her hand was so soft and feminine. "Delilah," he warned, closing both hands around her shoulders.

"This," she whispered in a sultry voice that coasted over him like rough velvet, "will feel even better."

He had to laugh, though it sounded more like an agonized groan.

She released him, patted his butt and said, "Now quit trying to distract me." Taking his hand again, she led him toward the kitchen, where she kept the pain pills. "I have the feeling you like to control everyone and everything, but I've been on my own too long for that nonsense."

She wasn't looking at him, so it felt safe to smile. She was the most endearing woman he'd ever met.

Her insight was also uncanny. It was true he liked to have control, but more than that was the fact he wanted to take care of her, protect her. He'd never even come close to feeling that with any woman other than Angel, and then it had been a clear-cut feeling. They'd both been going through bad times and had quickly learned to trust each other, to help each other. They were friends and there'd been no confusing possessiveness or lust or this irrational need to make her a part of him, to somehow meld her body and soul with his own.

He loved Angel, just as he loved Dane and their children, and by extension Alec and Celia and Tucker.

He'd protect any one of them with his life, but that instinct had never been put to the test. Dane and Alec were more than capable of taking care of their own, so Mick's sense of protectiveness was blunted by their presence.

Not so with Delilah. There was nothing and no one to soften the raw edge of volatile emotions consuming him.

He knew it was too much, too strong and overwhelming. It put him at risk, a risk he'd never faced before because he'd never met a woman who hit him so hard on a gut level.

He had absolutely no idea how to deal with her.

She stopped beside the kitchen counter, unmindful of her nudity, although Mick relished the sight of her under the bright fluorescent lights. While she filled a glass with water, he looked her over. Her shiny dark hair was mussed, half hanging over her brow, framing those incredible, bright blue eyes. Her lips were still slightly reddened from her climax, her cheeks still flushed.

Her nipples still tight.

He sucked in a breath and accepted the pill she handed him, tossing it back and washing it down with the entire glass of cold water. Delilah stepped behind him and peered at his shoulder.

"I think we should change the bandage."

He didn't want her taking care of him, and turned to face her. "It's fine."

She propped her hands on her slim hips and frowned up at him. He'd never had a naked woman remonstrate him before. It put a new slant on things.

"I'm changing your bandage, Mick." When he started to speak, she interrupted, saying, "It's early yet and I have a feeling you won't be falling asleep despite the pain pill."

"God, I hope not." He still smarted over the fact that he'd fallen asleep on her earlier.

"Then that means, being as you're so determined and you refuse to listen to common sense or a doctor's orders, we'll be making love for some time yet. You need to be comfortable and relaxed so that you don't hurt yourself."

He gave her a lazy smile, eyeing the glossy dark curls over her mound and the long length of her legs, now braced apart as if for battle. "Relaxed, huh? You think your lovemaking is so boring I'll be able to just sit back and yawn?"

Her eyes got heavy, her smile wicked. "I think you need to let me handle things. It'll be a novel experience for you. I'll be gentle…but thorough. I promise."

He must be getting used to her, Mick thought, because her boldness didn't shock him at all, it just fired his lust. He shook his head, but heard himself say, "All right."

Her soft smile broke into a triumphant grin and she turned, giving him a view of her saucy behind as she marched away. Crooking one finger, she called back to him, "Come along, now. I'll see to everything."

He was in so deep he could barely breathe, and strangely enough, he didn't give a damn. Everything would work out, he'd see to it.

Later.

DEL COULDN'T REMEMBER ever having so much fun. Mick was astounding, giving over to her and trusting her. At least as far as his body was concerned. His thoughts were still a secret, but she understood that. Her life wasn't one she openly discussed, either. Not that it had been bad, only that it had been different, and not many people understood her or her choices.

At the moment, she had Mick stretched out on his back, a pillow cushioning his head, his shoulder freshly bandaged. Together they had showered, touching and teasing anew, then taking turns drying each other. While she'd brushed her teeth, he'd commented on her body, complimenting her in the most outrageous ways.

She returned the favor, savoring the sight of him naked at her sink, his razor and aftershave there as if they'd always been a part of her home, as if they, as well as he, belonged with her.

He had an incredible physique, tall and strong and wholly masculine. While he brushed his teeth with amazing dexterity, considering he used his left hand, she watched the play of muscles in his shoulders and biceps. Still damp from the shower, his dark hair clung in curls to his nape and temples. Her blood raced at the beauty of him.

There wasn't a single flaw to his body—except for that obscene bullet wound.

Her heart nearly broke at the sight of it, and without thinking, she'd moved to kiss him above and below his stitches, where dark bruises marred his olive skin.

His groan, one of mingled awareness and physical pleasure, encouraged her. He'd braced his hands on the sink and allowed her to do as she pleased—and she pleased quite a bit.

After that, she'd spent a good fifteen minutes just touching him, caressing his aching muscles and hopefully massaging away some of the pain and stiffness from the injury.

Even with his head dropped forward and his body totally relaxed, Mick still looked so powerful, so strong and capable. It made her stomach jumpy to know he wanted *her,* desired *her.*

Had nearly died for her.

He grew impatient with the subtle touches and teased, "Is it your plan to taunt me all night? Because I'm a hair away from taking control again."

She laughed at him, then squealed as he hurried her to the bed. She had to regain the upper hand so he didn't do more damage to his injury, and it took her several minutes to convince him that she needed to wrap his shoulder again.

He'd finally given in, but only because she let him touch her anywhere he wanted while she saw to that chore. It was apparent that, even though she lacked his physical beauty, Mick felt the same fascination for her body that she felt for his.

Now he reclined in her bed, his eyes dark and hot, watching her as she leaned over to the nightstand and withdrew a condom.

"I hate to sound unsophisticated," she said, "but I've never put a rubber on a guy before. Tell me if I do it wrong."

He didn't reply, merely watched her as she tore the small package open and reached for him. She felt the subtle clenching of his muscles, the heat rising off him in waves. She glanced at his jaw and found it locked hard.

"Like this, right?" she asked, knowing she was pushing him, and enjoying it.

"Good enough," he growled, and his abdomen tensed as she slid the condom over the head of his penis and then midway down its length.

Del surveyed her handiwork. "Not bad," she announced, trying to drag out the anticipation as long as she could. It wasn't easy; already her hands were shaking and a weakness seemed to have invaded her bones. Mick was thick and hot and silky in her hand.

"I've always been really careful," she whispered, trying to regain lost control, "about protection. Not that I'd mind having children someday, but not until I meet the right man."

His body taut and expectant, Mick rasped, "I want kids someday, too."

Del soothed him, stroking his right arm, his chest and shoulders. She met his smoldering gaze and asked, "With the right woman?"

"Yes."

Sliding her leg over his hips, she positioned herself. "Well, this woman is going to make you crazy with pleasure tonight."

His back arched. "I'll get my turn," he told her.

She laughed. "Not until the doctor says you're able." Slowly, so slowly every nerve ending sparked, she lowered herself. He'd barely penetrated at all, just the thick head of his penis inside her, her inner muscles gripping and quivering around him, when she stopped with a gasp. "It's...it's been so long for me," she muttered, trying to explain, her words broken and breathless and fast. Already she felt stretched, uncomfortably tight, yet tantalized. "I'm...I'm not at all sure."

Mick strained beneath her, sweat dampening his forehead, his chest. Delilah knew she couldn't wait any longer or he'd hurt himself. Swallowing back her own discomfort and uncertainty, she braced her hands on his chest, drew a deep breath and pressed down until he was fully, completely inside her.

An explosive curse broke from Mick. She whimpered in response. For long moments, neither of them moved except for a slight trembling of rigid muscles and a spontaneous flexing of sexes as they each struggled to adjust.

Forcing her head up, Delilah looked at Mick through a sweltering haze of sensations. "Are you...all right?"

"No." His left hand lifted, spread wide over her hip. "I need you to move, baby."

Del licked her lips. "It's just that you're...bigger than I thought."

Without his permission, his hips rose, pressing into her, deepening his penetration. "I can't do this," he groaned.

And Delilah's heart tumbled over.

"Mick." Leaning down, she kissed his mouth, his throat, licked at his salty skin. Very gently, subtly, she rocked her hips. His fingers contracted on her flesh, biting hard as he urged her to continue.

She slid up, her wetness making it easy and

smooth, then all the way down again, harder and faster with each turn. Suddenly, despite his injury, Mick gripped her hips in both hands and pumped into her, holding her tight to him, not letting her retreat. He looked feral and explosive and so sexy she felt her own climax begin.

This was what she'd wanted, him filling her, his body a part of hers, wild and real with no reserve between them. She tipped her head back and cried out her pleasure, then heard Mick's answering moan of completion.

A few seconds later his fingers went lax and she lowered herself to nestle against him. He grunted, and she mumbled, "Did I hurt you?"

It took him a little while to answer, but she didn't mind. She felt the bellowing of his chest beneath her ear, felt his sex still deep within her. "Mick?"

Using his left hand, he smoothed her bottom. "I'm feeling no pain. Even my brain is numb."

She didn't want to, but she raised herself to her elbows. "Will it hurt you if I sleep here with you?"

His dark eyes opened. "It'd kill me," he said huskily, "if you didn't."

Tears clung to her lashes. She hurried to blink them away and sat up more. After a deep, calming breath that helped to chase away the excess emotion, she said, "I'm ready for bed. You?"

The way he looked at her told her she hadn't fooled him one bit. He knew she was mired in sentiment, that making love with him had thrown her for a loop. She'd had sex in the past, but this wasn't sex. This was… She wasn't sure what to call it. Sex had been easy to give up, but she couldn't imagine giving up Mick.

More tears clouded her vision, but he didn't seem to mind. In fact, he looked…satisfied.

Del snorted at herself as she swiped at her eyes. He'd come, so of course he was satisfied. "I'll just get rid of the condom and turn on the air conditioner and—"

Mick moved out of her reach. "I can take care of myself, thank you, and I'll set the air conditioner. I'd like to wake up without hypothermia."

"I set it too cold?" She watched him climb from the bed, and was gratified to see he shook just a bit, too.

He stood in front of her and touched her chin. There was a silly smile on his face, in contrast to the male triumph in his dark gaze. "Yeah. You set it too cold," he agreed. "I'm a man, not a polar bear."

Then he went down the hall to the bathroom. Del stood there, bemused, until she heard the water turn off and the toilet flush.

She rushed to straighten the bedclothes and reposition Mick's pillow. She'd sleep on his left side, to keep from injuring his shoulder, she decided.

He walked into her room, as comfortable with his nudity as she was. After setting the air conditioner a tiny bit higher, he got into bed as if sleeping with her were nothing. She wasn't sure if she liked that or not, considering it seemed like a very big something to her. But then he turned off the light and settled back, and when she crawled in next to him, he put his arm around her, drawing her close. The darkness added a new level of intimacy, filling her with contentment.

Her mind peaceful, her body sated, she kissed his chest and asked, "Will you tell me if you get uncomfortable during the night?"

"No." She pushed up to frown at him, but he only laughed and pressed her face back to his chest. "Shh. Go to sleep, Delilah. You've worn me out and I need to recoup so I can get even tomorrow morning."

Feeling smug, she said, "You'll have to wait to even the score. I have to go out in the morning."

His arm tightened. "Where to?"

"Neddie's funeral is tomorrow."

"Neddie?"

Because she'd already told Mick all about him, she sighed. "Neddie Moran, the man who helped me with my research."

A volatile silence followed her statement, then seemed to detonate. Mick turned, pinning her beneath him in one hard, fast movement, his expression furious. "Neddie *Moran* is the criminal who taught you how to steal cars?"

Watching him warily, she said, "Yeah, so?" He'd sounded ready to fall asleep one moment, then outraged the next. "Mick, you're going to hurt your arm."

For some reason, he looked astounded that she would even mention his arm. He jerked around and flipped the light back on. "Forget the morning. We've got to do some talking right now."

"We do?" Del scooted up in the bed and pulled the sheet over her breasts.

"Damn right we do. Do you know how Neddie Moran died?"

"He drowned."

"He didn't just drown. Someone else drowned him." Mick drew a breath. "Sweetheart, he was murdered."

CHAPTER EIGHT

MICK AWOKE TO AN EMPTY bed. Again.

This time, in light of everything he now knew, fear hit him before anything else. He glanced at the bedside clock. Three-thirty. They'd finished their talk almost four hours ago. Where the hell was she in the middle of the night?

He was out of the bed and heading for the door on silent feet before he'd even given himself time to think about it. The reality of her association with known criminals had his skin prickling with unease, his every sense on alert.

She saw no connection between Neddie's recent death and her own very near escape from death.

Mick, however, was positive that the two events were in some way related. She'd associated with Moran, formed a strange friendship even, and now the man was dead. It had been tricky, telling her what he knew of Moran's death without telling her how he knew, or giving away confidential information. The death was still under investigation, but thanks to reporters, it was public knowledge that Neddie had been drowned in the river, so Mick had no problem sharing those details.

Not that they'd swayed her. The most he'd been

able to get out of her was a promise that she'd let him escort her to the funeral. Mick planned to avoid even that, using a deception to keep her away, while he had men checking into any possible associations between Neddie and the robbers at the jewelry store. He didn't like himself for it, but he felt it necessary to protect her.

Hours of talking to her had proved that reason and logic wouldn't work. Not with Delilah Piper, and definitely not when she felt an obligation to a friend.

Mick went only a few steps down the hallway before he saw the dim blue light of her computer shining in the otherwise dark apartment. He heard the light tapping of her fingers on the keyboard, and peered around the hallway corner.

Sitting there in front of her computer, her glossy hair mussed, a T-shirt her only clothing, Delilah looked totally absorbed in her writing. Mick leaned against the wall and watched her, aware of a strange twisting in his heart.

Never had he allowed himself to consider hearth and home and a family of his own. He'd become so discriminating with women, so particular, that he'd doubted any woman would have ever appealed to him on that level.

But standing in a dark hallway looking at Delilah, he felt a contentment unlike anything he'd ever known. She was a woman of constant change and contradictions. She made him hot with her careless, comfortable air, and she kept his emotions turbulent with her daring and her stubbornness. And now that he'd laughed and argued and made love with her, he couldn't imagine not having her in his life.

Insane, he insisted to himself. But his pulse continued to riot and his lungs constricted, and only a small part of that reaction was due to lust. Hell, he shouldn't even have felt lust. It hadn't been that long since she'd wrung him out.

But he looked down at himself and, sure enough, he was already semihard. What could you do with a woman who affected you so strongly, except keep her close and make sure she didn't have the chance to affect any other man the same way?

Delilah paused, bit her lip, stared at nothing in particular and then smiled and began typing again. Mick shook his head. She amazed him, amused him, and she turned his libido red-hot.

Not wanting to startle her, he said softly, "Am I interrupting?"

She glanced up, then held one finger in the air, indicating she needed him to wait.

He should have been annoyed. They'd finished making love for the first time and she'd sneaked away to write, and now had the gall to make him wait. He smiled. No woman had ever treated him as she did, and damned if he didn't like it. Probably because her reactions, her responses, were all so real. Delilah didn't have a deceptive bone in her body. She said what she thought, did as she pleased, and that meant she could be trusted—the most appealing factor of all.

Mick sidled closer and stood behind her. He moved her heavy hair off her nape and used his thumbs to stroke her.

Delilah froze, then twisted to face him. "Um...I can't write with you there."

"Why not?"

She frowned, then turned off her monitor. Shadows closed in around them. "It makes me jittery for anyone to look over my shoulder. I don't want you to read anything out of context and think it's lame."

"I wasn't reading," he explained, still holding her neck easily between his hands. "I was considering the possibility of dragging you back to bed."

Delilah faced the computer again, her hands in her lap, her head bent forward. Finally she said, "I'm running behind, Mick. I need to finish up this scene, okay?"

"It's almost morning."

"I know. But the scene is there now, in my head." She twisted again, this time in a rush. "I'm sorry. I know this probably seems odd to you. But writers write...whenever. And I do have a deadline that is quickly closing in." She shrugged. "I've never had anyone live with me, so I've never had to not write when I wanted to. Know what I mean?"

Mick grinned. She meant that she didn't want him to interfere with her writing, but was trying to be tactful. He said only, "How long do you think you'll be?"

Again she shrugged. "I don't know. As long as the words are coming, I want to keep at it. Once this scene's done, I'll have some free time before I need to start the next one."

A thought occurred to Mick: if she stayed up all night writing, perhaps she'd forget about the damn funeral, and he wouldn't have to deceive her. "Okay, sweetheart. You take your time, okay?"

"You don't mind?"

"Of course not. There'll be times when I'll be gone all night working." Even in the dim shadows, he saw her scowl and had to fight from laughing out loud. "I'm sure you'll be understanding, too, won't you?" he teased.

Very grudgingly, she muttered, "I guess."

"Then I'll see you in the morning."

She continued to stare up at him. "Since you're here anyway, will you give me a good-night kiss?"

"My pleasure." Mick made it a kiss to singe her eyebrows—and felt himself burned instead. In that moment, he wondered if he'd ever get enough, if a lifetime of tasting and touching her would ever satisfy him.

He had his doubts.

"Wow," she said when he lifted his mouth. "You think I can work a kiss like that in with a murder scene?"

Mick stared at her blankly and she waved her hand toward the computer. "That's where I'm at in the book. All your talk about Neddie and connections and conspiracies gave me an idea for the murder scene. Do you think my hero would stop in the middle of trying to chase down the escaping madman to kiss the heroine?"

Mick shook his head. "If the heroine was you, I'm sure of it."

He saw the white flash of her teeth, then heard her chuckle. "You're outrageous. Now go on before I totally lose my train of thought and end up with them making love in the middle of the street instead of doing the responsible thing.''

Thinking of the ''responsible thing,'' Mick pushed any remnants of guilt from his mind. He'd do whatever was necessary to protect her. ''Take as long as you need,'' he said. ''Good night.''

As soon as he turned away, he heard the tapping on her keyboard resume. Madmen and making love and responsibility. Somehow they were all tied together with Delilah, and probably with her research pal, Neddie Moran, and the shooter, Rudy Glasgow, and the robbery.

All Mick had to do was find out how.

His mind filled with possibilities, both intimate and protective, so it was no wonder he slept fitfully. He had just awakened again when he felt Delilah slipping into bed beside him. He glanced at the clock and saw that it was only an hour or so until dawn.

Turning toward her, he slid his good arm beneath her head and murmured sleepily, ''Did you finish your scene?''

''Yes.'' She snuggled down, fitting herself to him as if they'd been doing this for most of their lives. That's how it was with Delilah, natural and comfortable and *right*. Her hand settled on his chest, her fingers twining in his body hair, caressing. ''I'm sorry I woke you.''

''You didn't.'' Mick pressed his mouth to her crown, drawing in the sweet scent of shampoo and Delilah. ''I've been thinking.''

''You should have been sleeping.''

"I'll sleep with you." He felt her smile against his chest. "What were you doing in the jewelry store, honey?"

Startled, she looked up at him, then with a shrug, nuzzled into his side again. "I was researching."

Their voices were both low, mere whispers over the hum of the air conditioner and the lazily twirling ceiling fan.

"What kind of research?"

Her fingertips sought and found his nipple, toying with him, making him stiffen even while half-asleep. "In this book," she whispered, "the hero has to break into a jewelry store and steal something that the madman is after, before he can get it. So I was trying to see how I'd break into that store if I was a madman."

Mick chuckled. "Neddie couldn't tell you how to do that, huh?"

"He told me a lot of things, gave me a lot of ideas, but not details on a robbery." She pressed her face against Mick in a show of emotion. "I'd contacted him about it, and even left a message, but he hadn't returned my call. I realize now that he probably couldn't."

Shit. If she'd left a message on a machine, then that could be the link that had led them to her. Mick squeezed her closer. No way in hell would he let anyone hurt her. "What exactly did you say on the message?"

"Mick." She rose up on one elbow to look at him. "I do like talking to you in the middle of the night like this, but—"

"Actually, it's morning," he said softly, pushing a curl away from her face.

"That's my point. I really would like to get some sleep."

He chuckled. "No sparing my tender sensibilities, huh?" That made her frown with concern, and he added quickly, "I'm just teasing."

"Are you sure? Because I guess I could stay awake and talk more about this if you really wanted to."

"Actually," he murmured against her mouth, "I was thinking about sports."

She again pushed away, peering at him through the dark with interest. "Are you an athlete?"

Snorting, he said, "Hell, no."

"You don't like sports?"

"I have no idea. I just never played any."

"But all little boys play baseball and football and—"

"I didn't."

She seemed to have forgotten all about sleeping, and her frown was back. "Well, why not?"

He didn't want to talk about his childhood, about his mother's shortcomings. Not now. Preferably not ever. "I was thinking about a sport you taught me."

Despite his best effort, there was an edge to his tone, a deliberately forceful change of subject that she picked up on. She might often be obtuse to her surroundings, but Mick found she was very attuned to him. It unsettled him, and turned him on.

She cupped his jaw in a gesture so tender, his heart ached. "What," she asked, lightly touching the corner of his mouth, "have I taught you?"

"Riding." He rasped the word, forcing it past an emotional lump in his throat, desperate to change his ache to a physical one, one that she could easily appease.

In the next instant, Delilah kissed him—everywhere. The emotional and the physical commingled, a variety of needs that stirred him on every plane.

After she rolled the condom onto him, she mounted him with a smile and leaned down to kiss his mouth. She slid her body onto his with a snug, wet fit, and whispered wickedly, "Giddyap."

DELILAH GROANED as she managed to get one eye open. Her entire body ached in places she hadn't known she had. And her butt was cold.

She forced her head up and saw that Mick had kicked the covers to the bottom of the bed. Her front, curled into his side, was warm enough. But her behind faced the air conditioner and was numb with cold.

When she looked Mick over, gloriously naked, she quickly heated. Until she noticed the alarm clock.

"Noon!"

Beside her, Mick groaned and he, too, opened one eye. "What is it?"

"I overslept!"

"Don't worry about it," he mumbled, and tried to draw her close again.

"But Neddie's funeral! I'll never make it now." She couldn't be sure, but Mick looked very satisfied over the situation. Del frowned. "Did you keep me awake all night on purpose?"

Both eyes opened and he stared at her breasts. "Yeah."

"Mick!"

"I'm not into making love with comatose women, so of course I had to keep you awake."

"Oh." She subsided, but only a little. "That wasn't what I meant."

"All I did," he informed her, reaching out to smooth his hand over her hip, then her belly, "was mention riding." He glanced up, his dark eyes unwavering. "You're the one who did the rest."

Because he was right, and because his hand felt too good on her body even now, she flushed. "I feel terrible," she admitted.

Mick cupped his fingers between her legs, fondling, seeking. His voice morning-rough, he crooned, "I think you feel very nice."

She frowned at him and said, "I'm sore, so forget it."

His smile made him look like a pirate. A dark sexy pirate, set on pillaging. "I'll be understanding," he promised, "and run you a nice hot bath. I'll even get the coffee." Then he added deliberately, "But forgetting about it is impossible."

"Mick." She said his name on a sigh.

His tone, his look, turned serious. "You're about all I can think of these days."

She melted. And she wasn't that sore, she decided. But he'd taken her words to heart and slid out of the bed. He stretched, careful of his wounded shoulder, and she sighed yet again at the sight of him. *Much*

more of this, she thought, shaking her head, *and I'll
begin sounding like a wounded coyote.*

"Since it's already too late to make the funeral,
would you like to come with me today?" He looked
expectant—and just a bit too watchful.

"Where are you going?" she asked.

"I need to set up something with a therapist for
my shoulder."

"I thought the doctor said to give it two weeks
first."

Mick shook his head. "I can't wait that long." He
flexed his right arm, winced, and added, "I don't like
being less than a hundred percent."

He started out of the room and she scurried after
him. He detoured into the bathroom, so she had to
pull back. Damn, he shouldn't be pushing himself.
But how could she stop him? He far outweighed her
and had double the stubbornness she possessed.

She waited in the hallway until she heard the bath-
water start. She called through the door, "Mick?"

The door opened and he snagged her, pulling her
inside. He looped his left arm around her waist, kissed
her pursed mouth and said, "You soak while I get
coffee. I'll shower when you're done."

"You're supposed to be resting!" she said, trying
for a stern expression.

"Making coffee won't tax my meager strength, I
promise." He kissed her nose and swatted her on the
behind left-handed. "Now, soak."

"Take your medicine!" she yelled to his back.

She was submerged in the hot water, letting it ease
her aches and pains, when Mick came in carrying two

mugs of steaming coffee. To her disappointment, he'd pulled on jeans, and she frowned at him. "No fair me being naked and you being dressed."

He handed her a cup of coffee. "It's the only way I can guarantee we'll make it out of here today." He grinned and added, "Otherwise I'm likely to join you in the tub. You're a helluva temptation."

She ignored his outrageous compliment and sipped—and moaned with pure, unadulterated pleasure. "Oh, that's good."

"Just what I wanted to hear. I'll take over all the coffee duties."

"You could just show me how to do it."

"I'm not quite that trusting."

Wondering just how trusting he might be, she splashed him. "So you're saying you don't like my coffee, either?"

"I had a hairless chest before drinking it."

Del tried to feign insult, but she ended up laughing instead. "Okay, so I made it stronger for you. I thought all men wanted their coffee strong and black."

He nodded. "So you know a lot of men with iron stomachs, impervious to the cold, fearless and reckless and invincible?"

"No, but that's how I write them," she teased.

Sounding far too serious, he asked, "Is that the kind of man you were looking for?"

Del considered getting serious, too. She considered telling him he was exactly what she'd been looking for, even though she hadn't realized it until she met him. Instead, she shook her head. "I know the difference between reality and fiction, but I don't have much experience with men's preferences. And for the record, I wasn't looking. I didn't really think there was room in my life for a man, not since I've kinda thrown myself into my writing.''

Mick put the toilet lid down and sat. ''You really enjoy writing, don't you?''

Her need to write wasn't always a pleasant one. ''I suppose it's a love-hate relationship. I feel the craving to write almost all the time. Sometimes it's inconvenient. People think I'm dumb because I plot a lot. They consider it daydreaming, and write me off as being too fanciful. But I doubt I'd feel like me if I wasn't writing.''

She hesitated, then tilted her head to look at him. ''I hope you can understand. There'll be a lot of times when I'm trying to listen, but my mind will go off track. And I get up a lot at night to write. It seems like as soon as I try to sleep, my brain starts churning and I just can't shut down.''

''I'll persevere.''

''It doesn't mean I'm not aware of you. It doesn't mean you're not important.''

''I understand.''

His acceptance was just a tad too quick, making her suspicious. ''Do you? Not many guys I've dated have.''

He gave her a measuring look, then asked, ''Have you dated many?''

''Sure. In my younger days, when I was curious about things.''

''Things?''

She grinned. "Sexual things, though the sex was never enough to keep me...engaged for long. I outgrew my curiosity and my fascination with men. These days, writing is more interesting, and more important than any guy—especially when I have a deadline, which I almost always do." She thought about that, and added softly, "Of course, those guys weren't as important as you."

Mick looked down at his coffee cup for a long moment. "Because I protected you?"

"Partly," she agreed. "No one has ever tried to protect me before. You blew me away, putting yourself in line for a bullet."

"What about your folks? Surely they're protective."

"I guess." She idly soaped her arm, thinking about her family. "They're wonderful, and they love me, but with two older, more serious brothers, I'm kind of the odd duck."

Mick didn't say anything to that, just continued to encourage her with his silent attention.

"You can imagine how they all reacted when I told them I wanted to be a writer." She laughed, remembering. "They told me to get serious, and when they saw that I *was* serious, they worried. Especially whenever I did research. Now, though, they're really pretty proud."

"Are you close with them?"

"Oh, sure. And my brothers are great. They're both married and have kids and houses. They still worry on occasion, but meeting you would probably fix that."

Mick went still. "Did you want me to meet them?"

She'd rushed things, she realized, and said, "Not yet."

He frowned. "You said I'm different than the other guys you dated."

"Well…yeah. I never invited any of them to move in with me."

"How am I different?"

She shook her head, lost to rational explanations when it came to her response to him. "I don't know. Everything just feels different with you, sort of sharper edged. Better. I hope that doesn't alarm you. I mean, I won't start pushing for more."

Mick set his coffee aside and stripped off his jeans. "What if I push for more?"

Del felt her mouth fall open as he stepped into the tub behind her, forcing her to move up while the water sloshed inside the tub and over the sides. His hairy legs went around her, and he tugged her back into his chest. Against her ear, he whispered, "Delilah?"

"Then…" She swallowed, trying to get her thoughts collected. "Then I guess we'll just take it one step at a time."

He cupped his hand and poured water over her breasts. "Are you still sore?"

Her heart swelled and her stomach curled in anticipation. She leaned back, closed her eyes and whispered breathlessly, "No."

CHAPTER NINE

THEY SETTLED INTO a nice routine. Mick didn't want Delilah in his house, where she might see evidence of him being a cop, so he had Josh and Zack alternately bring him more clothes as he needed them. Now her closet was filled with his things.

A dozen times he thought of telling her the truth, of explaining why he'd started the deception in the first place. But he'd only known her a little over a week, and working undercover made him more cautious than not.

Their relationship grew every day. He'd have a chance to tell her everything eventually.

Meeting with his sergeant had been difficult. Mick had set it up so that Angel and Dane would be visiting when Josh came by. They drove out for pickup pizza, and Mick slipped away to meet with the sergeant. He got a new gun, which he hid away, and an update on the robbery—which wasn't promising, since they hadn't discovered anything new.

He'd eventually have to see the shrink, as policy dictated anytime a shooting occurred. But under the circumstances, the sergeant was willing to give him more time for that.

Though he could have driven himself, Mick

claimed soreness to keep Delilah with him when he went to physical therapy. She took her laptop and wrote in the waiting room while he went through a series of increasingly difficult exercises meant to bring him back to full strength. It was slow going, and frustrating, to say the least, but he knew it wouldn't be much longer before he could make love to her as he wanted to, without concern for his injury.

Often he woke at night to an empty bed, and he'd hear her in the other room, tapping away at her keyboard. Rather than go back to sleep, he usually waited for her, and they'd make love when she crawled back in beside him.

Her unusual routine suited him just fine.

There didn't seem to be any dwindling of the devastating chemistry between them, but little by little they were both less alarmed by it, and now they wallowed in the near-violent sensations. Delilah proved inventive and curious, and she had no shyness with his body, taking everything she wanted and giving back as much in return.

Ten days had passed before his sergeant called and told him Rudy Glasgow was finally awake and coherent and ready to talk. But strangely enough, he only wanted to talk to Mick. He'd actually awakened from his coma a few days earlier, but had remained stubbornly silent and still too weak to leave the hospital. There'd been no sign of the other men, but Mick wasn't giving up, and neither was the police department.

His sergeant told him to give Detective Faradon, the lead investigator for the case, a call. Mick peeked in at Delilah, saw she was totally engrossed in her story, and punched in the numbers.

He spoke briefly with Faradon before requesting that the detective use Delilah's number only for emergencies. "Anytime you need to get in touch with me, just call my place and leave a message. I'll check the calls often."

"Running a secret life?" Faradon asked.

Mick ground his teeth together. He didn't want Faradon to know that he was still keeping secrets from Delilah. "I don't want her to overhear anything," he said as an excuse. "It could taint the case if she learned of anything important."

"Just telling you is risky," Faradon agreed. "We're only keeping you informed because you were shot, which makes you damned involved, from where I sit."

"Thanks." Mick rubbed the back of his neck. "I'm glad you understand. So, you got a pen handy?" He recited his home number to Faradon, then they briefly discussed the condition of the man in the hospital before hanging up.

Now all Mick needed was an excuse to get away from Delilah. He didn't want her to know that he'd be talking with Rudy Glasgow, yet he'd made such an issue of going nowhere without her, she was bound to be suspicious if he tried to leave on his own now.

As usual, she sat at her computer working when he finished making lunch and approached her. She was nearing the end of the book, and according to her, that's when she got most involved with the story. She had to tie up loose ends and wrap up the novel with a punch. Mick considered the way her mind worked, conjuring up so many twisted mysteries, and he shook his head. "Hungry?"

Glancing up, she asked, "Who was on the phone?"

Mick stalled, then said, "Just a friend."

"Josh? Zack?"

He hated lying to her, and often he didn't even need to. She hesitated to pry, so if he just shook his head, she'd let it go at that. Sometimes it seemed to him that Delilah went out of her way to give him his privacy, to not push. That bugged him, since it took all his concentration to keep from pushing her. She came to him willingly, accepted him in all ways, but there were still pieces of her that remained hidden. It made him nuts.

Instead of answering her specific question, he asked, "What do you have planned today?"

She accepted the sandwich he handed her and took a healthy bite while shrugging. "Writing. More writing. I hope to finish this weekend. Why? Did you need me to take you somewhere?"

It amused Mick to see how she dug into her sandwich. Sometimes when she wrote she forgot everything else, including food. When her hands began to shake, then she'd remember and grab a bite to eat.

Other times she did nothing but eat while writing. She kept a variety of snacks in her desk drawer—white-chocolate pretzels, caramels, peanuts, chips. She shoveled food away like a linebacker, yet she stayed so slim, even delicate. Her metabolism astounded him.

Settling his hip on the edge of her desk, Mick

shook his head. "No, I don't want to interrupt you today. Looks like it's going well."

"It is. I've thought about this scene for ages. It's a fun one to write. Really gruesome."

He laughed at that. "Then you stay home and finish up, but I do need to go out for just a little while."

"Without me?"

"Unheard of, I know, especially with how I've depended on you." He studied her face, seeing the hurt and something more. "You don't really mind, do you?"

She hedged, saying, "Why do you need to go out?"

Going with a sudden inspiration, he touched the end of her nose and smiled. "It's a surprise."

She flopped back in her seat and gave him a mock frown. "Not fair. What kind of surprise?"

"Now if I told you that, it wouldn't be much of a surprise, would it?"

She hesitated, fiddling with the crust on her sandwich. "You don't need to buy me things, you know."

He nodded gravely, playfully matching her mood. "I know."

She didn't look appeased by his response. "You sure you're okay to be on your own?"

"I'm a big boy, Delilah."

"Ha! Don't I know it." Her lecherous grin had him laughing again.

Damn, how he loved her shifting moods, how he loved...

Oh no. He pulled up short on his wayward thoughts, frowning at himself for letting such a deep insinuation intrude. He'd known her all of ten days—if he disregarded the two weeks prior to their formal meeting. He cared about her, more so every hour. No denying that. And he was drawn to her on the most elemental levels.

But it was far too soon to be thinking beyond that. Far, far too soon.

She mistook his frown and sighed. "Okay, I won't play mother hen, but please don't overdo it. It hasn't even been two weeks since you were shot."

Glad of the misunderstanding, he nodded. "Cross my heart."

Mick was ready to leave ten minutes later. He reminded Delilah to keep her door locked and not to let anyone in when he wasn't there. She was still skeptical about any personal threat, but she placated him by agreeing. She had few visitors, other than his friends, but she received mail from her publisher and agent regularly. She promised Mick she would be extra careful, and he finally left.

He was anxious to get some answers, anxious to face the man who'd put a bullet in his back.

The man who'd tried to kill Delilah.

The thought burned Mick, put a fire in his gut and a vibrating tension in his muscles. His sergeant had warned him not to overstep himself, to keep his cool, and Mick had agreed, even knowing it wouldn't be easy. The case was out of his hands, turned over to Homicide, and they could have refused to keep him involved. But they'd agreed to let him in to talk to Rudy Glasgow, in hopes he'd be able to get additional information.

Knowing Delilah would stay in her apartment alone all day made it easier to be away from her. She'd said she intended to write, and Mick believed her. Once she got involved with her stories, not much, including him, could pull her away.

He found her intensity rather endearing.

An around-the-clock watch had been placed on Rudy's room, even while he'd been unconscious. As Mick approached, the present guard came to his feet and set his magazine aside. Glancing down, Mick saw it was a periodical on martial arts. He smiled.

"Dawson, with City Vice." Mick held out his credentials for the guard to verify.

He nodded. "I was told to expect you."

"Has anyone else been in to see him? Has he talked to anyone else?"

The young officer rubbed the back of his neck. "Far as I know, he made a call to his lawyer and told the lead investigator that he'd speak with you. That's it."

"He called a lawyer?"

"Almost first thing after waking up. I heard he was real insistent about it."

Mick supposed that with an attempted-murder charge on Glasgow's head, getting a lawyer would be a huge consideration. "He's doing okay now? They expect a full recovery?"

"Yeah. He's a bit weak and shaky yet, and his leg is still healing, so they're planning to keep him another day or so, but then they'll ship him out." The guard grunted. "If you ask me, he's ready to go now, just dragging it out for the sake of a cushy bed."

Mick didn't doubt the probability of that. He pulled the door open.

The room was similar to the one he'd stayed in, only the shades were tightly drawn to keep it dim, and the TV played loudly. Mick took it all in with a single glance, then lounged against the wall. "You wanted to see me, Glasgow?"

Rudy Glasgow glanced over at him. His face was pale, his eyes shadowed, testimony to his physical state. It didn't move Mick one bit.

Rudy studied Mick for a long minute before grinning and motioning him closer. "I won't bite. Hell, even if I did, I doubt you'd feel it, I'm so damn weak."

Mick refused to respond to that prompt. He went straight to the matter most important to him. "Why'd you try to shoot her, Glasgow?"

He had to shout to be heard over the television, and it annoyed him. Rudy had soft sheets under him, plump pillows behind his head, a mostly eaten meal still on the tray beside his bed. Except for his elevated leg, wrapped in gauze where the bullet had struck, and the guard outside his door, he seemed to be pampered.

It grated that a criminal—an attempted murderer—should be treated so gently.

With a long, lethal look, Rudy said, "That bullet may have crippled me for life."

Mick bared his teeth. "No shit? That's the best news I've had all day."

"Screw you," Rudy suddenly said, lifting himself forward in a surge of anger. He kept his tone low, his voice a growl barely audible over the sound of the TV. His right hand twisted the sheet at his side.

Mick raised a brow, glad to see he'd riled the man. In his experience, information was always more forthcoming when your adversary was upset.

The information he got wasn't quite what he'd been expecting.

Slowly, by tiny degrees, Rudy's hand opened and he rested back on his pillows. He breathed deeply, as if that small fit of temper had taxed him, then a sardonic light entered his tired eyes and he actually chuckled. "But then," he said, "she's already doing that, isn't she?"

"Doing what?"

"Screwing you." He laughed again.

Feigning ignorance, Mick asked, "What the hell are you talking about?"

His laugh was bitter and mean. "That double-crossing bitch you protected. Oh, she covered her ass real good, I'll give her that."

Impatient, Mick barked, "Turn that damn television down. I can barely hear you."

"You heard me just fine, but I'll keep the set on so no one else hears. This conversation is between me and you. What you do with it after that is your own business."

"You planning on telling me something important, is that it?"

"Damn right. You," Rudy rasped, and thrust a finger at Mick, "are making cozy with an accomplice."

"Is that so?" Mick forced himself to speak casually, though a tightness invaded his chest. "And who would it be?"

"The woman you protected!"

"The woman *you* tried to kill?"

"She had it coming!"

Finally, Mick thought, finally he'd get some answers. He summoned a pose of boredom, when inside he seethed with anticipation—and something else, something damn close to dread. He blocked it; *he had to know.* "How do you figure that?"

"Because she was in on the robbery."

Mick laughed, though he didn't feel even an ounce of humor.

Rudy seemed beside himself. "Why the hell else did you think she was there?"

Mick stayed silent, not about to encourage him.

The man smirked. "My lawyer has been in contact with her, you know. He told me that she's got you moved in and under her spell. She even bragged to him that you wouldn't prosecute her, not while she's keeping you happy in bed."

"You expect me to believe this?" Mick knew Delilah hadn't talked to any lawyers. He'd been with her twenty-four-seven. Protecting her, he thought... No, he wouldn't let doubts intrude because of this scum! Delilah was an open, trusting woman. A gentle woman.

Who drove her car into rivers and learned how to hot-wire cars. A woman who kept company with criminals...

Mick shook his head. He knew every damn call she'd gotten. From her agent, her editor... But then, he'd just taken her word on that, when the strangers had called and she'd excused herself for a private conversation.

"You know she's a damn publicity hound," Rudy continued. "Don't you read at all? This is her biggest stunt yet, though we sure as hell didn't know about her twisted ending until we heard the cops coming. Then we realized she'd tipped them off. There was no other way they could have known we'd be there."

Icy dread climbed Mick's spine, chilling him on the inside, making his voice brisk. "A passerby claims to have seen you through the front window, and he called the police on his cell phone."

Rudy waved that away. "She set the whole thing up, including the guy who placed the call. Think about it—what was she doing there when she didn't buy anything? And why the hell would a real successful writer live in that dump she calls home?"

Mick had often wondered the same thing himself. But what did he know about a writer's salary, successful or otherwise? And for that matter, what did Glasgow know about how Delilah lived?

Feeling edgier by the second, Mick demanded, "Why tell me this?"

"Why?" Again Rudy leaned forward, and this time he shook a fist. "Because I'll be damned if I'll sit here and rot while she goes scot-free!"

"So you think I'll go to the police and have them arrest her? That I'll ask to have her prosecuted?"

"Cut the crap. You don't need to go to the cops because you *are* a cop. I know it, and more importantly, *she* knows it, regardless of your lame act about being a PI.''

Mick's heart thudded to a standstill. How did this man know what he'd said to Delilah, unless Delilah had told him? Feeling as if a fist was tightening around his windpipe, he managed to say, ''A cop?''

''That's right. You must really think she's stupid, but believe me, she's a clever one. She hadn't counted on you being in the jewelry store that day. She'd told us she just wanted to take part in the robbery, to experience it because of her twisted way of researching things. We'd get the goods and she'd get her insight. She promised to pay us nicely for our trouble.

''But then I guess she decided it'd work out better for her if she got rid of us. If anyone got wise to what really happened, she'd be off the hook. It would have been our word against hers, and she's fast becoming a celebrity, while we all have records. Without any proof to back us, she'd have walked away with a ton of fresh publicity, and we'd all have done time.''

''You still don't have any proof—or are you stupid enough to think I'm going to believe you?'' Mick had bluffed with the best of them, and right now he felt as if he'd gambled with his heart.

''Just hear me out.''

''Not if you're only going to spout bullshit.''

Again, Rudy's hands fisted in the sheets, and his face turned an angry red. ''When she realized I knew the truth about how she'd set us up, she saw you as a way out. I bet she came on real strong, didn't she? I can tell by your expression she did.'' Rudy laughed. ''She figures you'll protect her, but I want you to see justice done. That's what cops do, right? They arrest the criminals.''

Mick narrowed his eyes. ''Or shoot them in the leg.''

''Bastard!''

His shout was so loud, the guard stuck his head in the door. ''Everything okay in here?''

Mick didn't even look at him. ''Get out.''

Holding up his hands, the guard said, ''Just checking,'' and backed away, letting the door hiss shut behind him.

Mick took a step forward. His heart hammered, but he kept his expression impassive, blank. ''Give me one good reason why I shouldn't take you apart.''

''Why the hell would I lie? And think about it— how would I know all this otherwise?''

''Your buddies who got loose?'' He stood right next to the bed now, staring down at Rudy, fighting the urge to do him more damage. ''We haven't rounded them up yet—but we will.''

Rudy groaned, but more out of frustration than pain. ''Believe me, they're long gone. Not a speck of loyalty in their veins. No, the only one I've spoken with is my lawyer, and he gave me some gritty details that just about pushed me over the edge.''

Mick didn't want to hear any details. ''Give me the lawyer's name.''

''Not yet.'' Rudy absently massaged his leg. With deep satisfaction, Mick watched the pain cloud his face. ''Not until she gets what she deserves.''

''Why would she tell the lawyer anything? It would only incriminate her.''

The man shook his head. "He's in love with her. He would never do anything to hurt her, including sharing this information with you. He only told me because he wanted me to understand that she had no intention of getting involved in this mess, that I couldn't count on her to help me out."

"Ah." Mick made a tsking sound of false sympathy. "So you have no one to corroborate this ridiculous tale, huh? Too bad." The sarcasm didn't work as well as he'd hoped; he still felt ready to shout with rage. The *ridiculous* tale was far too close to sounding plausible to suit him.

"I don't need anyone to confirm my story. You already know it's true."

"Not so," he lied. "I don't believe anything repeated by an attempted murderer and bungling thief."

The man looked dumbstruck, then florid with rage. "She really did get to you, didn't she? I understand she wore you out that first night, drugged you, then used her mouth to put you to sleep. But you're a good sport. I mean, you paid her back in kind, right, once you'd gotten a little rest and your friends had all gone home?" Rudy jeered, his voice grating down Mick's spine. "For a wounded man, you were tireless, I'll give you that. But then with her in the saddle, what man wouldn't be?"

A red haze of pain and anger nearly blinded him. "You son of a bitch." Mick grabbed him by his hospital gown and twisted, lifting him a good six inches off the mattress. Disappointment threatened to buckle his knees. He had begun trusting her, caring about her, even lo—

No! None of that mattered now. The only way Rudy could have known the intimate details of Mick's first night with Delilah, especially the playful reference to riding, was if she'd told someone.

And why would she do that unless what Glasgow said was true? He couldn't believe he'd let his lust for her override his professional instincts.

Anguish tore through Mick, obliterating his reason, filling him with bitter regret.

On the heels of those overwhelming sensations was refreshing fury, a reaction he knew how to deal with, an emotion that gave him back his breath—and his strength. He let the rage overtake him.

He released Rudy with a wrenching motion that made the man choke and hold his throat.

Mick backed away, knowing he'd gone over the edge. He wouldn't let her hurt him like this. He wouldn't let her make him forget his duty, his responsibilities.

Goddamn it, he'd been the worst kind of fool, but no more. He didn't verify or deny Rudy's claims, he simply turned on his heel and walked out, but he heard Rudy alternately gasping and laughing behind him.

Hot purpose drove Mick, made his steps long and hard and impatient.

The guard tried to speak to him, but Mick's throat was all but closed, his thoughts, his feelings agitated, even violent. He had to collect himself, get himself under control.

And he had to see the lead investigator on the case.

He had evidence to share—and he wouldn't feel sane until he did.

DELILAH HEARD THE KNOCK and left her desk. Mindful of her promise to Mick, she asked, "Who is it?"

"Josh," a voice called back, and, leaving the chain on the door, she cracked it open.

Not only Josh stood there, but Zack, too. They made a mismatched pair, she thought, seeing them both smile at her. Josh with his dark green eyes and blond hair always reminded her of a slick cover model. He had cockiness stamped all over him, and he knew his effect on women. She shook her head. His effect was wasted on her. She had eyes only for Mick, and she liked it that way.

"Can we come in?" Zack asked.

If Josh looked like a model for *Playgirl,* then Zack, with his kind blue eyes and bone-straight, light brown hair, looked like a model for the Sunday ads, maybe for comfy house slippers. He looked warm and cozy, like a man meant for a family.

Josh was excitement. Zack was comfort.

Mick was both those things and more. He was everything. Too quickly, he'd become so important to her.

She held the door open so they could enter. "Mick's not here."

They both drew up short, and Josh, in the rear, almost ran into Zack. "What do you mean, he's not here?"

Delilah shrugged. "He said he had a surprise something or other to do and left at lunchtime, almost four hours ago. He didn't want me to go along.''

They shared a look. ''You promised to stay in?'' Josh guessed.

She shrugged. ''I had writing to do, anyway. But this overprotectiveness is getting absurd.'' She gave them both pointed looks to let them know they were grouped in with the overprotective absurdity. After all, they backed Mick up every time he warned her to be cautious. She wondered how they thought she'd lived this long without them all looking over her shoulder, protecting her every step of the way.

Zack put his arm around her. They were both overly familiar, treating her now as if she and Mick were a longtime couple. They'd come around almost every other day, and had learned to make themselves at home. ''Grant the guy the right to worry.''

''He doesn't return the favor.'' She didn't mean to sound complaining, but it sure came out that way.

''Meaning?'' Zack asked in a gentle tone.

''Meaning he doesn't want me to ever worry and he looks annoyed if I do.''

Josh dropped onto her couch. '''Course he would. He's a guy.''

Del warned him with a look. ''Your sexist attitude is going to get you into trouble someday.'' At first Josh's attitude had rubbed her the wrong way, but now she accepted him, even liked him. In small doses.

Zack nodded. ''I've told him the same, but this time he's right. Mick can take care of himself.''

She laughed at them. They saw everything in black-and-white, especially where men and their roles in life were concerned. Men were supposed to protect, to defend, to cherish. Even Josh, with his variety of girlfriends, treated them all as special. And Zack made his beautiful little girl the center of his life.

That thought brought another, and she asked, "Where's Dani?" She enjoyed visiting with the child. Dani wasn't the average four-year-old. She was too precocious, too aware of her surroundings.

"Gone to the movies with a neighbor and her daughter. She said to give you a hug from her." So saying, Zack pulled Del close and squeezed her, rocking back and forth.

She laughed and pushed herself away. Never in her life had she been touched so much. Her parents, once they'd realized she was different, had given her space—not necessarily space she wanted, but evidently space they needed. They hadn't known how to deal with her, so they'd dealt with her less.

Not so with these guys. The less they understood her, the more determined they were to figure her out. And in the process, they coddled and cuddled her a lot. They made her laugh, made her exasperated, made her feel important, wanted.

She enjoyed it all, the intimate, hot touching she and Mick shared, the friendly touching and camaraderie she got from Mick's friends, and the emotional touching, the acceptance, the welcome. Not a day went by that she didn't hear from one or another of Mick's family or friends.

It had never occurred to her how isolated she'd become. She wrote in a void, emerging only for research and publicity. But then Mick had saved her life, and in the process, changed it irrevocably.

"When do you expect him back?" Josh asked, even as he picked up the TV remote control and started looking for a sports channel.

Zack turned the television off. "Dolt, did you consider that she might be busy?"

Josh glanced at her. "You busy?"

Feeling rather conspicuous now, Del gestured at her desk, littered with small sticky notes and research files. "I was just writing the last chapter."

"Then we can hang out and wait for Mick?"

Zack groaned. "Writing is work to her, you idiot. How can she work if you're here disrupting her?"

Josh looked totally bemused by the idea that he might be a bother to anyone, and Del relented. "Not at all," she said. "I'll enjoy the company. I really don't know how much longer Mick will be, though." She glanced at the wall clock and saw it was nearly five. "I thought he'd be back by now."

Zack glared at Josh, which made Josh raise his brows in a *what?* expression, before asking, "You're sure you don't mind?"

"I've been writing all day. My legs are cramped." Then a thought hit her and she said, "I haven't been out running once since Mick moved in. I miss it."

Again they shared a look, and it was Josh who said, "It's not safe for you to be out traipsing around until they catch those other guys."

"Yeah, right," she scoffed. "Who's to say they'll ever catch them? Am I supposed to stay cooped up forever?" Josh opened his mouth and she rushed to say, "Don't answer that! I know what *you* think already."

He grinned shamelessly. "I was just going to say to wait until Mick is completely healed and I'm sure he'll run with you. In the park. Or someplace else that's safe."

"But not here," Zack added.

"No, not here."

Del sat down on the couch next to Josh. "Why not here?"

Josh frowned, measuring his words. "Being the intense writerly type that you are, you may not have noticed, but this area is pretty hazardous."

"Hazardous how?"

He glanced at Zack for help. Zack sat on her other side. "Unsavory types live around here."

"Really?"

"Well, yeah…you never noticed?"

She chuckled at his disbelief. "Of course I did. I also noticed the variety of people who live here, old and young, black and white and Hispanic, male and female, friendly and hostile. I love the atmosphere, the constant chaos. No matter what time of night I'm up to write, there's something going on outside. People feed my inspiration, and I write better in places like this."

Zack reached over and tweaked a tendril of her hair. "You're a nut, sweetheart."

She swatted at him, laughing.

Josh agreed. "Most women I know want to avoid the criminal element as much as possible. You're the first person I've heard who wants to embrace it."

"I write about the criminal element, remember? Most of my mysteries revolve around a villain. Besides, I go where my villains go. And that makes for some fun travel."

"Yeah?"

"Yup. I love moving."

They were just getting into that discussion when Del's doorbell rang. She glanced at both Zack and Josh, then started to get to her feet.

Josh stopped her with a hand on her arm. "Mick?"

Shaking her head, she said, "Not unless he lost his key."

Zack moved past them both. "I'll get it."

Del smiled at their determination in keeping her safe. She didn't bother telling them that she received a lot of special delivery packages from her editor. No, she just sat back and indulged them in their maleness.

When Zack opened the door, she saw two people there, a man and a woman dressed in suits. The woman gave a faint, stony smile. "Is Ms. Delilah Piper in, please?"

"Who's calling?" Zack asked suspiciously. At the same time, Del stood to better see.

The woman looked past him. "Ms. Piper?"

"That's right." Del started toward the door, but Josh kept pace at her side.

The woman flipped open her bag to display a shiny, very official badge. "I'm Detective Darney, with the city police department. This is Detective Breer. Would you mind coming with us to answer some questions?"

Josh bristled, eyeing the badges as if to verify their authenticity. "What's this about?"

At his tone, the male officer spoke up. "She's wanted downtown for questioning. That's all…for now."

Confused, Del asked, "Questioning about what?"

Both Josh and Zack flanked her, and Del appreciated their solid, comforting presence. She felt off balance and a little frightened.

Detective Breer ignored Josh and faced Del instead. "For possible involvement in the jewelry store robbery," he intoned, his voice so deep Del felt her skin prickle.

"*What?*" She thought she shouted the word, but it came out as only a vague, rusty whisper.

Detective Darney looked sympathetic. "You've been named as an accomplice," she gently explained. "But before any charges are filed, we'd like to talk to you."

Del had no idea what to do; she'd never faced a situation like this! She turned to Josh with a blank stare, hoping for direction. He looked furious and concerned. "Don't worry, sweetheart. We'll be right behind you."

"Mick…"

Zack gave her a squeeze. "We'll get hold of him. I promise."

She nodded, reached for her purse, and then Detective Darney had her arm, leading her out the door.

CHAPTER TEN

AT LEAST THEY HADN'T handcuffed her, Del thought with a struggling sense of humor to temper her despair. Her throat felt tight, her chest hurt and her stomach was queasy. She almost faltered as she was led through double glass doors and into a long corridor, but the police station wasn't a place to make a scene.

Detective Darney's heels tapped on the tile floor on one side of her, while Breer's heavy steps echoed as solid thuds on the other. They had her caged in—guarding against her escape? Absurd, almost as absurd as the interrogation room where they stopped.

Detective Breer pulled a chair out for her. "Would you like a cup of coffee?"

Numbness seeping in, Del shook her head. The proffered courtesies, in light of the situation, were almost laughable. She drooped down into the chair.

The plastic-covered seat squeaked beneath her. Her blouse stuck to her back from the heat and her tension, forcing her to lean forward. Sweat gathered between her breasts. The unmarked car she'd ridden in had icy-cold air-conditioning, but this room was hot, stuffy, closing in on her. Suffocating.

Once while doing research, she'd been in a room

just like this. She knew the procedure and the protocol, and tried to calm herself with the fact that she knew what to expect, though she'd certainly never thought she'd find herself in the position of being an actual suspect.

Still, she wouldn't panic. It was all a misunderstanding. And thinking that, she said, "If you get hold of Mick Dawson, he could explain to you that I was just a victim."

As if she'd summoned him, Mick strode in. He had another man behind him, and both of them wore frowns, but Mick's was darker, and very grim. Del didn't understand, and she couldn't stop herself from saying in some surprise, "Mick!" and then, as relief washed over her, "Thank God you're here."

His black-eyed glance lacked any emotion as he took a seat at the end of the table—a good distance from where she sat.

Anxiety smothered her. Mouth dry, pulse racing, Del looked down the expanse of the table to Mick. It meant something, that awful distance he'd instigated, but for the life of her, she couldn't imagine what. When he'd left her at the apartment that afternoon, everything had been fine.

He'd even told her he planned to get her a surprise gift.

Thinking this wasn't exactly the surprise she'd hoped for, Del twittered nervously. The silly sound just sort of escaped on its own, a girlish giggle, a forerunner to hysteria, making her edgier. She slapped a hand over her mouth. She didn't understand…any of it.

She swallowed hard and reached for composure. "What's going on?"

The man who'd entered with Mick held out his hand. He was large and beefy, and had salt-and-pepper hair neatly trimmed above his elongated ears. Watery, pale blue eyes were closely spaced to an overlarge nose. His suit fit his square frame loosely, and a wrinkled tie hung crooked around his neck.

He looked like a wonderful character, Del thought, someone she could put into a book. She knew she shouldn't be thinking such inane thoughts at the moment, but all other thoughts cut like tiny razors, and her mind naturally shied away from them.

She couldn't bring herself to accept the man's hand.

He eased back, putting his hand in his pocket. The other held a clipboard. "Ms. Piper, I'm Detective Faradon, lead investigator on the robbery you were involved in." He checked his clipboard, then rattled off the date and time and location.

Del concentrated on finding her breath and centering her thoughts. She had to deal with this—whatever it might be. "Could you please tell me what this is all about?"

Rather than sit, Faradon propped his hip on the edge of the table. Del expected the table to collapse under his weight, but it held.

She skipped another glance at Mick. He was staring at her with such stony concentration that it struck her like a physical blow, forcing her to flinch away.

The other two detectives watched her as well. It

was like being on display, or caught in a hangman's noose, and it hurt.

"Ms. Piper, are you acquainted with Rudy Glasgow?"

She shook her head, then stopped abruptly. "Yes, he's the man in the hospital, the man Mick shot."

"So you do know him?"

"I know of him." Her heart beat too hard, too fast. "I've read the accounts since the shooting. His name has been in the papers. He's...he's unconscious."

"Not anymore." The man surveyed her through lowered, bushy brows. His expression turned speculative, calculating. Finally, he said, "He claims to know you."

Forgetting her sweaty blouse, Del dropped back hard in her chair. Her spine offered less support than an overcooked noodle. "He's wrong," she replied flatly.

"He claims," the man continued, glancing at his clipboard, "that you set the whole thing up as a publicity stunt."

Del's gaze shot to Mick and locked with his. Neither of them blinked. Dear God, surely he didn't believe such an idiotic story.

She shook her head. "No."

"That's it?" Mick asked, his voice harsh and loud in the closed room. "No other explanations?"

Del searched his beautiful face, his once gentle face, and her heart crumbled. The flat, compressed line of his mouth, his locked jaw and dark flinty brown eyes showed his distaste.

For her.

Del winced with a very real pain. *He'd already found her guilty in his mind.* She wanted to reach out to him, to touch him, but she couldn't. She didn't think he'd let her.

"Mick?" she whispered.

His expression hardened even more and he looked away.

It hurt worse than anything she'd ever felt. She murmured to his averted face, "I can't believe you just did that. I...I really can't."

He gave her another sharp look, but this time she dismissed him.

Looking down at her hands, Del said, "I don't know Rudy Glasgow, and I didn't set up the robbery for a publicity stunt. I don't do that."

"You have been known," Detective Breer pointed out, "for your extravagant research tactics."

"Tactics that have never hurt anyone or broken any laws." She felt hollow, stiff. Wounded. "I was there that day, as I've already said, to see how a robber would set things up, but—"

"Isn't that something of a coincidence," Detective Darney asked, her voice soft in comparison to the men's, "that a robbery would take place while you were doing your research for a robbery?"

"Yes." Del's stomach churned with an awful dread. "It's an incredible coincidence."

"You've spoken with him."

Del jumped at the lash of Mick's accusation. She didn't quite look at him when she asked in a small voice, "Who?"

He rounded the table until he faced her from the

other side, giving her no choice but to meet his gaze.
"Glasgow. I saw him today." He slashed a hand
through the air, impatient, provoked. "He knows
things."

"What kind of things?"

After glancing at the other people in the room,
Mick narrowed his eyes on her. "Things you and I
have done. Intimate details that he couldn't have
guessed at."

Detective Darney turned away. The men stared at
her, their attention burning hot. Embarrassment hit her
first, then a wave of remorse for what Mick had
clearly thrown away.

And finally her temper ignited in scalding sensation. It chased away the numbness and burned away
the hurt. Her heart raced, her pulse pounded.

Very slowly, she came to her feet. "I haven't spoken to anyone about anything we've done."

"He knew it all, Delilah. He knew *details.*"

She stared over his shoulder, her mind racing as
the ramifications of that sank in. "Then he...he found
out some other way."

"How?"

"It's not my job to figure it out." She turned point-
edly to Faradon. Sweat gathered at the base of her
spine. She itched from the prickling of fear, mortifi-
cation, loss and anger.

"All of you," she said, addressing the whole room,
"you are looking at the wrong person. I don't know
Rudy Glasgow. I haven't spoken with him."

"You've told no one?"

She glanced at Mick, overcome with sadness. His

distrust would not be easy to forgive, and he would be impossible to forget. But she had no choice now. "What we've done, Mick...well, it was special to me." She got choked up and despised herself for the weakness. She wasn't used to declaring herself in front of a crowd, especially a hostile crowd. And she didn't delude herself; this crowd was hostile. They'd already condemned her.

She cleared her throat and made a last stab to reach him. "I would never have discussed our personal situation with anyone, much less the man who shot you."

For a long, sizzling moment, Mick stared at her, and she held herself still, hoping he'd smile, that he'd tell her he believed her. That he'd apologize.

He jerked away, cursing softly. His back to her, Mick ran a rough hand through his hair, and Del found herself stupidly concerned for his injury. She could feel his tension, his anger.

She ignored everyone else in the room. At the moment, the only one who mattered was Mick. What the others thought could be straightened out later. She said steadily, "If you just think about it, you'll know I couldn't have done that. That I wouldn't have done anything like that. You know me."

"Barely," he said, still not facing her.

She wavered on her feet. That he could say such a thing after everything they'd done together, after everything she'd felt for him...

She called herself a fool, even as she begged, "Don't do this."

His gaze cut toward her, accusing. "He said you

were counting on our relationship to keep you safe from the law."

Mick's insinuation was clear. He chose to believe a man who'd shot him in the back, rather than her. Del forced herself to straighten. Later, she'd have to decide how to deal with her broken heart.

Right now, she had to figure out what to do to make the detectives believe her. That had to be her top priority.

But how? She looked around at them—and saw pity from the lead investigator, interest from Detective Breer and understanding from Detective Darney. Del hated it all, and accepted that they all considered her guilty.

"Are you arresting me?" She was proud of her steady voice, the strength in her demand.

Faradon tapped his clipboard against the table. "Not just yet. But I don't want you to leave town."

"Fine." Del turned to walk out on wobbly legs, but he stopped her.

"Ms. Piper?"

She froze.

"I may have more questions later. I trust you'll cooperate with me?"

She turned to face him. "The man wanted to kill me—or so everyone keeps telling me. Now that he's come up with this outrageous tale meant to incriminate me personally, I have to believe it was a deliberate act against *me*. Of course I want him convicted and his cohorts found. I'll help you any way I can."

Looking a little bemused by that heartfelt speech, Faradon murmured dryly, "Thank you."

Del pushed the door open and walked out. Her neck hurt, her stomach coiled. Tears burned behind her eyes, and she fought them back.

She wanted to run, as fast as her legs could carry her. Just as she hadn't known such wonderful elation existed until she'd met Mick, she hadn't known anyone had the power to hurt her so badly.

But she held her dignity intact and walked, head held high, back down the long corridor. She was more than a little aware of Detectives Breer and Darney following behind her.

When she reached the front desk, Josh and Zack stood there, impatient and worried. Zack reached for her first, pulling her into a warm, tight embrace that was just what she needed, but not who she needed it from.

"Hey," he said, squeezing her a bit tighter, "are you okay? You're shaking."

Swallowing back a choking sob, she nodded against his chest and allowed herself the luxury of being held by him for one moment more. Then she pushed away.

Josh touched her cheek. "Mick didn't return my page yet."

It took two attempts before the words would come out. "No need to page him. He's here."

Josh and Zack frowned, their expressions mirroring each other. The irony struck her, and she almost laughed. Not only would Mick not help her, but...

"He was the one," she said, trying for a note of self-mockery in place of desperation, "who evidently brought the new evidence to the police."

Josh didn't appear convinced. "Honey, are you all right?"

"No, no I'm not." Any second now she was going to throw up. Not because of Rudy or the robbery. She was innocent, and sooner or later they'd all realize it.

No, she was sick at heart, and sick inside, because she loved a man who'd just turned his back on her, and she had no idea how she was going to recover.

A deep breath, then another, didn't really help. "Being that you're Mick's friends, not really mine, and being that he now thinks I'm a... Well, I'm not sure what he thinks." She shook her head, understanding now why he'd kept his thoughts so private—because he'd never trusted her. "All I know is that it's ugly, that everything has changed, and I have no doubt you'll both back him up as you always do. So—" she fashioned a smile out of her stiff lips and tried not to notice the concern in their eyes, the caring "—I guess this is goodbye. It's been swell, guys."

She hurried out front, with both of them rushing behind her. A taxi rounded the corner onto the adjacent street, and she jogged across the parking lot to hail it, just wanting to escape, to be alone—as she'd accustomed herself to being. She had the cab door open when Josh grabbed her arm.

"Delilah, wait."

She looked up at him—and saw Mick standing in the station doorway. "He can explain," she said, tears filling her eyes to the point where everything blurred. "Goodbye."

Josh had no choice but to release her. She didn't look back to see them talking. She knew what Mick would tell them, what he believed, and she couldn't bear to see them turn on her, too. She'd finally gotten comfortable with them, accepted them as a part of her life, a disruptive, unruly, fun part.

And now it was over.

She dropped her head forward and covered her face. *How?* she wondered, wishing she could understand what had happened, how it had all gone so wrong in the blink of an afternoon.

The man Mick had shot was no longer unconscious. And he'd told Mick something, found some way to convince him that she was involved. Mick had said he knew personal things, intimate things. That had to mean details of their lovemaking.

Judging by the way Mick had looked at her, *he* hadn't told a soul, so he'd assumed that she had done the blabbing. To a criminal. To a man who'd tried to kill her and had shot him.

And then the shock of it hit her. She felt chilled to the bone, shivering with realization, revulsion.

The cabby pulled up to her apartment, and Del handed him a twenty, not even thinking about getting change, or how much she'd tipped him. She stumbled to the steps leading to her apartment and stared up at the front door.

There was only one thing for her to do.

She had to leave.

MICK HATED TO ADMIT IT, but he was relieved to see that Josh and Zack had followed Delilah to the station. That meant she hadn't been alone when the detectives took her. He'd regretted sending for her almost immediately, but then he had a lot of regrets, and they all centered around her. He had to stop thinking with his emotions and start using his head instead.

He turned to Josh as he approached, but wasn't prepared for the solid pop in the left arm his friend delivered.

"Ow, goddamn it!" Awkwardly, he rubbed his arm and glared at Josh. "That hurt."

"Good." Josh looked ready to take another swing, this one at Mick's head. "What the hell did you do to her?"

"To Delilah?"

Zack rolled his eyes. "No, to Queen Elizabeth. Of course to Delilah. She came out of here nearly in tears."

"Not *nearly* in tears," Josh accused, his nostrils flared like a charging bull. "She was crying, damn it."

Mick hurt from his hair to his toenails, and not all of it was physical. The idea of Delilah crying only added to his pain, making it more acute when he'd thought he couldn't hurt any worse. Dully, wishing he could undo the past, or somehow change it, he said, "She's not who you think she is."

Zack went very still, then stiffened. "What did you do?"

To see his two best friends rallying to her defense added one more bruise to his already battered conscience. He'd wanted them to accept her, and vice versa. But now it hardly mattered.

In the briefest terms possible, Mick explained the

situation. He hated going through it again, hated re-hashing all the ways he'd been duped, all the ways she had lied.

When he finished, Josh popped him again.

Mick squared off, unwilling to let Josh's hostility continue. "Will you quit that!"

Pushing himself between them, Zack said, "Josh has a point."

"A point?" Mick stared at him, incredulous. "All he did was hit me!"

"Because you needed to be hit," Zack explained, always the cool one, always the peacemaker. "Jesus, man, you don't know anything about women. I realize you don't date much—"

"Look who's talking."

"—but I figured you'd have picked up some things just from being around Josh, if only by osmosis."

"I know more than I care to," Mick grumbled in return. He knew that he was a lousy judge of character, that he'd allowed his gonads to overrule his good sense. That few people could be trusted, but he was too damn stupid to learn that lesson.

"Not," Josh said, pressing forward again, "by a long shot."

Mick was amazed by Josh's red-eyed, aggressive attitude, which went well beyond defensive friendship for Delilah. *He was acting territorial.* Mick closed the space between them in a heartbeat. "What the hell does she mean to *you?*"

"More than she does to you, obviously!"

Again, Zack wedged into the middle, chest to chest with Mick, forcefully moving him a few feet away from Josh. "Quit baiting him, Josh. And Mick, he's right. Why the hell didn't you talk to her privately?"

"I'm a cop," he reminded them, with an enormous dose of sarcasm and a chip on his shoulder so large his knees almost gave out. "I'm supposed to bring in the criminals." No sooner did the words leave his mouth than he winced. He sounded just like Rudy.

Josh shook his head and all but shouted, "You're also in love, you ass."

Mick stared at him, and wondered if he could reach him before Zack intervened. Probably not, judging by Zack's watchful attention. Mick settled for saying, "Go screw yourself."

"Oh yeah, that'll fix things." Josh threw up his hands. "Do you have any idea how rare a woman like Delilah is?"

Possessiveness bristled along his nerve endings, despite what had just transpired in the interrogation room. "Not more than a few days ago, you were calling her strange!"

"Strange, unique, rare." Josh shrugged. "But that was ten days ago, before I really knew her."

"You're keeping count!"

"She's damn special."

Zack nodded. "Very special."

"Did either of you hear me?" Mick demanded in a shout, so frazzled and confused he knew his hair should be standing on end. "She's dealing with Rudy. She was in on the whole thing."

Zack leveled him with a pitying look. "I don't believe it."

"Neither do I," Josh added. "If you'd talked to her privately, maybe she could have explained."

"She had a chance to explain in there," Mick roared, stabbing a finger toward the station, "and all she did was deny any connection to him."

"Maybe because she has no connection, and maybe because you threw her for one hell of a loop." Josh squeezed his eyes shut. "God, she looked so hurt, it's breaking my damn heart, and I'm not the one in love with her."

Zack raised a brow over that, but refrained from saying anything.

"She's crazy about you, Mick. She trusted you." Disgust filled Josh's tone. "And you just tossed her to the wolves."

Mick looked away from the accusation in Josh's eyes. "All I did was have her questioned."

"All you did," Josh said, grabbing him by his shirtfront and shaking him, "is show her that you don't care two cents for her feelings, that you don't trust her and that you'll gladly believe a man capable of murder rather than hear her side of things."

Put that way... Mick shook Josh off and paced across the parking lot. Heat rose from the blacktop in waves, adding to his frustration, making him sweat.

His first sight of Delilah in the interrogation room had showed her to be wilted, stunned. By the time she'd walked out she'd mustered up a bit of stiff-backed pride. But the incredible vibrancy that he'd thought an integral part of her had been gone. He shook his head, wanting to dispel the image of her beautiful blue eyes clouded with distress. "I was…sick when I got done talking to Rudy."

"Sick and stupid," Josh sneered.

Zack grabbed Josh. "Will you knock it off! This isn't helping, and to be frank, I'm beginning to be a bit suspicious of your interest myself."

Josh glared at him, then at Mick's questioning gaze. Finally, he shrugged. "If Mick wasn't interested in her, I'd have been hot on her trail. So what?"

Already on a short fuse, Mick exploded. "You miserable son of a—"

This time Zack had to leap between them, shoving at both men hard to keep them from coming to blows. "You're both causing a scene, damn it!"

Around Zack's body, Josh taunted, "What's it matter to you, buddy? You just threw her away." And then, as if that wasn't enough to curdle Mick's blood, he added, "I think I'll go *console* her."

Another struggle ensued, while Zack did his best to keep the two of them apart. Josh, muttering a sound of disgust, finally gave up and stepped away. "Fine, you still want her? Well then, go after her. But *listen* to her. And don't you dare make her cry again."

Mick, red in the neck and teeth gnashing, subsided as well. He didn't really want to take his rage out on a friend. It took him several moments, but he finally got the words out. "You honestly think there might be another explanation?"

They both nodded at him. Josh said, "I believe in her. She may be good at coming up with elaborate plots for her books, but she'd never hurt someone she cared about."

Mick wondered if, after what he'd just put her through, he could still be counted among those she cared for.

"And no way," Zack added, "would she take a chance on innocent people getting caught in the cross fire just for publicity."

Mick groaned, hearing the ring of truth in their words. Josh walked away from them both and went to stand near a telephone pole. Zack squeezed Mick's uninjured shoulder. "Yep, I'm afraid you might have blown it. Better to get there as quick as you can and start your apologies. If you give her too much time to consider what you've done, she may not be able to forgive you."

Mick stared at his feet. "I can't imagine what explanation there could be. Rudy knew things that no one should have known."

"It would be easy enough for him to guess that you were sleeping together. That doesn't take an Einstein."

"He knew...details. Specific details that went beyond—"

"I understand," Zack rushed to say, before Mick could stumble on. But Mick noticed there was a gleam of curiosity in his eyes, too.

He straightened. "I'll give her a chance to talk to me, one on one. And I hope like hell you're right, that she can clear this all up."

"Ha. I think you better do more than that. You better get down on your knees."

Mick glared at him, but as he walked away, he didn't rule out the possibility of begging. He'd never felt so miserable in his life—not when Angel had been threatened and he knew he couldn't protect her, not even when his mother had died in a stranger's shack, an empty whiskey bottle beside her. No, the thought of losing Delilah was a gnawing ache that kept expanding and sharpening until his guts felt on fire and his chest threatened to explode.

Even if she had been in on the scheme, he didn't want to lose her. He'd find a way to keep her out of jail, keep her straight, even if that meant keeping her in bed, under him, from now on.

Before he reached his car, he was running.

It occurred to him with a blinding flash of insight that if his friends were right, if Delilah was in fact innocent, he'd just left her alone and vulnerable. Anything could happen to her.

He stepped on the gas and made it to her apartment in record time.

JOSH SAW ZACK GLARING at him and he grinned, though his grin felt more sickly than not. "What?"

"Don't use that innocent tone on me. What the hell were you thinking?"

Forcing a chuckle, Josh shook his head. "I just worked him into a lather. He needed to be shook up or he'd have stood around here pondering all the possibilities, and by the time he realized we were right, it would have been too late. I saved him some time and heartache, that's all."

"So everything was an act? You're not hung up on her?"

Josh winked, and lied through his teeth. "Not at all. You know I like to play the field."

"Huh. I know you've never had a woman show complete and utter disinterest in you before."

"True." Delilah had gone from not noticing him, to grudgingly accepting him as Mick's friend, to displaying a fondness that bordered on sisterly. From the start, she'd made her preferences known, and it had been Mick all the way. Josh laughed. "I tell ya, I can live without it ever happening again."

Zack turned to look at the road. "I hope Mick doesn't kill himself getting over there."

"I just thought of something," Josh said, and reached for the cell phone clipped to his belt. "Since we both know Delilah didn't have any part of sharing that information, someone must have been spying on them."

"But how?" Zack asked. "Mick claims it was very personal in-the-bedroom stuff."

Josh grinned. "Yeah, I wish he'd elaborated on that." Zack laughed, never guessing exactly how big a lie that was. The last thing Josh wanted to hear was the personal sexual details between them. It ate him up.

Delilah, with her contrary ways and openness and brutal honesty, had stolen a piece of his heart. It was the damnedest thing he'd ever experienced, and while he was thrilled all to hell and back for Mick, he couldn't help wishing that he'd found her first.

He shook off his melancholy. Right now, all he wanted was for Mick and Delilah to be happy, and that meant Mick had to get her to forgive him. To that end, Josh wanted to figure out what had gone wrong.

"You think someone could have seen in through the bedroom window somehow?"

"I don't know," Josh admitted, "but I know who could find out."

Awareness lit Zack's eyes. "Alec?"

"You betcha." He punched in a series of numbers and waited until the call was answered. "Alec Sharpe, please. Yeah, it's an emergency."

Only a few seconds passed before Alec took the phone. "Sharpe here."

It would have taken far too long to explain, so Josh merely said, "Hey, Alec, this is Josh. Mick is kind of in trouble and you need to get over to Delilah's apartment."

To Josh's surprise, Alec didn't ask any questions, didn't ask for details of any kind. He said only, "I'm on my way," and the line went dead.

Zack looked at Josh as he closed the cell phone. "Well?"

Josh shrugged. "He, uh, he doesn't say much, does he? But he's heading over there now." He glanced at his watch. "Figuring he was at the office, I think it'll take him about forty-five minutes."

Zack frowned in thought. "With what I've heard about Alec, I wouldn't be surprised if he made it in thirty."

Then they stared at each other. Josh shifted, looked up at the broiling afternoon sun and then the glare off his car's windshield. He propped his hands on his hips and tilted his head at Zack. "You got anywhere you need to be?"

After glancing at his watch, Zack said, "Not for a few more hours. Dani was going to the pizza parlor after the movie."

They'd been friends so long, they often shared thoughts without words being spoken. "Think we should?" Josh asked.

Neither one answered, then in unison they said, "We should."

CHAPTER ELEVEN

MICK SAT OUT FRONT for several minutes, stewing in his own misgivings. He hated to admit how much he hoped, prayed, that Delilah could come up with an alternate explanation. Even now he wanted to hold her, to tuck her close and tell her everything would be all right, that he'd keep her safe and keep scum like Glasgow away from her.

He groaned. It was entirely possible that she'd set up the whole robbery, that he'd gotten shot because of her.

It was even probable, given the facts at hand.

Cowardly bastard, he accused himself, and jerked his car door open. He'd face the outcome, whatever it might be, just as he'd faced everything in his life, good and bad.

He took the concrete steps two at a time. The long flight of stairs leading to the upper level didn't slow him down, either. He bounded up them, anxious to speak to Delilah, to figure things out.

He started to knock, then decided to use the key she'd given him. She might refuse to let him in under the circumstances, so he unlocked the door and stepped quietly inside.

The apartment was silent, causing his instincts to

scream. Mick reached to the small of his back and pulled out his gun. He'd armed himself right after seeing Rudy in the hospital. He hadn't worn the gun before that because he hadn't wanted to make Delilah suspicious, and he was only a mediocre shot with his left hand. But he'd felt naked without it.

Every light in her apartment blazed, and things were scattered everywhere—boxes on the floor, cushions pulled loose from the sofa.

Fear for her clawed at him. Mick crept forward, away from the open door, then quickly ducked as the chopping block from the kitchen whooshed past him, barely missing his head. It fell to the floor with a clatter, the wood neatly splitting down the middle. He whirled and aimed.

Thrown off balance by the impetus of the attack, a small body tumbled forward and landed against his chest, warm and familiar. Mick automatically raised his gun to the ceiling while catching her.

He and Delilah stared at each other.

Slowly, Mick lowered his arm to his side, watching her warily. She stepped back and away from him, then covered her mouth, breathing hard. "Ohmigod." Her fingers over her open mouth trembled. She shook her head. "I'm sorry. I didn't know it was you."

All color had leeched from her face. Her eyes appeared huge and distressed. Everything inside Mick melted, all the suspicions and the worry and the anger temporarily replaced by the need to protect her. "Are you all right?"

Seconds ticked by while they stared at each other. She shook her head again. "No."

That was all she said before turning away and heading for her bedroom. Obviously, no one else was in the apartment, given the way she went about her business.

Mick followed her into her room, and the first thing he saw was the suitcase opened on the bed, partially packed.

His knees locked; his healing shoulder pounded with a renewed ache. "You going somewhere?"

She didn't look at him again, though her face remained pale and he could see her hands trembling. "Yes."

His throat tightened. "Where?"

"I can't tell you in here."

A frown pulled at his brows. "In here in the bedroom?" he asked, perplexed by her odd behavior.

She shifted impatiently. "No, here in my apartment."

"You heard what Faradon told you." He strode toward her, uncertain but determined. He wouldn't let her get away from him. "You're not to leave."

Her scathing glance stopped him in his tracks. "I can't very well stay here. But don't worry. I'm not skipping town. I'll still be around for you to persecute."

"Prosecute," he corrected automatically, then caught himself, realizing she'd said it on purpose. He clenched his teeth, counting to ten. Attempting a softer, more reasonable tone, he said, "I don't want to prosecute or persecute you, babe."

She went to her dresser, picked up an armload of items and dropped them haphazardly into the suitcase.

"Get out of my way," she said as she started past him to the hallway. "What are you doing here, anyway? And why are you creeping around with your gun out? Were you going to shoot me?"

She didn't wait for an answer to that outrageous insult, but marched into the hall.

"You know damn good and well I wouldn't shoot you! I wouldn't do anything to—"

"Hurt me?" She stopped abruptly. "It's a little too late to make that claim, isn't it?"

"Delilah…"

In a hurry to finish packing, she rushed off. Was she leaving her apartment rather than throw him out? Did she think he intended to stay with her still?

Actually, he hadn't thought that far ahead, but the idea of leaving her, of not having her next to him at night, her soft body his to touch, her gentle breath warming him, gave him a lost, sick feeling in the pit of his stomach.

He put his gun away, then knotted his hands to keep from reaching for her. She looked…breakable. Fragile.

She stopped in the middle of the floor, as if uncertain what to do next. Her gaze landed on her computer, and she dove toward it with a purpose, quickly pulling cords and disconnecting the monitor.

Mick used that opportunity to clasp her shoulders. Touching her made him feel better. "Delilah, listen to me."

She jerked away so violently, she almost lost her balance. "Don't touch me," she said in alarm, her eyes huge and round and filled with wariness. "Don't you ever touch me again."

They watched each other in silence. Mick was the first to finally speak. "Tell me what's going on."

For a long minute, she stared at her hands. "All right." She took a deep breath, met his gaze defiantly. "I fell in love with you. I trusted you. I knew it was too soon for that, but I couldn't seem to stop it. And you've broken my heart. I really don't think I can ever forgive you."

Her words were damn difficult to take, filling him with elation—because she loved him—and the heavy weight of sadness, because he didn't know if he could do anything about it. He chose his words carefully, watching her, gauging her reaction. "Because I turned you in?"

Her eyes closed and a tiny, very sad smile appeared. "No, because you'd think that about me at all." She looked at him again. "Here I was, letting myself go crazy for you, and you hadn't really learned anything about me at all."

The need to hold her was a live thing. He barely resisted it. "Can we back up just a bit?" When she didn't answer, he asked, "Why are you in such an all-fire hurry to leave now?"

She gave a broken sigh. "And here I thought you were so smart. Smart and brave and honorable." She reached for his hands and enfolded them in her own. Leaning so close he thought she would kiss him, she whispered near his ear, "I didn't tell anyone anything. I figure you didn't, either. That means my place has to be bugged."

Mick stood there, stupefied, watching her lean back, watching her wait for his reaction. Bugged?

A stillness settled over him, slowing his heartbeat, squeezing his lungs. *Of course her place was bugged.*

But it would have to be worse than that. Just listening wouldn't have given anyone such specific details of their first night together. No, that was something that had to be seen, too.

Almost in slow motion, Mick looked around, heart pounding with acceptance. He caught Delilah by the shoulders. "Come on."

"Where?"

"To my car. I want you out of here."

She dug in her heels, resisting his efforts. "I'm not your responsibility anymore. I can take care of myself, just like I've always done."

"We can't talk here," he insisted.

And she added with a note of sadness, "We don't need to talk anywhere. We're through."

He hadn't been willing to accept that when he'd thought her an accomplice; no way in hell would he accept it knowing she was innocent and in danger. And he didn't doubt her now, not at all. Maybe he was too anxious to find an alternate explanation, one that didn't incriminate her in any way. But this time he was going by his heart, by his guts, not by his damn pride or his conscience.

He gripped her shoulders tighter, opened his mouth—and heard someone say, "Am I interrupting?"

They both whipped around, and Mick shoved Delilah behind him. Alec lounged in the doorway, one black brow quirked in question, his equally black eyes speculative.

Mick caught Delilah's hand, dragged her resisting behind him, and stepped out into the hallway. Without a word, Alec followed. They moved to a corner and there, where no one could possibly hear, Mick asked, "What the hell are you doing here?"

"Josh called and said you needed my help." He looked at Delilah, his gaze speculative. "What's going on?"

"Damn." Mick quickly explained the possibilities to Alec. Several times Delilah tried to wiggle her hand away from him, but he held tight, and she seemed reluctant to make a scene.

Alec didn't appear the least surprised by any of it, but then he was a specialist when it came to espionage equipment. "Probably a Minicam," he said. He put his large hand on the side of Delilah's neck and bent to look her in the eyes. "You okay?"

She didn't so much as glance at Mick. "I'll survive."

Alec considered that, holding her gaze for a stretch of time, then shook his head. "I think you should go on home with Mick. Let me check things over here and... No?"

She shook her head. "I'm not going home with Mick."

"Yes, you are," Mick told her. "Alec, I just need a sec to talk to her."

Her gaze glued to Alec's, Delilah bared her teeth in what she probably thought looked like a confident smile, but instead showed her tension. "I'm *not* going home with Mick."

Alec raised his brows, waiting for Mick's response. He was saved from that fate when pounding footsteps sounded on the stairs. They all moved at once, Mick again shoving Delilah behind him while drawing his gun, and Alec stationing himself in front of them both.

Josh and Zack skittered to a halt at the sight of them blocking the hallway.

"Uh, we decided you could use some backup," Josh explained.

Mick growled, knowing Josh thought he couldn't apologize to Delilah correctly on his own.

Delilah mistook him, though. From behind Mick she muttered meanly, "Some watchdog you are if you need those two."

Mick turned to frown at her.

Alec sighed.

More footsteps sounded. Dane, gun in hand and arm extended, reached the top of the stairs in a crouch. Everyone blinked at him.

Alec said, "You got my message."

"Yeah." Dane came to his feet and tucked the gun away in a shoulder holster. "What's going on?"

Delilah stepped around Mick, glaring at all five men. "Do you all run around town armed?"

Josh and Zack shook their heads. "Of course not."

Alec, Dane and Mick said at the same time, "Yeah."

She turned away in exasperation. "I need to finish packing."

"Packing?" Josh asked, his tone filled with alarm.

"You're going somewhere?" Zack tried to step in front of her.

Alec caught her by the back of her shirt, then quickly held up both hands when she rounded on him. "Don't slug me, just listen up, okay? You can be pissed off at Mick all you want. Hell, I would be, too."

"Me, too," Josh and Zack said almost in unison, earning Mick's glare.

"But," Alec continued, "you have to think here. Don't go putting yourself in danger just to spite yourself. I don't know where you intended to go, but with everything we've just found out, even you have to realize you need someone who can protect you."

Dane crowded closer. "Just what the hell is going on?"

Mick groaned. "God, I'm getting tired of explaining this."

"Then let me." Delilah drew herself up, and she wore the meanest expression Mick had ever seen. It relieved him, because at least some of the shock, some of the hurt, had been replaced. "Mick went to the hospital to see Rudy Glasgow."

"He's awake?" Dane asked.

"Yeah," Mick said. "Unfortunately, he is."

"While there," Delilah continued, "Rudy convinced him that I was part of his little gang, a criminal to be arrested."

Her tone was so nasty, the men all held perfectly still as if frozen by her censure.

"You see, Rudy knew personal stuff—and no,

none of you need details—about what we'd done here in the apartment."

"In the bedroom," Zack supplied, earning a hot glare from Delilah.

"So, of course," she practically sneered, "Mick had to believe the worst about me."

Mick swallowed hard. She'd have them all lynching him before she finished. Already Josh was seething again, and Zack kept giving him reproachful looks. Dane and Alec just seemed resigned. "Delilah—"

"He convinced his connections in the police department to have me picked up for *questioning*."

Everyone looked at everyone else. Dane ventured, "Connections?"

Mick shook his head. "Never mind." Delilah didn't yet know he was a cop, and he had a feeling now wasn't a good time to tell her. He had enough amends to make without confessing his own deception.

"She thinks her apartment is bugged," Alec finished for her, cutting to the chase, "which would explain things."

"Ah." Dane nodded. "That'd make sense, I guess."

"It explains it better than thinking she had a hand in that damned robbery," Josh pointed out unnecessarily.

Zack elbowed him hard.

Defensive, Delilah crossed her arms over her middle and repeated, "I am not going home with Mick. I can take care of myself."

"You know," Alec said, his lowered brows making him look more than a little fierce, "this could have all been a ploy. Why tell Mick you were involved unless someone wanted him to get angry with you, to walk away from you?"

"Which would leave you alone and unprotected," Dane finished for him. He nodded. "Someone wants to get to her, but that's impossible with Mick watching over her. So they instigated this little separation."

Still determined, Delilah said, "I have a deadline."

"Good Lord," Mick muttered, unable to believe she'd be concerned with that now.

"I don't have time to debate with you. I just want to get settled down and finish my work."

"Someone is after you, damn it!"

Even when Mick shouted at her, she didn't meet his gaze. She stared down at her feet and said, "I'll be very careful."

She turned toward the apartment door, and again she got pulled up short. Josh, standing tall and resolute beside her, held her arm. "If you don't want to go home with Mick, come to my place."

Raging jealousy shot through Mick. Growling, he took an aggressive step forward, and both Alec and Dane flattened a hand on his chest, stalling him.

Delilah smiled in regret. "I can't do that, Josh. I'd drive you crazy in an hour."

"Not so."

She shook her head stubbornly. "No, it's out of the question. I wouldn't consider imposing on you."

"Then come home with me," Zack said. "Dani would love to have you there."

"No," she answered gently, looking a little amazed by the offers. "I don't sleep regular hours, and I'd be disruptive and—"

Dane shrugged. "You know you're welcome to our place, or to Alec's."

Alec nodded. "Absolutely."

"But either way, Delilah," Dane continued, "you can't be alone. It isn't safe."

Mouth open, she shook her head. "I don't believe this. You people hardly know me. You can't really want me underfoot. And if there is some type of danger, I could be bringing it to your homes!" She shook her head again, more violently this time, as if making a point. "No, I could never do that."

Dane turned to Mick. "Why don't you go in with Alec and look around? I'd like to speak to Delilah alone a second."

"About what?" Mick asked suspiciously, afraid Dane might bury him further. He was beyond pleased that everyone had jumped to her defense, had rushed to assist her, but he'd have been happier if she'd had no alternative but to give him another chance.

"About life and love and reality."

Josh grinned. "Can I listen in?"

"No." Dane caught Delilah's arm and dragged her toward the steps. "This'll only take a minute."

DELILAH WENT GRUDGINGLY. Truth was, she didn't know what to do. Her only plan had been to get out of the apartment. She felt...dirty. Not just from Mick's impossible and hurtful accusation, but by the sickening possibility that someone had been watching her, someone had seen her making love to Mick. She shuddered with revulsion.

Dane put his arm around her shoulders and stopped at the landing at the bottom of the stairs. It was slightly cooler here, but not much. She felt hot and irritable and irrevocably wounded.

"You asked why any of us would want to take you in."

"I've never known people like you," she admitted, glad for something to think about besides the invasion of her privacy.

"We'd do it for Mick. We love him, and it's obvious you're important to him. He'd go out of his head if he screwed up this badly and something happened to you. I don't want to see him hurt that way. He's been hurt enough in his life."

The thought of Mick suffering because of her made her sadder than ever. Damn it all, she still loved him—and that was sheer stupidity on her part. Nursing her hurt, she said, "Yeah, he cares so much he thinks I'd get him shot."

"Men in love do stupid things. Our brains get all muddled. It's not what we expect, and we don't know how to deal with it."

"He's not in love."

"Wanna bet?"

"He's never said so."

"In words, maybe. But from the start he's been fascinated with you."

She scoffed, and Dane added gently, "Delilah, he took a bullet for you."

She shrugged off that irrefutable fact. When he'd

thrown himself on top of her, he hadn't even known her name, so he couldn't have had feelings for her then. And since then…well, since then everything had been too fast. She was confused, so no doubt he was, too. "Mick is a hero," she reasoned. "He'd do that for anyone."

Dane laughed. "I agree, he's pretty damn heroic. But he's still human, so you have to allow him some human faults. Like bad judgment on occasion, and jumping to conclusions. And acting before he's really thought things out—which is what I think happened today."

"Do you have any idea how badly it hurts for him to think that of me?" Her heart, once full to bursting with love for Mick, now felt cold and hard, a dull ache in her chest.

"Yeah, I do. I made the same mistake with my own wife once."

That got her attention. Delilah stared at him, fascinated.

"It's a long story," Dane said, "and I won't bore you with the details now, but I let her think I was my deceased twin, because I thought she'd had a hand in trying to murder him."

Delilah felt her mouth drop open, her eyes widen. "That sounds more outrageous than the stuff I put in my books."

Dane winced. "I know." Then he smiled. "I fell in love with Angel before I got around to telling her the truth. When it all came out in the open, she hated me. Or at least I thought she did. *She* certainly thought she did. Circumstances not a lot different from what you're dealing with now kept her with me. And it gave us a chance to work things out.''

"You think I should go home with Mick so he can make amends?''

"I think you should give your relationship every chance to work out the ugly mistakes. It's not like you two met under normal circumstances. You've been shot at, he's been wounded, someone is obviously after you for some reason—that's enough in itself to make any relationship difficult.''

"I guess.''

Dane hugged her close. "One more thing. Mick wouldn't risk his life for just anyone. From what he said, he was already mesmerized by you before the shooting. He'd watched you, and thought about you. I understand it happens that way sometimes.''

She rubbed her face, so tired and washed-out and confused she could barely order her thoughts enough to keep talking. "I don't know.''

"You're feeling muddled, too,'' Dane pointed out, while gently rubbing her back. "All the more reason you should give things a chance. Go to his place, rest up, talk. I'm not saying to forgive him tonight, but at least let the opportunity exist for him to make it up to you. Give him a chance to explain. Who knows? Maybe he'll say something profound and you'll be able to forgive him.''

They heard a noise and looked up the stairs. Mick stood at the top. Had he heard their conversation? His gaze on Del, he said, "We found something.''

"We'll be right there.'' Dane put his arm around her and started her walking. "It's been a rough day.

Wouldn't you like to go sit down and let your mind rest for a few minutes?''

Mick waited for them, watching Del closely with his intense, probing gaze. He almost seemed to be holding his breath, he stayed so still.

"Delilah?"

The gentleness, the hope in the way he whispered her name, broke Del's resolve. She nodded. "I'll go with you."

He let out his breath in a rush.

"But this doesn't mean I forgive you."

He nodded. "I haven't forgiven myself. For now I just want to get you settled and know you're safe." Then to Dane he said, "It's an optic fiber Minicam. High-tech stuff, run from the apartment next door."

Dane halted in midstep. "Next door?"

"Led in through the vents on the connecting walls." He glanced at Del, and she could feel his suppressed rage. He held himself in check for her, but he was more furious than she'd ever seen him. "Which included all the rooms except the kitchen and the bathroom."

Thinking of the eyes that had been on her, watching her while she wrote, slept, while she made love with Mick, made her stomach lurch. In the next instant Mick was there, gathering her close despite the trouble between them. "I'll find them, babe, I swear."

Giving herself a brief respite from her pride, Del rested her head on his shoulder. God, it felt good to have him hold her again.

When Dane went ahead into her apartment, Mick led her toward Josh and Zack. He touched her chin, bringing her gaze up to his. "I think it'd be best if you waited in my car. I'll only be a minute."

Josh threw his arm around her shoulder—and Mick promptly removed it. He said under his breath, "You've pushed enough today, Josh."

Josh just grinned, and Del had no idea what they were going on about.

"Have you ever noticed the neighbors next door?" Alec asked Del as he reentered the hall.

She gathered her scattered emotions. Now was no time to fall apart. "I know most everyone else in the building, but I thought that apartment was vacant."

"Does your landlord live here?"

"Afraid not." She wrung her hands, still shaken by having her worst suspicions confirmed. "I can call him if you want to check it out."

Mick shook his head. "We'll need to notify Faradon. He'll get a search warrant."

Del looked from one male face to another. "So what do we do now?"

"We get you settled and safe." Mick's eyes narrowed. "And then I'm going to see Rudy again."

CHAPTER TWELVE

DELILAH WAITED INSIDE Mick's house while he carried in her computer equipment, which she'd insisted on bringing along. Alec had checked the hardware and software for bugs and declared everything clean, so there was no reason for her to miss her deadline.

A severe headache left her somewhat nauseous, but she wasn't sure what to do. She'd never been in Mick's home before. Whenever he'd needed something, she'd offered to bring him home, but he'd always gotten someone else to take care of it.

Now she realized why. He hadn't wanted her inside his personal domain. That would have been too close to suit him. He wanted to keep her as distant as he could while still being intimate with her. And she, like a fool, had given him the perfect opportunity by moving him into her apartment.

"Where would you like me to put it?"

She turned to see Mick standing in the doorway, his arms filled with her monitor and keyboard, watching her. Josh and Zack stood behind him, loaded down with more equipment.

Del glanced around and shrugged. "I guess the bar counter would work as well as anywhere."

Mick didn't move, even though Zack and Josh

were making impatient noises behind him. "You can use my desk."

"No, thanks." She walked away. The last thing she wanted was to further invade his privacy.

Almost an hour passed before they had her settled in. Dane had trailed them during the move, watching to make certain they weren't followed. The whole thing seemed very cloak-and-dagger to Del. Despite her profession, she'd never expected to be on the receiving end of a real mystery. Mysteries were figments of her imagination, not reality.

Mick's house, moderate in size, probably forty years old, had a quaint coziness about it. Del stood at the kitchen sink looking out the window. His backyard faced a cul-de-sac, and some distance away she could see a pool filled with playing children, another family grilling out on their patio. It all seemed so...domestic. Hard to believe she was here because someone wanted her dead.

Zack slipped his arms around her and rested his chin on top of her head. "You'll be all right."

She patted his hands where they crisscrossed her waist. One thing she'd realized through all this was that Josh and Zack were now her friends, too. She cherished that fact. "You think so?"

"I know there's no way in hell Mick's going to let anything happen to you."

She laughed at that. "Oh, I dunno. He just might decide I'm a criminal again and hand me over to them."

"Nope, ain't gonna happen. You've thrown him for a loop is all, and believe me, that's not easy to do." He kissed her temple, then asked, "Did I ever tell you how hard it was to make friends with him?"

She shook her head.

"He was so closed off, so damned isolated from everyone and everything. Because the fire department and the life squad are located right next door to each other, Josh and I were friends before we ever met Mick. But we all ate at Marco's and every day we'd see Mick sitting there alone. He'd just eat and leave."

It wasn't a pleasant image, his self-imposed isolation, and Del's heart softened in spite of her efforts to the contrary.

"One day some guys came in drunk and started causing problems." Del heard an odd note of enthusiasm in Zack's tone. "They were loud, disruptive, making a mess and scaring off customers. It was interesting, watching Mick go on alert, seeing how he took it all in and waited to make a move, without even appearing to notice. A waitress asked the men to leave, and one of the guys stood and took an aggressive stance. There were four of them, but Mick never hesitated to jump to her defense.

"He told the guy—nicely—to back off. A punch was thrown, and within seconds, Mick had the guy flattened. The others tried to rush him, three against one, but Mick didn't have any problem handling them." Zack chuckled. "He sure got Josh's respect that day."

"You two didn't help him?"

"He didn't give us a chance," Zack claimed defensively. "At least not with the actual fight. But afterward Josh insisted on buying him a drink—*insist* being the operative word, because Mick was hell-bent on keeping to himself—and the rest is history. It still took us half a year to get him to loosen up, to finally realize we weren't in cahoots with the bad guys. But we've been pretty close ever since.''

"You're saying Mick doesn't come by trust easily?''

"You have to get him there kicking and screaming.''

She smiled, thinking that a pretty apt picture. "Why?''

"Now that's something you'll have to ask Mick.''

"I'm glad you're not telling *all* my secrets, Zack.''

Zack gave Del a reassuring squeeze and turned to face Mick with a grin. "Just trying to help out.''

Josh stood next to Mick. "Good luck. I just got read the riot act for that very same thing.''

"You," Zack said, "had it coming.''

Mick actually smiled. "You know, Zack, sometimes it's hard as hell to tell whose side you're on.''

"I'm on the side of the right and just.'' He saluted Mick. "I suppose you're ready for us to make our exit?''

"I wouldn't be that rude.''

Josh snorted. "He told me to get the hell out.'' So saying, Josh went to Del and hugged her right off her feet. "If he gives you any problems, call me.''

Over Josh's shoulder, Del saw Mick's expression harden, and she quickly disengaged herself. "I'll be fine.''

Josh teased, "But just in case...''

Zack grabbed him by the back of his shirt and

dragged him away. "I need to get home for Dani, so we'll see you both later. Mick, if you need anything, just let us know."

Mick didn't answer; he was too busy watching Del.

She shifted uncomfortably, then heard the front door close. *Now what?* she wondered.

Mick came a step closer to her. She felt hemmed in by his imposing silence and the cold sink at her back.

She wasn't sure what she expected, but he only said, "You look exhausted. Why don't you take a warm shower while I hook up all your computer stuff? Or are you hungry? I can fix you something to eat."

She shook her head, very unsure of herself and the situation. "A shower sounds nice. But I...I don't know where it is."

Appearing pained, he closed his eyes, then opened them with a rueful sigh. "I'll show you around."

It was a two-bedroom house with hardwood floors and a small cream-and-black tiled bathroom. He showed her his bedroom, his air watchful, then the guest bedroom across the narrow hallway. Del peeked into both rooms.

His dark gaze pierced her careful reserve. "You can use whichever room you want." Unnamed emotions deepened his voice.

"Where will you sleep?"

"Wherever you want me to."

Well, heck. That put the decision back on her, and she felt too unsteady to force the issue at the moment.

She gestured toward the smaller room. "I'll use this one."

With no inflection whatsoever, Mick said, "All right. I'll put your things in there." He led her back into the bathroom. "Towels are in the linen closet right here, and shampoo and stuff is already on the tub ledge."

He started to turn away and she reached for him. The muscles in his forearm tightened when her hand closed around his wrist. "Mick?"

He looked from her hand to her face. "Yeah?"

Del wanted to groan. He was so stiff, so...formal. She had a feeling he was trying not to pressure her, but she wished he would... No, she didn't know what she wanted.

"Is there any chance they know where you live?"

"No. We weren't followed today. Dane made sure of that, and I trust him. And only my closest friends, and the people I work with, have my address."

"But..."

In the briefest of touches, his fingertips grazed her cheek. "I've got a lot of explaining to do, honey. I wanted to wait until I got you here, so you couldn't change your mind about staying with me. But now I think I have to come clean."

Del stiffened. "If you're going to hurt me again, Mick Dawson—"

"No." His fingers tunneled into her hair, stroking her warmly. "I swear, I'll do my best never to hurt you again. But what I have to say will probably make you madder than hell."

She could deal with mad, she supposed. "All right."

"Take your shower, get comfortable, then we'll sit down and lay everything out in the open."

She wasn't at all sure she liked the sound of that, but figured he was right. From here on out, she wanted, demanded, honesty. If he couldn't give her that, they had nothing.

MICK GAVE A SATISFIED NOD. He'd managed to accomplish a lot while she showered. But then, she'd stayed in there forever. Too many times to count he'd wanted to check on her, to make sure she wasn't crying or upset, but he knew getting too close to her while she was naked and wet would be his downfall.

So he clenched his teeth and worked. He had her computer, printer and fax machine all set up in a neat little organized corner. He'd given her his own padded desk chair, and taken one from the dinette set for himself. He'd hung her clothes in the closet, changed the sheets on the guest bed—a bed that had never been used. Canned chicken noodle soup simmered on the stove.

He'd called his sergeant and explained things, and spoken with both Faradon and Dane. Unfortunately, the apartment next to Del's was indeed empty, but they had been able to get some fingerprints. Running them would take some time.

Mick had just finished cutting two sandwiches into halves when Delilah walked in.

Her wet hair was combed straight back from her forehead and she'd pulled on loose shorts and a

T-shirt. Barefoot as usual, she padded toward him and pulled out a chair. "I hadn't realized I was hungry, but the soup smells good."

Mick was so tense even his knuckles hurt as he put some soup in a bowl and set it before her. They ate in silence. When she was almost finished, he said, "I'm not a private investigator."

Her head lifted, her eyes wide and cautious. "You're not?"

Because he couldn't stop himself, Mick pushed his bowl aside and took her hand. "At first I lied out of necessity. I can't tell everyone the truth, that's just a fact of my job. Why I continued to let you believe the lie, I'm not sure. I told myself that we didn't know each other well enough. Too many things didn't add up." He met her beautiful blue eyes and admitted, "Actually, I think I was just afraid."

"Of me?"

He looked down at their clasped hands. She was so small boned, so delicate despite her height. She had a willowy appearance, and he wanted nothing more than to protect and cherish her. "It isn't easy to admit, but you scare the hell out of me."

Time stretched taut while she pondered those words. She turned her hand in his and returned his hold. After taking a deep breath, she said, "Okay, so what do you really do?"

"I'm a cop. I work undercover."

She stared at him, silent.

"I'd just finished a bust when I met you, which is a good thing, since I don't have a medical release to get back to work yet, and I hate turning over a case to someone new. It screws up the work that's already been done.''

Still holding his hand, Delilah rested her free arm on the table and leaned forward, her animosity and distrust replaced by curiosity. ''That's why you were armed?''

''Dane and Alec really are PIs. But yeah, I never go anywhere without my gun. Used to be a gun would make you stick out as a cop, but these days *not* having a gun would be a bigger giveaway. The world has turned into a nasty place.''

She chewed her bottom lip. ''What you do, is it dangerous?''

''Sometimes.'' Lying to her was no longer an option. ''I mostly deal with prostitutes and drugs and gambling. Because of what I do, I live well away from where I work.''

''I noticed.''

Of course she had. Delilah was no dummy, he thought with a sense of pride. Even more encouraging was the fact that she hadn't yet pulled away from him. He took hope. ''Rudy knew I was a cop. He said you knew and had told him.''

He felt her slight emotional withdrawal when she stated, ''But now you know that isn't true.''

He rubbed his thumb over her knuckles, trying to soothe her. ''I assume he heard me on the phone, talking to my sarge while I was at your apartment.''

''Where was I?''

''The shower, the bed, involved in writing.''

''Oh.''

''Delilah…I'm sorry.''

"No, I understand."

"Do you? Because I sure as hell don't." Self-disgust rose in his throat. "That first night I spent with you, I should have told you the truth."

"As I remember it, that first night I was too busy seducing you," she said, her tone lighter, more accepting.

"And here I thought I was the seducer."

Her face suddenly paled and she swallowed. "All the while, someone watched us."

"Don't think about that." Mick wanted to pull her into his lap, to hold her close. Instead, he redirected her thoughts. "If one of Rudy's cohorts did hear me, they still wouldn't know I was undercover. The station protects my identity."

Mick could see her researcher's mind at work. She frowned thoughtfully and said, "I think I understand how all this works, although I've never interviewed an undercover officer before."

"Now's your chance," he teased, so relieved that she wasn't angry, he almost felt weak.

"You drive your personal car to the station, but then trade up for an undercover car?"

"Not exactly. No uniforms ever know who's undercover. There's a special place where we switch cars, provided by the city. Once a car gets burnt up—"

"Burnt up?"

"Recognized." She nodded and he continued. "Then we get a new car."

"Something old and disreputable?" she asked, her

nose wrinkling at the thought even as her eyes lit up with interest.

He shrugged. "Sometimes. But sometimes we get a fancy car. You never know. It depends on the case."

"You work with a partner?"

"Not exactly, but no one ever works without backup. We all carry pagers and cell phones—another common tool among criminals, thankfully. If something goes wrong, we have special codes we can dial to get help fast."

They talked for over an hour. Delilah surprised him with her understanding. But then maybe it was just her desire to learn about his profession that swayed her. He told her about how wires could be detected with special devices that ran through TVs. If the TV reception got wavy, meaning it had picked up the wire's reception, a perp might know he'd been set up, and things could get hazardous real quick.

Mick told her about his jump-out bag. It held a mask to cover his face when he made arrests, so the perps wouldn't recognize him. And about his vest, which he wore even when it was ninety degrees outside. He described the SIG Sauer guns some punks carried, and the hollow-point bullets used to make a bigger wound.

Everything he told her, no matter how gruesome, only made her curious for more. In so many ways she delighted him, excited him, alternately brought forth his lust and his protectiveness.

When she started yawning, Mick stood to put their bowls in the dishwasher. "I think it's time for you to get some rest. After everything I put you through to-day, you have to be exhausted.''

He turned to see her rubbing her eyes tiredly. ''I'm wiped out.'' But she didn't stand, didn't make a move to go to bed. She just stared at her hands.

Mick closed the dishwasher and stood at her side. ''You don't have to be nervous here, Delilah. My house is secure, and Faradon has someone driving by every fifteen minutes. You're safe.''

''I know.'' Still she didn't move.

Mick knelt down beside her. ''What can I do?'' he asked. He searched her face, and wished like hell he had some answers. ''I know I can't make up for not trusting you, but I'll do whatever you need me to.''

She stared at his hand on her knee. ''You don't owe me. What you did…it's understandable. I just wish you'd talked to me first. Together we might have…''

''I'm a bastard, I know.'' He worked his jaw, then pointed out, ''You haven't yelled at me at all.''

Her slender shoulder lifted in a halfhearted shrug. ''At first I was too devastated to yell. Then too hurt. Now…well, now I understand.''

''I'd feel better if you'd yell.''

Her soft mouth curled at his words, which weren't quite facetious. ''There's no point to it.''

And Mick had to wonder if that meant she considered him a lost cause, not worth the effort of a good yell.

Time, he'd have to give her time. ''Come on. I think I'm ready for bed, too.''

Looking at him through her inky lashes, she stood.

He couldn't decipher her mood, and hated the helplessness he felt.

They went down the hall together, and Mick allowed himself to hold her for just a moment. He kissed her forehead and stepped away. "If you need anything, or want anything, I'm right next door."

She nodded. "Good night."

Mick stared at that damn closed door for far too long before taking himself off to bed. He doubted he'd get any sleep, and in fact, he wasn't tired at all. His body hummed with tension, with leftover adrenaline.

He left his door ajar so he'd hear her if she called out. Lying there in the darkness, he went over all the possibilities, but couldn't come up with a good reason why Rudy would want her dead.

It had to be linked to Neddie Moran somehow. It was just too much of a coincidence for her to have known Neddie before he was killed, and for Neddie's death to have taken place so close to the attempt on her life.

Mick turned to the bedside table and picked up the phone. Hitting the lighted numbers, he called Faradon.

"It better be important," Faradon grumbled. It sounded to Mick like the man was eating, but then Faradon probably ate a lot. He was as big as a bear.

"Did you find any connection between Neddie Moran and Rudy Glasgow yet?"

"Nope, not a thing so far. But then it could be Neddie knew one of the other guys, and without their names, we're lost. The prints'll probably help. Don't worry, we'll keep digging. We're bound to turn up something soon.''

Frustrated, Mick had just replaced the receiver into the cradle and settled back when his door squeaked open.

Delilah's silhouette was outlined by the faint light coming through his windows. ''Mick?''

Mick's body thrummed to life as he propped himself up on one elbow. Unless his eyes deceived him, she wore only a T-shirt. He forced the raw hunger from his tone and asked as gently as possible, ''You okay, babe?''

She crept closer, hesitated. ''I don't want to sleep alone.''

Those softly spoken words had a startling effect on his libido, an even bigger effect on his heart. Mick lifted his sheet, inviting her into his bed.

She hurried the rest of the way to him and slipped in by his side. For a second, she kept a slight distance between them. Mick didn't move, didn't breathe, and then she turned to him and gripped him tight, and all the pent-up tension inside him exploded.

''CHRIST, I'M SORRY, so damn sorry,'' he murmured into her hair. His hold was tight and infinitely gentle.

Del cuddled closer, comforted by his scent, the warmth of his skin.... ''You're not wearing anything?''

He stilled, then said, ''I can put something on if you want.''

''No.'' She loved touching him, and she needed the feel of him right now. All of him. The hair on his chest provided a nice cushion for her cheek, and she nuzzled into him. "Just hold me, okay?"

He turned to face her, drew her closer into his body so that he surrounded her, protected her. Always. Del felt a fat tear sting the corner of her eye. God, he was always trying to protect her.

"Does it bother you?" she whispered into the darkness, into the safety of his nearness.

"Hell, yes." His large hand opened on the back of her head, his rough fingertips sinking in to cradle her scalp, massage, soothe. "When I think of those bastards looking at you, I want to kill them. I *could* kill them."

Del sniffed and laughed and continued to cry softly. She was so damned confused. "No," she chided, wanting to hear him, to borrow some of his strength. "I meant does it bother you that they saw *you*. Your privacy was invaded as much as mine."

"I hadn't thought about it," he said. "At first I was just blind with…"

"Rage? Because you thought I had lied to you?"

He shook his head, then nuzzled her shoulder and squeezed her until she squeaked. "I hate to admit it," he rumbled against her throat, "but you deserve the truth. Ugly as it might be, regardless of how damn asinine I feel about it."

"The truth?"

"It wasn't rage I felt first, but this awful drowning hurt." He pressed his mouth to the skin of her throat, her shoulder. "There aren't many people in this world who could hurt me. But thinking that you'd used me, that you were laughing at me…it knocked my legs out from under me. It was all I could do to get the hell out of Rudy's hospital room without ripping him apart.''

Del turned her face to his. "I'm sorry," she said very softly, and meant it.

"Oh God, don't. Don't apologize to me!" He sat up and switched on a light, shocking her, making her blink against the glare of it. "You should slap my face, Delilah. Or curse me or…hell, I don't know what. But don't apologize."

She looked up at him, her eyes welling with emotion, and his expression crumbled.

"Oh, babe, no, don't cry."

That got her laughing again, a wobbly, pathetic laugh. "Don't apologize, don't cry." She sniffed, and gratefully accepted the tissue he handed to her. She blew hard before continuing. "I've thought about it, and I can see why you believed Rudy. We haven't really known each other that long, not long enough for unconditional trust."

She scooted up to sit against the headboard. "Trust doesn't really come easy to me, either."

"Tell me what to do," Mick said, touching her cheek to remove one lingering tear. "Tell me how to prove to you that I *do* trust you."

She blinked. "Do you?"

He settled himself beside her, and their shoulders touched. Del had the sheet to her chin, but Mick barely had it covering his lap. Even now, in a vortex of emotions, he stole her breath away. He folded his hands over his abdomen and stared at the far wall.

"Damn right I trust you," he said. "I think it was

myself I didn't trust all along. But you...almost from the minute I saw you, I wanted you. You drew me like no one ever had, and that shook me because I wasn't used to anyone affecting me like that." He glanced down at her. "It's scary the way you make me feel."

Del lifted his left arm over her shoulder and curled into his side again. "Okay?"

His arm tightened. "Better than okay."

"Will you tell me about your childhood?" She felt him stiffen, felt the stillness that came over him, body and mind.

"Why do you want to know?"

"To try to understand. I've gotten the impression it wasn't great, but that kid's a part of you."

"No."

"You can't run away from your past, Mick. All you can do is deal with it."

"I've dealt with it," he muttered.

Del knew she was pushing, but it was important to her to know all of him, the good and the bad. "Then you shouldn't have any problem sharing with me." To force the issue, she added, "Since you trust me."

"That has nothing to do with trust."

"Of course it does!" Again she twisted to look at him, but he pressed her head back to his shoulder. Del grinned. "You know, even Neddie trusted me enough to confide in me. He told me about his past and things he'd done, things he regretted."

This time Mick turned her face up to him. His fingers were hard, firm on her chin. "What things did he tell you?"

"You first."

"Delilah…"

She only raised a brow, waiting.

He sighed, gave a slight shake of his head and then kissed her forehead. He settled back, and though his pose was relaxed, she felt the rigid way he held himself. "Family services took me away from my mother twice. The first time it happened, I was about five. She'd gone out partying and hadn't come back, and a neighbor reported her."

Covering her shock and her sympathy, Del asked, "How long was she gone?"

"All weekend. In those days, other than her disappearing every now and then, it wasn't so bad. The house stayed kinda picked up and she had a regular job and she still seemed to…like me."

Seemed to like me. Del's heart cried out at the hurt he must have felt. She smoothed her hand over his chest and kept quiet.

"They gave me back to her easy enough, and I was glad. Sometimes being with her was rough, but it was nothing compared to not knowing what would happen, or being stuck with strangers. My mother promised to take some classes, to get into rehab for her drinking, and voilà—I was back home."

"Were things any better then?"

He laughed. "They got worse, actually. She was embarrassed that her neighbors knew I'd been taken away, so we moved. She got a new boyfriend and started drinking even more, but she was careful to put on a good show for the folks who checked up on her.

It was another couple of years before things really went down the toilet.''

Del cringed at the idea of something worse than a mother neglecting her son for an entire weekend, but again she kept silent, wanting him to talk.

"My mother had an affinity for drink first, and men second. She moved them in and out of our house, but none of them ever contributed, and most of them didn't care to see me too often. Until I was about twelve, I tried to just stay out of sight. But then her liver went bad and she got really sick, and the guy who was with her at the time took her to the hospital. She had to stay awhile, and he skipped out, so family services had me again. That was the worst. I mean, at five I probably needed looking after. But at twelve? I'd have been fine on my own, and when they finally let her out of the hospital I knew I had to take over or I'd get taken away from her for good. Not that I'd have missed her much, but…'' He shrugged.

"The familiar," Del said, "is almost always easier than the unfamiliar."

"Yeah." He smoothed his fingers up and down her bare arm for a few minutes, thinking. "I was bigger than her by then, so she couldn't close me off in my room anymore or use threats against me. I could outrun her, and smacking me hurt her worse than it did me. So I told her how things were going to be."

Del shivered at the harshness of those words, at the awful reality he'd faced at such a young age. "At twelve years old, you took charge?"

"Damn right. And she listened, and did as I said, because she knew otherwise I could get her arrested."

"How?"

"She had men in the house who were thieves and cons. She'd done a lot of stupid stuff while drunk, including prostituting herself for drinks, gambling with money we didn't have, accepting stolen goods in exchange for a room—usually to someone busy dodging the law. Our television, and for a while our car, were both stolen."

Del wondered if that was why he'd chosen to work Vice, because he'd already seen the other side of it.

"A lot of the men would make big promises, some even to me. They'd talk about taking care of her, buying things, but they all lied. Family services lied, too, always telling me things would get better. And she was the worst of all—she lied every damn time she said she loved me. After that, she'd always tell me not to say anything to anyone because she'd be taken away and I'd be left all alone." He laughed, a rough, humorless sound. "I knew it was bullshit all along. Whatever maternal instincts she'd had got drowned in a bottle early on. By the time I was twelve, she'd already pretty much wiped her hands of me, but my new conditions really finished things off."

He drew a long breath. "She did as I told her, and she hated me in the bargain."

Del hugged him tight. "What, exactly, did you tell her to do, Mick?"

CHAPTER THIRTEEN

"WE SOLD OUR HOUSE, which we were about to lose anyway, since she missed more and more work from drinking and couldn't make the payments. I didn't want to end up on the street, and neither did she. I checked around and found an apartment building—the one right next door to where you rent. It was a terrible area even then, but I used the money we made off the house to buy it, and the rent from the other apartments was income. I was in charge, taking applications from renters, collecting the rent, running ads when necessary."

"You did all that at twelve?"

"There weren't a lot of choices." He smiled down at her. "But it wasn't bad. Hell, it was the best it had been for a while. She stayed drunk and ran around with every Tom in town, but she knew better than to screw with the bill money. When I got old enough, I got a job and that helped, too."

"When did you meet Angel?"

His gaze brightened with a smile of genuine warmth. "She moved in when I was sixteen. Her first son, Grayson, was just a little-bitty squirt, and she'd been in a car wreck and was barely able to get around herself. I helped her out, and she started tutoring me in the school subjects I had problems with. Angel was...she was the type of woman I hadn't seen before. She didn't lie or make things up. If something needed to be done, she found a way to do it.''

Del felt more tears gather and quickly swiped them away. "I know she loves you."

"Yeah. She does. She thinks of herself as a big sister, or a surrogate mother, I guess." Mick reached over and tweaked Del's nose. "Now, you talk about a role model, that's Dane. Alec, too. They're both great guys."

She caught his hand and held it to her cheek. "They say the same about you."

Del kissed his palm, and he asked, "Delilah, will you forgive me?"

She hesitated to be totally honest with him. She knew that she loved Mick, and she'd rather die than hurt him. But the night was quiet, the light low, and he deserved the truth. "I can forgive you, because I understand." *I love you too much not to.* "But I don't know that I'll ever feel the same again."

He went rigid. "What does that mean, Delilah?"

She wished he hadn't turned the light on. She'd have preferred the concealing darkness, which made confessions so much easier. "Since the day I met you, I've seen you as bigger than life, a knight in shining armor, fearless."

He snorted. "That's nonsense. Hell, I just told you, *you* scare the hell out of me."

She shook her head; nothing really scared Mick, she knew. And she certainly didn't have that type of power over him. If she had, he wouldn't have turned on her so easily. "I write about heroes every day, but I didn't know they existed. I didn't think any man would deliberately risk his life to keep someone else safe. I didn't know a stranger would risk his life, not for me."

He frowned over that.

"I saw you as…" she shrugged helplessly "…the best of everything."

Mick shoved away the sheet and stood. Gloriously naked, he stalked to the window and looked out at the black, balmy night. A large oak blocked what little moonlight there might have been. No leaves stirred; all was silent except for the bumping of her heart.

The faint light from the bedside lamp threw a glow along one side of his body, causing shadows to dip and swell over his muscles and bones, exaggerating his strength, which she already knew to be considerable. She wanted to touch him everywhere. She wanted to eat him up. And nothing, not even her hurt, could change that.

"I come from nothing, Delilah." His voice broke the night, harsh and raw. "For most of my life, I was nothing. Despite how they feel about it, I'm like a stray that Angel dragged home and everyone accepted. I owe Angel and Dane and their whole goddamn family for showing me what family is, for letting me know how a real life could be, and for helping me to get that life. I owe them for who I am now. But if you stripped them away and left me with just myself, with just the bare bones of *me,* I'd be back at square one. And that sure as hell isn't a white knight.''

''No!'' She struggled to her knees, clutching the sheet to her throat. ''You are who you are, Mick Dawson, a strong, capable man with or without anyone else.''

He whirled around. *''I am not a damn hero.''*

He looked livid, his eyes red, his nostrils flaring. Del stared.

''Don't you dare put me on some fucking pedestal,'' he growled, ''because I'm guaranteed to fall off. I'm human, and I blunder my way through life just like everyone else.''

When she remained silent, wide-eyed and stunned, he stomped back to the bed, caught her upper arms and lifted her from the mattress, causing her sheet to fall. She worried for his injured shoulder, and his injured soul.

''You thought I was impervious to cold, too, that I had insides made of iron.''

Del sputtered. ''Don't bring up my coffee now!''

''You don't know what I go through, how I fight every day to make sure I stay deserving.''

Deserving of what? she wanted to ask, but she couldn't. ''Mick...''

''To a lot of people, right and wrong are clear-cut values. But not to me. I force those ideologies into the front of my mind all the time—that a woman strung out on drugs is wrong, not just desperate. That a young man with a gun is a criminal, not a kid trying to survive. I don't even know what a white knight is, but I know what the rules tell me, and I follow those rules to the letter.''

Del swallowed her hurt. Looking at him, seeing his pain, hurt even more. ''Did those rules tell you to protect me when you knew it might get you killed?''

His jaw clenched; his entire body tightened. But his hands didn't hurt her. She knew without a doubt that Mick would never, ever physically hurt her.

''An officer has to take action when he sees a civilian threatened.''

She barely heard what he said. ''Did those rules insist you turn me in because you thought I was breaking the law? Or did you do that because you thought I'd used you?''

He tipped his head back and groaned. ''Both.''

''Mick?'' She needed to touch him, to soothe him, but his hold didn't allow for that. So she gave him the only words she knew that might help. ''I forgive you.''

His gaze jerked to hers, hot, burning, filled with relief, with satisfaction, greed, elation.

She saw the pulse racing in his strong throat, saw the muscles in his shoulders quiver, saw the glaze of relief in his eyes.

''I want you,'' he groaned. ''More than I've ever wanted anything. More than I wanted my mother to care, more than I wanted Angel to be safe.'' He shook her slightly. ''More than I want my next breath. But I'm just me, and if you try to make me more than that we'll both be disappointed.''

Del licked her lips. It sounded to her like he loved

her, though he hadn't quite said so. "Do you want me now?"

He lifted her a few inches more until his mouth ground down on hers, bending her head back. His tongue thrust deep. Her body came into stark contact with his, making her aware of all his hard angles and firm muscles, and the long, hard length of his throbbing erection.

Just as quickly his kiss eased and he gentled his hold. His velvet tongue licked, teased, then slowly withdrew. "I'm sorry," he murmured against her mouth, nibbling on her lips, softening them. *"I need you."*

"Your shoulder," she said in alarm, fearing he'd hurt himself.

And Mick groaned again, a sound of half humor, half awe. "Even when I act like a marauding bastard, you don't put me in my place." His expression was less strained, and a half smile curled his mouth. "You're something else, Delilah Piper, you know that?"

"Something good?" she asked.

He smoothed her hair, stroked her lips with his thumb. "Something wonderful," he whispered, and then he kissed her again, this time with such sweetness, such love, she didn't even need to hear him speak the words. She couldn't resist him. He'd tell her what she wanted to hear sooner or later, but for tonight she had him, she had his confidences, and that was more than enough.

THE SECOND MICK AWOKE, he knew the other side of the bed was empty. He sat up in a rush, panic closing in—and saw Delilah sitting in the chair by the window. He eased back, but his heart continued to stutter and his stomach still cramped. "You couldn't sleep?"

A dark shadow made up her form in the gray, predawn light, and still he sensed her smile. "Watching you is more fun than sleeping."

He realized the sheet was around his ankles, and he cocked a brow at her. It was easier to breathe now, with her so obviously teasing. "Taking advantage of me?"

"Yes."

Mick stretched and yawned. With his initial alarm gone, he realized he felt better today, less frazzled, but not completely satisfied. He didn't think he'd be content until he had Delilah committed to him one hundred percent. And that meant getting a ring on her finger and hearing her say the vows.

When she was officially his wife, then maybe he could relax.

He'd made progress last night, though he hoped like hell she'd never put him through anything like that again. He hated rehashing the past. It shamed him, reminded him of how weak he'd been, how far he'd struggled. And whether Angel admitted it or not, he always knew he'd never have made it without her. If it hadn't been for Angel, he'd be on the other side of the law right now, the one being arrested for God only knew what, rather than a cop doing the arresting.

It was an emotional struggle he dealt with every day.

He heard Delilah sigh as he stretched his left arm

high, and grinned. She was so blatant about enjoying his body, both by touch and sight. He was glad he hadn't spent his life chasing women and screwing around like so many males seemed driven to do. It made their relationship that much more special. She was the only woman who'd ever lived with him.

"I thought you'd be writing," he said as he stood and went to his dresser to get some shorts.

She turned to watch him. He knew his way in the dark, but still he flipped on the wall switch, wanting to see her better.

She looked...dreamy.

"I didn't even think about writing."

He frowned, stepped into his gray boxers and went to her. She wore his shirt, and that turned him on. Of course, if she'd been wearing nothing at all, or the sheet, or her own T-shirt, he'd have still been turned on. She couldn't breathe without making him hard.

He stood looking down at her, dreading the question he had to ask. "Did I interfere with your work?"

"How so?"

He smoothed her glossy dark hair behind her ears, touched her arched brows. "You were so upset, I thought..."

"Oh, no. When I'm upset, I usually work through it at the computer. Same when I'm excited. Or sad."

Mick shook his head. Not much got in the way of her writing.

"It's just that last night was so wonderful. *You* were so wonderful." She sighed again, a sigh of repletion and fulfillment, making him feel like that damn white knight she'd spoken of.

Then she added, "I've been thinking, too, about Neddie, about some of the stories he told me."

Slowly, Mick straightened. "Let's do this over coffee."

"Do this?"

"I have a gut feeling that whatever you're going to tell me will be the clue we've been missing. I need caffeine to digest it all, so I don't miss anything important."

Delilah stood and did her own stretching. His pulse leaped. If this wasn't so important… He eyed the bed. But no, it *was* important, and he had to see to her safety first.

"This gut feeling of yours," she asked, "is it like a cop's sixth sense?"

Mick put his arm around her and led the way to the kitchen, flipping on the lights as he went. It was only five-thirty. It'd be another hour or so before the sun lit the sky. "I just know that somehow all this stuff is related."

She nodded, took a stool at the counter—evidently more than willing to have him wait on her, which he was glad to do. "I think it has to do with the story I'm working on."

"Your newest book?" He measured coffee and turned on the machine.

She nodded. "You got anything I can snack on? I'm starved."

He remembered she'd been too upset to eat much the night before, and guilt washed over him. He scrounged around until he found her a few cookies.

"I can put some eggs and bacon on, too," he offered, and she accepted with a mouthful of cookie.

"You talk while I cook," he said.

She waved the second cookie at him. "Neddie was trying to go straight, you know? A condition of his parole was that he continue to be counseled, and part of his counseling was to own up to the things he knew he'd done wrong. So he sometimes talked to me."

"You were supposed to absolve him of guilt?"

"Not even close." She chewed on her cookie, thinking, then shuddered. "He told me some gruesome stories," she admitted. "Stuff I could never use in a book. It was too...real, and you know what they say about truth being stranger than fiction. But in a way, Neddie had this odd code of honor. He didn't hurt anyone that he didn't think needed to be hurt. I mean, he didn't just choose innocent victims."

"He hired himself out, honey. He did what he was paid to do."

"I know." She brushed the remainder of the crumbs from her hands and watched Mick lay bacon in a hot skillet. "But he only took jobs that his conscience would let him take. Like this one guy he snuffed—"

"Snuffed?" Mick eyed her, appalled at the casual way she said that.

She shrugged. "It's part of the lingo."

Didn't he know it. "Go on."

"Anyway, the guy he killed had some huge gambling debts, but Neddie said he took the job because the guy also abused his wife."

Mick made a face. "What a discerning fellow."

Delilah laughed. "That's what I said to him. And he knew it was still wrong, but he said he half enjoyed beating that guy up and then dumping him for dead, because he hated anyone who would hit a woman."

"We're in agreement on that."

In a voice as soft as butter, she said, "I know."

Mick poked at the bacon with a fork. He couldn't take her hero worship on an empty stomach, so he steered her back to the subject at hand. "What does any of this have to do with your story?"

"Well, Neddie told me that these guys tried to hire him to kill a man because the guy knew too much and wanted to come clean. They were afraid he'd turn evidence on them or something, so they wanted Neddie to kill him, then sink his car in the river."

Mick jerked around, staring at her. A limp piece of uncooked bacon dangled from the fork in his hand.

"Neddie refused. Not only because he was out of the business and trying to go straight, but because he said he sympathized with the other guy. He said they were alike, both of them wanting to be legit, and there was no proof the guy would rat. After all, Neddie said he'd never ratted anyone out before."

This is it, Mick thought with a surge of triumph. *This is the link.*

"I told Neddie about how I'd learned to escape a car that had gone into the river, and he said I couldn't have escaped if I'd been dead before it went in." Delilah tilted her head at Mick, her beautiful, light blue eyes filled with a heavy sadness. "Is that what happened to Neddie? You said he was murdered, and I know he drowned. Did someone kill him, then drive his car into the river? The paper didn't give all the details. I didn't know you were a cop, so I didn't think you'd know, either. After all, it was supposed to be confidential stuff for the ongoing investigation.''

For the first time that he could remember since becoming an officer of the law, Mick didn't even consider what was right or wrong. He set a cup of coffee in front of Delilah and pulled out the stool next to her. Their bare knees touched, his on the outside of hers. ''Neddie's wrists,'' he explained carefully, ''had bruises on them, evidence that he'd been tied up, though there were no ropes or anything on him when his body was found.''

Delilah reached for his hand, and Mick squeezed her fingers.

''He had a wound on the back of his head, too. The coroner said he'd been struck with a blunt object, knocked out just before the car went off the bridge— or possibly as the car went over. It'd be impossible to tell for sure, but as you just said, he wasn't given the chance to escape the car and swim to the surface. We're thinking whoever did it hoped the car wouldn't be found until time and the natural effects of water and cold had done enough damage to disguise a deliberate murder.''

''He had a suicide note in his pocket?''

Mick nodded. ''Yeah.''

Her lips quivered, and she drew a ragged breath. ''That's exactly what Neddie described, what he said the men wanted him to do.'' She blinked away a sheen of tears, and whispered raggedly, ''I used that whole scenario in my book.''

"The book you're working on now?"

"Yes. In the last book, the hero got away by keeping his head and doing the things I'd learned from submerging myself in a car."

Mick shuddered. He could *not* think about that now. Somehow he'd figure out a way to temper Delilah's more dangerous inclinations, without stifling her.

"But in this book," she continued, oblivious to his turmoil, "he was knocked out, a suicide note planted on him, and the heroine had to save him."

Just like Delilah to twist things around, Mick thought. But then, if any woman were capable of a rescue, it'd be Delilah Piper. He wouldn't underestimate her on anything, once she set her mind to it.

It was an enormous long shot, but Mick asked, "That whole scenario is too damn close to the truth to be comfortable. Does anyone know what's in this book?"

She nodded. "Tons of people, I'm sure. Remember I told you I was on the news, discussing my current project? We talked about that whole scene. I…I was laughing about it, bragging that it could happen, and that a woman might indeed be a hero. I never once considered that I could be putting Neddie in danger."

"Neddie didn't know about the interview?"

"I don't know." She covered her face. "He died shortly after that. He…he might have died because of *me*. Someone could have heard that radio program, someone who knew we'd become friends, that Neddie coached me on my research."

"And they might have assumed he'd told you too

much, and that you could repeat it." If Mick thought he'd felt fear before, it was nothing to what he felt now. Someone wanted to shut her up, to make certain she couldn't repeat details that might be incriminating. But he didn't know who, and until he did know, until he could get the bastards, her life was at stake.

Delilah rocked slowly back and forth in her seat as the ramifications settled around her. "I'm to blame."

With a new fury, Mick tipped up her chin. "*Wrong.* Don't even go there, babe. When you live the type of life Neddie did, then you run the risks. That's just how it is."

"He was changing."

"Maybe just a little too late." Mick pulled her into his lap. "Did Neddie give you any names, anything that might connect him with the killers?"

She thought hard, staring down at her hands. Slowly her gaze rose to his. "You know, he did say something, but I'm not sure it'll help."

"At this point, it'd have to be more than we've got."

She nodded, her brows drawn. "He said the guys who wanted to hire him should have known better, because they'd been in prison with him in '86, all of them convicted for car theft."

It took several moments for it to sink in, before Mick allowed himself to believe. "Bingo."

"You think?"

"I think it'll be easy enough to check prison records. That might do it, with your testimony. Especially if the fingerprints from the apartment next to yours match up. We should have those today."

"Is that why they tried to kill me? They knew Neddie had been talking to me? They knew he'd...told me things?"

Mick hugged her. God, she was precious to him. And she was also smart, so there was no point in hoping to protect her. Besides, he didn't want her feeling guilty for Neddie's death, not if he could help it.

"The bruises on Neddie's wrists showed that he put up a hell of a fight, that he tried to work himself free. But he didn't make it." Mick kissed her temple, her ear. "Could be they promised to let him go if he named everyone he'd talked to."

She shook her head, adamant in Neddie's defense. "No, Neddie would never have done that, not if he thought they'd hurt me."

Her innocence amazed him. "How long did you know him, sweetheart?"

"A few months. But we were friends, Mick," she said staunchly.

"That's not enough time to really judge."

She leaned back and gave him a level look. "It's longer than I've known you."

Mick scowled, not appreciating that comparison at all. "He was an admitted murderer. A car thief. Those things are not synonymous with ethics, and any man could cave when his life was on the line."

"I won't believe that."

Mick decided to let it go. She'd been hurt enough, and disillusioning her now wouldn't accomplish a thing. "Let's finish up breakfast and shower, then I'll call Faradon. He should be up by then, and if not, well, he'll get up."

"You really think any of this will make a difference?"

"I know it will."

"I hope so," she said. "I want this behind us. I want us to take walks in the park and go to the zoo, and I want to get back to my research."

Mick groaned. He didn't know if he could live through her special brand of daredevil study.

But he knew he didn't want to live without her, so he supposed he'd find a way to get used to it.

CHAPTER FOURTEEN

THE PHONE RANG while Mick was in the shower. He'd insisted that Del go ahead while he cleaned the kitchen, and when she'd protested, he claimed it had to be that way. If he showered with her, they'd never leave his house.

She accepted that he probably was right.

With her hair still wet and her feet bare, Del picked up the phone. "Dawson residence."

"Faradon here. Is this Ms. Piper?"

"Yes," she said shortly. Detective Faradon still wasn't one of her favorite people, not after the interrogation she'd been through.

"We got the fingerprints back and have some photos to go with them. We'd like you to come to the station and take a look, see if you can ID anyone. How soon can you be here?"

She bristled at his demanding tone. At the very least, she felt the man owed her a few apologies. "Actually, Mick and I were coming in, anyway." She didn't mention her new "evidence" because she wasn't convinced it would help. Mick could explain everything.

There was a pause, then he asked, "How soon?"

"Mick is about done showering now. I'd say we'll leave here in the next fifteen minutes."

"I'll be waiting," he said, and rudely hung up.

A few minutes later Mick came out looking nicely rugged and sexy as sin in faded, well-worn jeans and a soft gray T-shirt. He wore scuffed, lace-up black boots. As Del watched, he checked his gun.

She inched closer. "Can I see?"

He glanced up. "What? My gun?"

Nodding, she said, "A Smith & Wesson, right? Semiautomatic?"

Mick held the gun out of her reach. "No one touches my gun but me."

She rolled her eyes. "I'm not going to fire it. And I do know a little about guns."

"Research, I suppose?"

"Yes."

"Well, then you know enough to understand how dangerous they are." With a dexterity that proved how quickly he was healing, he tucked the gun into a holster at the small of his back, and smoothed his T-shirt over it. "And," he said again, "*no one* touches my gun but me."

"Fine. Whatever."

He caught her before she could turn away, and kissed her neck. It was shameful, but she immediately softened, just as he'd probably known she would.

"Who was on the phone?" he asked against her throat.

Sometimes it was annoying, loving Mick. She couldn't seem to stay angry with him, especially when he kissed her. "Your buddy, Faradon."

"He's not my buddy, he's just the lead investigator on the robbery and shooting." He kissed her again, this time nuzzling beneath her ear. It felt like her toes melted. "What did he want?"

Struggling to get her brain in gear, she succeeded in saying, "He has fingerprints and photos, and he wants us to come take a look for a positive ID."

Stepping back from her, Mick looked at the chunky black watch on his wrist. "Hell, it's barely eight o'clock. He's at it early."

Feeling hopeful for the first time, Del asked, "Do you think that means we're close to having this wrapped up?"

Mick took her arm and headed for the door. "Even with an ID, we'd still have to get hold of them, but it'd sure make it easier to track the bastards down. It's tougher to hide when everyone knows who you are. There's also the possibility that Rudy'll be more willing to talk once we have names."

The sun never did quite rise. Instead, as they stepped outside, they saw that fat purple clouds had rolled in, leaving the air heavy with the scent of rain. In the distance, lightning flickered.

Mick cursed. "Did you want to grab a jacket or umbrella?"

"I won't melt."

She saw his surprise, then his smile, as he opened the car door for her. "I'd forgotten your affinity for rain," he said.

When she raised a brow, he explained, "The day I finally met you, the day of the robbery. Everyone else had an umbrella, but you didn't even seem to notice how soaked you'd gotten." He slid his hand over her waist and squeezed suggestively. "I noticed."

Del smiled at that. It was nice being reminded that the awesome attraction went both ways. If Mick had indeed noticed her when she looked like a used rag mop, then his interest was as keen as hers. Maybe more so, because she hadn't paid him a bit of mind until the shooting.

Once he folded his big body behind the wheel, she told him, "I love running in the drizzling rain. It's peaceful and it stimulates my muse."

He started to make a nasty crack, no doubt about stimulating her, and Del elbowed him. They both laughed and she thought how nice it was, how right, to be with Mick this way. She wondered, once everything was settled, what would happen. When it was no longer necessary for her to stay with him for protection, would he ask her to leave? Would he ask her to stay?

Half an hour later she was still pondering that when the sky opened up. No slight drizzle this, but a raging summer storm full of power. The stuffy, humid air came alive with electricity, crackling and snapping all around them. Trees bent and dipped, leaves and debris danced across the rain-washed roadways.

Del slanted Mick a look. "Rainstorms are sexy," she whispered.

"You're sexy. Rain or no rain," he replied, keeping his gaze on the road.

She grinned, about to tell him how she'd like to spend the afternoon once they finished at the station, when they were blinded by a sudden glare. In the darkness of the morning storm, an approaching car's bright lights reflected off Mick's door. He flinched, throwing up a hand, but it didn't help. The car came from an empty side street, and rather than slowing, it accelerated to a reckless speed across the slick roadway, coming right for them.

Mick glanced out his window, gripped the wheel tightly and muttered with icy calm, "Hold on."

The car struck the back side-panel, throwing them into a spin. Del's seat belt tightened; she yelped in alarm, barely keeping her wits enough to twist around, trying to see what happened.

At the force of impact, Mick first overcompensated, and the car slewed off the road and into the mud before grasping the slick pavement again.

Del, assuming it was an accident—a result of the rainy conditions—wondered why Mick didn't just pull over. She looked over her shoulder, wide-eyed, in time to see the other car straighten and shoot toward them again.

Mick's hand flattened on the top of her head, and he shoved her down in the seat. "Stay there!"

The rear windshield exploded, glass flying everywhere. "Dear God!" Del held Mick's thigh, her face pressed into his side. This couldn't be happening! She tried to sit up, wanting only to protect Mick.

"Keep down," Mick barked, again flattening her in the seat. It suddenly hit her who was after them and why.

Del felt another impact, this time to the rear fender of the car, and there was no way to steer out of it. The car swerved off the road, slinging mud and fishtailing, and finally colliding with a scrawny tree, jarring them both hard.

Mick's head hit the wheel and he slumped.

"Mick!" She screamed his name, scrambling to get her seat belt off, to reach him. Her heart leaped into her throat, her vision clouded with fear. Before she could reach him her door was jerked open. The thunderous roar of the storm intruded, along with a spray of rain and turbulent air. Hard hands grabbed her, yanking her back. She fought them, seeing the trickle of blood on Mick's forehead, the stillness in his body.

He needed help, a hospital! But already her feet were being dragged through the mud, and no matter how she fought, she couldn't escape. The hands holding her only tightened with bruising force.

Someone grabbed her hair and wrenched her head back. "Do you want me to go back and put a bullet in him to make sure he's dead?"

That voice was rough, familiar, and Del froze, choking on her terror. "No."

"Then come along and be quiet."

A hard shove landed her facedown in the front seat of the other car, and she barely had time to right herself before two men squeezed in around her. The battered car had been left running, idling roughly. The interior smelled of smoke and stale liquor. It was dirty, cluttered.

The man on her right pressed a gun to her ribs, hard enough to make her groan, and with enough intent to scare her witless. She recognized them as the same men from the jewelry store—the men who wanted her dead.

"What do you want?" she asked around her fear, wanting, needing Mick. *Dear God, please let him be all right.*

"Shut up."

The car lurched away, tires squealing, zigzagging with a distinct lack of caution for the weather and road conditions. Wet tendrils of hair stuck to Del's face and throat. She swiped them aside and twisted to see Mick's car as they made a screeching U-turn and sped away. Right before he was out of view, she could have sworn she saw him lift his head, but it was hard to tell with the rain streaking the dirty windows and the strobing effects of the electrical storm.

Del closed her eyes on another silent prayer. Mick *had* to be okay. The gun prodded her when they made a sharp turn, keeping her own danger in acute perspective. She felt icy cold inside and out, and couldn't stop the racking shakes that made her teeth chatter and her head hurt.

Keep them talking, she thought. "How did you know where to ambush us?" she asked.

Smirking, the man lifted his hand to his head, finger and thumb extended as if it were a phone. "This is Faradon," he mimicked. "We need you to come to the station."

Her stomach roiled. "You had us bugged again?" Had these disgusting men heard Mick's heartfelt admissions about his past? She couldn't bear it.

"Nope. I didn't overhear the call, I *made* the call. Your protector was rather accommodating, sharing his home number with Faradon and asking him to leave any messages concerning the robbery on his message machine. He didn't want you to know he was a cop, you see, but he still wanted to stick his nose where it didn't belong. The son of a bitch was determined to get hold of us.'' He shrugged. ''He called his house and took his messages that way, and you went on in blissful ignorance, thinking you screwed a PI, not a cop.''

Reality sank in. One more lie Mick had told. Strangely enough, she felt more concern for his guilt, if he should find out, than she did for the lie. She understood him. She knew why he hadn't confided in her. She'd meant it when she'd said she forgave him for that. ''You got Faradon's name and Mick's number from a call he made at my place.''

''That's right. So, no, Faradon isn't expecting you. He won't send out the cavalry.''

Del looked through the mud-spattered windshield and saw they were headed toward the river. Not the Ohio—no, that would be too obvious. This was a much smaller, much dirtier river. But it was deep. And fast. Mostly isolated excepted for the occasional fisherman. But not today. Today the river was deserted.

And she knew why they were going there.

Do not get hysterical, she told herself, even as her breath hitched and her lungs constricted. She could smell the two of them in the stuffy, steamy interior of the car. She could smell her own fear and their excitement. Bile rose in her throat.

They pulled off the main road and drove through

a patch of weeds and scrub. A ramshackle outbuilding sat to their right, and a long wooden pier, probably private, stretched along the shore, then angled out into deeper water. The car bumped onto it, tires thumping along the uneven, weather-worn boards.

Though they moved slowly now, edging nearer and nearer to the end of the dock, Del felt time speeding past her. A cabin cruiser docked to their right blocked them from view of the road.

Over the river, lightning danced, temporarily illuminating the sky and emphasizing the blackness of the deep, churning water. They meant to drown her, to kill her and sink the awful, dirty car with her inside it.

The driver laughed, reaching for her upper thigh and giving her a lecherous squeeze. "It's a shame we have to end this so quickly," he sneered. "Watching you with that cop makes me want to taste you myself."

Del slugged him.

She didn't think about it, didn't weigh the wisdom with the folly. She simply snapped, then reacted on instinct. Using a technique she'd learned in self-defense classes, she brought her elbow up and back. Hard, fast. Right into his face.

"Fucking bitch." The driver grabbed for his bleeding nose and temporarily lost control of the car. The other man grabbed Del by the neck, squeezing as he shouted orders.

In that single moment of chaos, everything became clear for Del, and she knew what to do.

She ignored the fist clamped around her throat,

making it impossible for her to draw air, and instead put her efforts into a hard shove on the driver. He lost his balance, and Del wedged her foot down to the floorboards. She found the gas pedal and jammed down.

With a loud roar of the engine, the car lurched forward. The driver shouted, gripping the wheel, but Del had clamped both hands on it. They wrestled, but he sputtered blood and went blind with panic.

The hand at her throat let go to grab her shoulder. It felt like her arm had been wrenched from the socket—but it was too late. The old car went airborne off the far end of the dock, suspending time and sound and reality, then dumped hard into the icy river with an enormous splash. Hissing and sputtering, the car tipped, engine first, and began sinking.

Both men forgot about Del in their panic. They pounded at the windows, screamed as the blackness engulfed them and water began rushing in.

Del concentrated on regaining her breath. Her throat felt crushed; it hurt to swallow, even to breathe, but she did it, slow, deep. The gun had dropped onto the seat beside her, forgotten. She tucked it into her pocket. The man to her right got the window open, and a great gush of frigid river water knocked him backward into Del. His elbow caught her shoulder, his foot dug into her thigh as he scrambled frantically to get to the window again, bent only on escaping the car.

On her knees so that her head stayed in the pocket of air inside the car, Del inhaled deeply, then slithered to the back seat. Water closed over her face just as her fingers found the window handle.

She thought of Mick, thought of everything she wanted to tell him, and did what she had to do.

MICK WIPED BLOOD from his face with one shaking hand and maneuvered the slippery, winding road with the other.

After smacking his head on the steering wheel, he'd come to in enough time to see the car leaving with Delilah—but not in enough time to stop them.

Going seventy miles an hour to diminish their lead, he'd called for backup. His actions had been by rote, because both his mind and his heart stalled the second he'd realized what had happened.

He reached the river just in time to see the car sail off the dock and hit the churning water with crunching force. Terror blinded him. He wasn't aware of slamming on his brakes. He wasn't aware of the other police cars pulling up at the same time, sirens blaring and lights flashing.

He threw open his car door and hit the ground running, his only thought to get to Delilah. The storm surrounded him, lashing his face, making his feet slip in the wet weeds and slimy mud. Just before he reached the end of the dock, he got tackled hard and then held down. He fought the restraining hands without thought, hitting someone, kicking another.

"No, goddamn it," Faradon shouted when Mick almost wrenched loose. "Hold him!"

Mick barely heard. Three men gripped him, twisting his arms, making his wounded shoulder burn like fire, but it was nothing compared to the agony in his heart.

They jerked him to his feet, and all around him men shouted orders, while sirens continued to squeal and blue lights competed with the white flashes of the storm.

Numb, Mick continued to strain against the arms holding him. Faradon stepped up close. "We have a team preparing," he said not two inches from Mick's face. "Dawson, do you hear me? They'll be in the water in ten minutes tops."

Mick shook his head. In ten minutes she would be dead.

With renewed strength he lurched forward, taking the men by surprise. They lost their footing on the slippery, weathered boards and their holds loosened. Mick broke free.

He'd taken two running steps when someone shouted, "Look!"

A spotlight searching the surface of the water reflected off Delilah's inky-black hair. She sputtered, coughed. Mick went into the water in a clean dive. With several hard fast strokes, he reached her.

When he closed his hands around her, she at first fought him.

"It's all right, baby," he said, spitting dirty water, "it's me."

"Mick?" She dog-paddled, swallowed some of the water and choked, then cried, *"Mick!"*

She clung to him. Mick felt so weak it was all he could do to drag in air. Then several men surrounded them, catching them both and pulling them to the docks.

He hoisted Delilah up first. Faradon himself leaned down. "Give me your hands, miss," he said, and Delilah reached upward.

Sloshing, shivering, she landed on the dock, and someone rushed to put several blankets around her.

"M-M-Mick?"

He heard the shivering alarm, the need, and helped to drag himself out. Officers tried to cover him, too, but he wanted only Delilah. Weaving on her feet, she reached for him, and then he had her, tight in his arms where she damn well belonged and where she'd damn well stay.

He heard her crying, and his knees went weak. He tangled his hands in her wet hair, knowing he was too rough, but unable to temper his hold. "I've got you," he said gruffly, and crushed her to him.

"Mick, c'mon, man," said a gentle voice. "Let's get her out of the rain."

As if from far away, Mick heard Faradon speaking to him. He wrapped Delilah closer and allowed them both to be led to the outbuilding. It was dry inside, that was the best to be said for it.

Faradon stood there, looking slightly embarrassed. "We're, uh, fetching some dry clothes."

Mick gulped air, swallowed choking emotions and a love so rich he couldn't bear it. Delilah clung to him, and he didn't know if he'd survive the fear of thinking he'd lost her. He lifted his head. "The bastards who took her?"

"We're looking for them. If they surface, we'll fish

them out. If not, we'll start diving until we find them.''

Delilah struggled for a moment, and Mick loosened his hold.

"Take this," she said, digging a gun out of her baggy jeans pocket. She held it out to Faradon, and he carefully accepted it.

"You disarmed them?" he asked, his voice heavy with awe.

Mick pressed her face to his shoulder. "She can explain to you later."

Faradon didn't look like he wanted to wait until later, but then a cop wearing a slicker stepped into the doorway. He held out a bundle of clothes, wrapped in another slicker, then nodded and excused himself.

Mick said to Faradon, "Get out. And don't let anyone else in."

Half grinning, shaking his head, Faradon said, "Right."

The door shut behind the detective, and Mick forced himself to loosen his arms from around Delilah. The small building was dim, crowded with boat trailers, ski equipment, tools. Mick bent, touched his nose to hers and whispered, "Let me get you dry, okay?"

She nodded. "I'm all right now."

"I know you are." He strangled on the words and had to stop, had to draw in a shaky breath. His hands trembled as he stripped away her sodden blankets and started to work on the fastening of her loose jeans.

"I lost my shoes in the river," she said.

Mick wondered if she was in shock. He needed to get her warm and dry, needed to get her to a hospital.

He needed… Swallowing hard this time didn't help. He hated it, hated himself, but tears clogged his throat. He felt unmanned, vulnerable.

Without the gentleness that he intended, he removed her clothes and turned to rummage through the bundle inside the slicker. He found a loose jacket, two more blankets.

"Lift your arms," he murmured, and she obliged. The jacket, apparently donated by one of the officers milling around outside, hung to her knees. Mick shook out another blanket, this one thankfully dry, and draped it over her.

Delilah clutched the edges together and said, "It's not really cold. I mean, it must be eighty-five outside. I'm just chilled…." Her teeth chattered, making her explanations difficult.

"Shh," Mick said, and stripped off his own shirt so he wouldn't get her wet. There was nothing he could do about his pants. He sure as hell wasn't going to run around bare-assed. He pulled one slicker over Delilah's head, then another over his own. "Let's get you to the hospital so you can be checked over," he said, deliberately concentrating on only one thing at a time.

Her fingers clutched at his arm, gripping the slicker with surprising force. "Mick, I don't…I don't want to go back out there yet."

His heart hit his stomach with her trembling words. He turned to her, opened his arms.

And she launched herself into him. "I was so—so scared," she said on a wail.

Mick wanted to absorb her into himself, to surround her always and keep her from ever being hurt again. Those damn tears got him again, and he squeezed her tighter, assuring himself that he had her, that she was okay.

Rain drummed on the metal roof of the shed and wind howled through every crack and crevice in the aged boards.

Then Delilah said something that made his knees give out. "I thought I'd lost you."

"What?"

She sniffed, shook her head while tears mingled with the wetness on her cheeks. Her words were broken, scattered and rushed. "I saw the blood on your forehead and I thought you might be dead or dying. You've already been hurt so much because of me." She leaned back to gently touch his face. "Are you all right? Truly?"

Mick dropped to his knees and stared up at Delilah, not caring that he cried, having totally forgotten about his own cut head. "*You* almost died," he groaned.

"Oh no. I knew what I was doing." She smoothed his sodden hair, her hand tender, loving. "I was afraid at first. Terrified really. But I kept thinking about you. I kept thinking what if I survived and you didn't? When I realized it was you in the river with me, I went weak. I was…well, I was doing fine until then."

Mick pressed his face into her belly. The chill had left her body and she felt warm, smelled musky and damp, and he knew he couldn't stand it, knew he was going to embarrass himself.

He held her tighter but it didn't help.

Faradon rapped at the door. "You two about done changing?"

"Go away!" Delilah yelled impatiently. "We'll be out in a minute."

Faradon grumbled something, but he didn't open the door.

Mick felt her cool hands cup his face, but he couldn't let her go, couldn't unclench his muscles. He hated feeling like this, powerless and weak and... He opened his hands on her behind and squeezed her closer, grinding his face into her, trying to absorb her.

He heard Delilah's smile as she said, "I love you, Mick Dawson. More than anyone or anything, now and forever."

He drew a shuddering breath and rubbed his face over her belly, on her borrowed blanket, drying his eyes and attempting to regain control. He had to get hold of himself. He had to...

"Tell me you love me, too," she whispered.

"I do," he said without hesitation. Only a trace of tears remained in his raw voice, not that he gave a damn. Delilah deserved to know everything about him.

"You do?" she asked.

"So much it hurts."

"I don't want you to hurt."

"Then don't ever leave me."

"Never." She slipped to her knees in front of him, still cupping his face. She kissed him, then kissed him again. She even smiled. "Will you stop calling me Delilah and call me Del?"

His shoulders shook. "No."

"Oh." She sounded surprised and disgruntled, and that went a long way toward helping him regain his discipline. Even at the worst of times, she amused him.

Finally she asked, "Well then, will you marry me?"

He actually laughed, but it turned into a groan. "I was going to ask you, you know."

"Sorry."

He touched her face, her sodden, tangled hair, her small breasts and narrow hips and long thighs. "God, I love you, every inch of you. I'll always love you, I swear it." When she gave him a brilliant smile, he added with more strength, "You've stolen forty years off my life with that last damn stunt!"

Her smile never wavered. She stood and held out her hand to him. As if *he* needed *her* assistance to stand!

He did.

He still felt wobbly, but as long as he didn't think about the moment that he'd seen that car go into the river...

He shuddered, took her slender hand and let her help haul him to his feet.

She put an arm around him and leaned her head into his shoulder. "I lost fifty years, leaving you behind in that car, bleeding. Nothing has ever scared me like that."

They headed for the door together. Just as Mick opened it, someone shouted, "I've got one of 'em!"

They followed the spotlight, and saw several cops converge on a man trying to crawl onto the muddy, thickly weeded shore. He was promptly handcuffed.

It wasn't until the next day that the police finally found the other man's body and confirmed his death. But they had two of them, Rudy Glasgow and the driver. They also had fingerprints, both from the apartment next to Delilah's and the gun she'd retrieved from the car.

It was over.

DEL FLITTED from one person to the next. She loved being in a large family, even if most of that family was male and not really family at all. They felt like family, treated her as such, and they loved Mick to distraction. That in itself made her more than a little fond of them.

At the moment, Angel and Celia were perusing Mick's new bookcases, now holding her books. Del had pretty much taken over his house. His spare bedroom served as her office, and he'd already had an extra phone line put in.

The kids were all outside playing, but they could be heard through the open windows. Every minute or so one of the adults went to check on them.

Dane and Alec were seated on the couch, Josh and Zack in adjacent chairs, all of them watching a sports channel. Now that Del was used to them, Dane no longer seemed so imposing and Alec was nowhere near as frightening. But they were still fascinating characters.

Grinning, Del dropped down on the seat between them, using each hand to pat a hard masculine thigh. The two men looked at her warily. "Now that I've finally finished my current book and got it all turned in," she said, "I've been thinking of doing a book about two PIs who—"

Mick, who'd sauntered over to stand behind the couch, covered her mouth with a large hand. Del froze.

"If either one of you wants to remain in my good graces you won't tell her anything about any-thing…dangerous."

Alec saluted Mick with his cola. "Sorry, but Celia knows everything dangerous involved in my job, and she's been chewing Del's ear for the past hour."

True enough, Del thought, appreciating both Ce-lia's forthright information and the way everyone had taken to calling her "Del," once she'd explained that she only used the name "Delilah" for writing.

Everyone except Mick, that is, who swore he loved her name as much as he loved her. The charmer. He even claimed "Delilah Dawson" had a very nice ring to it. Del couldn't wait for that to become her name in fact.

Dane nodded. "Yep, I'm afraid you're preaching to the choir here, Mick. You should have gagged the women, not us."

Mick groaned with heartfelt sincerity. He'd prom-ised to be understanding about her research, though

Del knew he wanted to keep her in a cotton-lined box so she didn't so much as stub her baby toe.

Del pulled his hand away and tipped her head back to see him upside down. "How'd you sneak in here behind me?"

Mick rolled his eyes. "Sweetheart, when your brain is plotting, a herd of buffalo could tramp through and you wouldn't notice."

Since that was true, she said instead, "But I thought you were outside playing with the kids."

"They did me in. They're vicious little brutes who keep singing about how I was saved by a woman."

Del frowned, feeling a good dose of jealousy. "What woman?"

Mick leaned down to kiss her. "You."

"Me?" He nodded, and Del said, "But I didn't save you."

The awful nightmare of the car wreck, of Mick's head injury and her dousing in the river was two weeks old now, but she still shivered whenever she thought of how close she'd come to losing him.

Angel sidled up behind the couch, too, and hugged Mick. Celia joined her, resting her hands on Alec's shoulders. Zack and Josh twisted in their seats to face Del. She felt hemmed in by them all—but now the feeling was nice, sort of comforting.

She was surrounded by friends and family.

Mick smoothed his hand over her hair, something she was now more than familiar with. "Of course you saved me," he said. "You love me, right?"

"Absolutely."

"There, you see?" Alec chimed in, nudging her

with his rock-hard shoulder. "You saved Mick from being a cynical fool who didn't believe in love."

Del looked at Mick again. With the way these people adored him, she found that hard to believe. "You didn't believe in love?" she asked skeptically, but at the same time she thought it probably explained his reticence in admitting his feelings to her. Now, of course, he told her how much he cared in a thousand different ways—including the simple words *I love you.*

Mick just smiled.

Dane nudged her next, almost knocking her into Alec's lap. "You saved him from being a control freak, too."

Del righted herself and laughed; Mick was still very much a controlling man, and she doubted that would ever change.

Zack said, "You saved him from living his life like a monk."

With a very slight blush, Del said, "Okay, you got me there." Everyone laughed.

Mick was a voracious lover, and he couldn't seem to keep his hands off her. Which she appreciated because she loved when he touched her. He'd also become a voracious reader. He'd devoured her books and claimed he couldn't wait for the next one. She'd been nearly beside herself with his praise.

Josh tossed back a drink, then asked, "So when is this wedding we're all anticipating?"

Mick frowned at his friend, but said, "I just got the church reserved for the first Saturday of next month."

"You're all invited," Del announced, "as long as you know it won't be too fancy. No tuxes, and definitely no long white lace gowns." She pulled her jeans-clad legs up onto the couch and hugged her knees. "I hate dressing up."

"I'll be lucky to get shoes on her," Mick teased, and Angel promptly corrected him. She'd been with Del when the dress *and* matching shoes were bought.

Del noticed Josh heading for the kitchen, his head down, his hands shoved into his pants pockets. She smiled at Mick, rose from the couch and went to her friend. She found him standing at the sink, watching the children play through the window. "Josh?"

He turned to her, but said nothing.

"You're happy that Mick's marrying me, aren't you?"

He looked surprised, then wary. "Why?"

"Because you're one of his best friends. I don't want to come between you."

That made him laugh. "You belong between us, honey. Mick's a lucky guy, and yeah, I'm happy for you both."

"I hesitate to point this out, but you don't exactly look happy."

"No?" He studied her face, his green eyes dark, his slight smile crooked, chagrined.

She shook her head. "*Morose* might be a better word."

Mick's arms slid around her, lacing over her stomach. "*Defeated* might work, too," he said gently.

Josh snorted.

Mick tightened his hold, surprising Del, then said, "There are plenty of women out there, Josh."

"Yeah?"

Zack stepped up. "That's right, and I intend to find one."

All eyes turned to him. Del grinned. "You're bride hunting?"

"Why is that such a surprise?"

Josh said, "Because you seldom date? Because you're the quintessential bachelor? Because no woman will ever come before Dani?"

Del slugged Josh, making him jump and rub his shoulder while grumbling.

Still frowning, she said, "No *good* woman would want to come before his daughter! Children should always be first. At least until they're self-sufficient. Besides," she added, patting Zack's chest and smiling, "Zack has enough love for a wife and several children."

"One daughter is enough! All I want now is the wife to complete the set. After all, Dani is crazy about you, Del. It made me think about what she's missing."

"Like what?" Mick asked. "You take great care of her."

"I try," Zack admitted, "but she needs a female role model. Someone quiet and intelligent and sincere."

"And sexy?" Mick asked.

Zack shrugged. "I'd rather she was domestic, if you want the truth."

"I wish you luck," Josh said with mock sincerity.

"I don't need luck, because I already have a plan. And I'm starting tomorrow."

Mick and Josh groaned, but Zack just smiled, confident in himself and his eventual success.

The rest of the family filed into the kitchen, including the children. Zack scooped up his daughter, hugged her tight.

"Time for us to go," Dane announced. "Tomorrow is a school day."

There were kisses all around, and everyone gradually left except Zack and Josh. Zack's daughter had fallen asleep on his shoulder, her blond curls disheveled, her mouth smooshed on her daddy's shoulder.

Zack pulled Del close with his free arm and gave her a smacking kiss on the mouth. "Congratulations again on the engagement," he whispered. He patted her cheek and stepped aside.

Josh set down his drink and reached for Del, catching her shoulders in his hands. He gave her the softest look she'd ever seen from him, leaned forward—and Mick's hand was suddenly between them, covering her mouth.

Mick bared his teeth at Josh and said, "Out."

Laughing, Josh pushed him aside and kissed Del on the forehead. "Your future husband is a jealous lout, did you know that?"

She waved his comment away. "Nonsense. He knows I'm crazy about him."

Josh and Mick exchanged a certain look that Del didn't understand in the least.

Shaking his head, Josh gave her a squeeze. "I'm glad you're so happy."

Holding his daughter to his shoulder, Zack grabbed Josh's collar and hauled him toward the door. "Let's go. Dani is starting to snore, and you're pressing your luck."

After they'd gone, Del asked Mick, "Okay, what was that all about?"

"What?" he asked, pretending innocence.

"That business with Josh. What's wrong with him?"

Mick looked briefly harassed. "Nothing that he won't get over," he said, and it almost sounded like a threat.

Before she could ask any more questions, he took her hand and herded her toward the bedroom.

"What do you think about Zack wanting a wife?" she asked.

Mick lightly pushed her down on the bed, then covered her with his body. He touched her cheek, her chin, the corner of her mouth. "I think he's a little jealous, too."

"Too?"

Mick kissed her. "Everyone knows I'm the luckiest man alive. When I think about the fact that you're mine, I almost can't bear it, it's so incredible. I want to tell the whole world." He smiled. "I love you, Delilah Piper."

"I'm lucky, too," she said softly. "I have you. And I did tell the whole world."

Startled, Mick leaned back. "You did?"

"Wait until you see the dedication in my next book. It's to my very own hero, the finest man alive."

She cupped his face. "And everyone knows that's you."

Mick frowned for just a moment, then his frown lifted and he shook his head. "Damn, I do feel like a hero. After all, the hero always gets the girl in the end, right?"

Del laughed. "In my books, he sure as heck does."

*Mick Dawson may be taken after being
CAUGHT IN THE ACT,
but if you loved him, you'll definitely
want to catch up with his friends.*

*You met Zack Grange, the sexy EMT
and single dad. Now meet Wynn Lane,
the amazon of a woman who moves in
next door and turns his life upside down.
Literally!*

*Don't miss Harlequin Temptation 852,
TREAT HER RIGHT,
in bookstores next month.*

*And in November,
Harlequin Temptation 856
brings you the unlikely but totally
delightful coupling of Josh Marshall and
Amanda Barker. She wants the macho
firefighter to pose for a calendar...but
MR. NOVEMBER
wants a whole lot more!*

Here's a preview of Zack's story...

_____ 1 _____

"YOU ARE A PAIN in the neck, Wynn, and a pain in the ass and everywhere else. But you know why." And with a small laugh, "What b.s. to say I'm not attracted to you."

She blinked at him, so startled she almost toppled over.

He shook his head. "You're not blind and you sure as hell aren't stupid. You know I want you."

"You do?"

"I do."

He briefly kissed her, but it was enough to make her breathless.

"Even now," she questioned, "with us standing here in my kitchen and everyone else right outside? Even though I haven't just jumped you and dragged you to the ground?"

"Is that what you thought?" A sexy smile played with his mouth, making her heart punch. "That because you took me by surprise and actually got me flat on my back was the only reason I acted as I did last week?"

Ignoring the part about taking him by surprise, Wynn nodded. The how and why of their interlude last week wasn't important. Not right now when all she really, really wanted was for him to kiss her again. But he simply kept staring at her mouth while his big rough thumbs stroked her cheeks. That was nice, too, so she held still and didn't dare complain or ask for more.

"Wynn, you did take me by surprise, you know that, don't you? You're strong, honey, but there's no way in hell you'd best me in a physical confrontation."

"Okay."

He laughed, a low husky sound, and shook his head. "You're placating me." And he kissed her again. "You're something else, you know that? I've never met a woman who wanted a man, yet continued to insult his manhood with every other breath."

"Your, ah, manhood?" Her gaze skipped down his body to his lap. He lifted her chin, keeping her from that erotic perusal while making a "tsking" sound.

"My machismo," he explained, "my masculinity." He tipped her face up and kissed her throat, the soft spot beneath her ear.

Wynn's toes curled inside her gym shoes.

"One of these days," he added while licking her ear and driving her insane, "I'm going to prove it to you."

"Yes." She had no idea what he wanted to prove, but whatever it might be, she was all for it.

His laugh was a little more robust this time. He looked at her, studied her dazed eyes and nodded. "All right. So, the challenge is made. What am I to do? I'm just a man after all, and I can only take so much without caving in."

He said all that with a wicked smile.

"What?" she said.

"Will you be at your hammock tonight?"

That caught her attention. Hope and excitement flared inside her. "Yes. Sure, of course."

"So anxious." He grinned and kissed her bottom lip.

"I know this is wrong, I swear I do. But damn I want you. You're making me nuts, woman."

His machismo sounded just fine to her attuned ears. She smiled dreamily. "You're making me nuts, too. I tried to leave you alone, to let you get used to the idea of me..."

"Ha!" Shaking his head, smiling, Zack said, "That'd take a lifetime."

She liked the sound of that. A lifetime with Zack. With each day, with every damn minute, she was more attracted to him, in a million different ways.

Seeing her expression, his hands gentled and he waggled her head. "Wynn, I'm not making any promises about anything. If we meet tonight, it's strictly for sex."

Her hopes plummeted, but the excitement was still there. She bit her lip, undecided what to do. On the one hand, she'd never been a woman for casual sex.

But on the other, she'd never wanted a man like she wanted Zack.

Brimming with passion and sensuality,
this collection offers two full-length
Harlequin Temptation novels.

Full Bloom

by *New York Times* bestselling author

JAYNE
— ANN —
KRENTZ

Emily Ravenscroft has had enough! It's time she took her life back,
out of the hands of her domineering family and Jacob Stone, the
troubleshooter they've always employed to get her out of hot water.
The new Emily—vibrant and willful—doesn't need Jacob to rescue
her. She needs him to love her, against all odds.

And

Compromising Positions

a brand-new story from bestselling author

VICKY LEWIS
THOMPSON

Look for it on sale September 2001.

Montana Matchmakers

Bestselling author

Kristine Rolofson

invites you to Bliss, Montana,
and the annual matchmaking
contest! Look for this sexy,
fun new trilogy:

#842 *A Wife for Owen Chase*
(August 2001)

#850 *A Bride for Calder Brown*
(October 2001)

#858 *A Man for Maggie Moore*
(December 2001)

MONTANA MATCHMAKERS
*Find the perfect match
in Big Sky Country!*

If you enjoyed what you just read,
then we've got an offer you can't resist!

Take 2
bestselling novels FREE!
Plus get a FREE surprise gift!

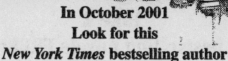

In October 2001
Look for this
New York Times bestselling author

BARBARA DELINSKY

in

Bronze Mystique

The only men in Sasha's life lived between the covers of her bestselling romances. She wrote about passionate, loving heroes, but no such man existed...til Doug Donohue rescued Sasha the night her motorcycle crashed.

AND award-winning Harlequin Intrigue author

GAYLE WILSON

in

Secrets in Silence

This fantastic 2-in-1 collection will be on sale October 2001.

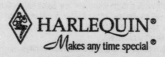

HARLEQUIN®
Makes any time special ®